The Lobster
Lady'

The Lobster Boy And The Fat Lady's Daughter

By

Charles Kriel

Fahrenheit Press

For my father, The Amazing Dick Kriel

Chapter 1

Charlie Koontz balanced on the edge of the golf cart's seat before pitching his body down onto the carnival midway. He made a three-point landing on two legs and a claw, his chin nearly smacking the ground. He pushed himself backward and upright on the dirt and grass, balancing his body across haunches and the whorled mess of flesh below his knees. His lungs heaved the Georgia air, hot and dark.

He stared at the dead battery under the "Amazing Lobster Boy" logo printed across the rear of the cart — he'd have to walk. Late for the meeting. Late for the payoff. *Let them wait.*

Charlie worked one thumb under the muddy elastic of one kneepad, and wrenched it around the first bend of one of his own short legs. He whistled low at the dog still in the cart, and started the long struggle across the midway. Charlie took a breath and threw one leg forward.

He counterbalanced with a wild push off the side of the cart, wheeling from the opposite arm and shoulder.

Moving now, he repeated the motion. His odd limbs rocked forward in turns, giving him the look of a turtle struggling to walk upright.

The dog followed. Charlie's gyrations pushed him through grass and packed mud toward the party at the cook wagon. A woman's arced laugh trebled over the lot from the cluster of lights across the dark midway ahead. Charlie had sent word for the kooch girls to leave their tent early, clearing it out for the payoff meeting. Now the women gathered around the cook wagon and slipped under the arms of ride jocks, lining up for feather steak sandwiches, corn dogs and dollar bowls of macaroni and sausage. Charlie listened to their shouts and the loud murmur of the party crowd — the wet click of popped tops followed by streams of effervescence.

Charlie twisted one fleshy claw to touch the bankroll in the shirt pocket, checking it was still there. Payday. Better that he pay the carnies first, then use what was left to graft the townies.

From the gathering of light, a tall man's silhouette walked toward him. Slim, wearing a knee length robe and sandals tied around his calves, the man could have been mistaken for a woman, but Charlie recognized his smooth gait. His body moved with an efficiency and grace Charlie appreciated, but would never experience.

He stopped in front of Charlie, his clothes glowing orange and white close up. Charlie rose barely to the man's waist. The man handed Charlie a longneck from the two he carried.

"Fancy a boost?" he asked. His rough Boston accent shocked against his shaved head and costume.

Charlie took the beer. "Fancy fucking yourself?"

They turned toward the cook wagon, moving with a practiced side-by-side rhythm, the tall man walking slow and patient as Charlie flailed his way across the midway, sloshing beer.

The dog loped behind, biding her time, stopping, sniffing, catching up again with the slow-moving pair.

"My joint give away beer now?" Charlie said. "I thought you monks took a vow of poverty."

The man laughed. "You're confusing my vows with the wages you pay," he said.

"It sure ain't paeans to chastity I hear you people whooping all day."

Over the years, the men had fallen into a pattern of teasing banter — an expression of real affection and respect, even when it left no room for insecurity.

Charlie had first spotted Matt "Monk" Clay on the net. He was the leader of a Chinese Shaolin act that failed to make it through the first round of a reality TV show pitting ethnic dance troupes against one another. Flamenco couples rapped the floor hoping to overwhelm the bells and ribboned batons of Welsh Morris Dancers, while the mighty force of a Russian neo-Cossack troupe danced a circle around them.

Handsome and unfazed by either the cameras or the rejection, Monk had learned his black skin and American accent disqualified his otherwise Asian troupe from representing the Chinese. Charlie was generally surprised at the new, out-loud racism he kept hearing since the election of a black president, but even he was shocked when one of the faded micro-celebrity judges asked the troupe if they were from Boston. "Because you Boston people all look alike to me."

The comment hadn't made it on the air, but the traffic it generated online guaranteed Monk's humiliation would be as complete as his failure.

The man had taken it in stride. Charlie went back to the clip day after day, amazed at Monk's gentle composure — his ability to find humor in the face of aggression.

After that, the troupe disappeared.

Charlie had tracked Monk to a one-room Boston flat furnished with a broken Salvation Army recliner and a mattress on the floor. Unopened bills filled the wire basket beneath the front door's mail slot. The rest of Monk's pick-up troupe had gone home.

The men had liked one another immediately. Monk thought Charlie the most committed showman he'd met, and Charlie felt a simpatico with Monk that he could only explain as a shared "otherness". In Monk, the world created a unique man. Charlie understood that, and had set about making a special place for him, just as he'd created one for himself.

From his face, Charlie looked normal, even handsome. His short-cropped hair brushed the back of a muscled neck, his shoulders rounded with curves and line from his ongoing struggle to move.

His chest and biceps gave nothing away until they led to his aborted limbs, signed off in Vs of bone, flesh and nail.

Charlie Koontz was ectrodactyl — a lobster man with claws of flesh for feet and hands. And he was the owner of The Lobster Boy's Mermaid Parade, a mixed show of human anomalies and mechanical attractions.

On one end of the midway, monstrous spiders of steel drizzled flashing lights, their spangled fiberglass buckets ready to swing hillbillies in never-ending circles.

At the other end, Charlie's carnival rides were set off by a bright one-ring-circus and the dark of tents filled with distortions of human dignity — a real freak show in a 21st century setting. That Charlie was a freak himself half accounted for his success skirting local laws banning the exhibition of human anomalies. Payoffs took care of the rest.

The two men passed the closed kooch tent, a skin show revue Charlie liked to call his *KoontzKammer* — his personal Chamber of Wonders. Inside, his *mermaids* performed an underwater strip show, often with Charlie seated on the edge of a tank so large it took two 18-wheelers to move it from town to town, empty. He used a flying rig to lower himself onto a hidden seat on the tank's lip where he touted the act. It was his best attraction — something the locals couldn't see on the internet — and the tank itself kept his women safe, away from straying towny hands.

Beyond the kooch tent, a banner promoted Charlie's act — born from the union of innocents and devils, cursed to the seventh generation, made to crawl the earth with claws for feet and hands, here was The Amazing Lobster Boy.

Dick in the dirt, a roll of bills in his breast pocket, Charlie wished he could just hand out wages and stay for the party, rather than carry on making his way to pay another redneck their price for allowing freaks and mermaids over the county line. Charlie liked to hold these meetings in his trailer, but the locals had insisted they meet in the kooch tent.

Charlie usually took these kind to the kooch, but afterward, as a complimentary treat.

That they'd demanded it pissed him off. *Fuck them.* He'd told his girls to clear out. Let the townies take his money and fuck off back to whatever dirt-farm or ball-and-chain they thought made their lives worth living.

He and Monk worked their way past The Lobster Boy tent, then edged up to the party, the crowd parting to let the show owner through. Charlie struggled himself up onto the bench of a folding metal picnic table. Beers began to arrive, but Charlie waved his short arms in the air for quiet.

"Now, you all know that I am fond of each and every one of you. Especially you, Jalinda." He scanned the crowd for the new mermaid he'd picked up in Alabama, two hundred miles back.

The group laughed, Jalinda blushing at the wolf whistles. "But I got business with the town marks tonight. Need to make this one quick. So y'all line up. Let's see how much of this money we can liberate before I contribute the rest to the brotherhood of the *poh*-lice."

The carnies cheered and fell into a loose line, according to the tradition of an immutable pecking order. Charlie started with the freaks — Toby the Giant and "Chesty" Chester, a half-and-half hermaphrodite act. They were paid first, along with the show's other real freaks. Next, Charlie counted out bills to Edgar the Electro, an ex-electrician from Chicago who pretended to screw lightbulbs into his mouth. Standing on a slab of powered steel, he passed electricity through his ungrounded body, channeled it to the glowing bulbs. Edgar was followed by Claude, a French human blockhead whose act began with nails hammered into his nostrils, and ended when he hung pig-iron from his nipples with a pair of rubber-coated clips. Last of the sideshow acts was the geek from the drug abuse show, his shirt stained with chicken blood — his mumbled name forever escaped Charlie.

The order moved from freaks to the star performers, starting with the mermaids. Most of the women were double-threats, working as acrobats, wire walkers or contortionists in the one-ring circus tent before taking their turn in the mermaid tank.

With a wink and wide bow, Monk received the collective wages for what the other carnies called the "Shallying Monks", another group of double threats. Charlie paid the animal trainers and the clowns, and dished out a bit extra for the hobo clown who doubled as a DJ, saving him the expense of a circus band.

Then came the carnies. Most shows charged carnies frontage — rent to put up their rides and games — but Charlie ran things his own way.

The Mermaid Parade was a fence-to-fence operation. Charlie owned everything — rides, games, sideshows, all of it. He preferred it that way. His people earned a flat rate, and despite Monk's remark, Charlie's carnies made more on a bad day than any percentage-worker could hope for at a hot spot on another show.

It kept the family happy.

Charlie paid down nearly to the end of the bankroll, counting out a final small stack of bills to the old couple who worked the toilets before tucking what was left of the wedge in his pocket, ready to leave.

He turned around on the picnic bench, and found Monk standing behind him.

"You want me along on this one?" Monk asked.

"Have I ever?"

"Doesn't mean you might not be open to a new experience."

"You got a feeling?"

"You usually do this in your trailer," Monk said.

"Like you said, new experience."

"Why not go all the way? Take me along. I could help."

Charlie looked the man up and down — the orange and white robes, his shaved head. "This is south Georgia, Monk. You're a bald-headed black man in a dress. How do you think that's going to help?"

Chapter 2

Charlie stopped, the dog starting to whine at his side. He could hear the party carrying on behind him. The dog looked back. Charlie never walked the midway without the cart. He wasn't built for it and he knew it, but the meeting was important. The Lions' Club sons-of-bitches in this town — they called themselves The Committee — they always asked for too much. If he offered five books of tickets, they wanted ten. Ten thousand cash became twenty. One year he'd offered them all a night with the mermaids. They'd come back wanting a weekend in his winterquarters — his own home in Gibtown, Florida — plus mermaids for the whole group. Charlie had to make this payoff. The Committee wouldn't cut him any slack.

Charlie could see the kooch tent up ahead. Red flags snapped the dark sky. A building-sized canvas stretched across a scaffold frame, touting the underwater skin show. In front of the thin stage, a ticket booth shaped like a clown's head hid in the canvas' moon-shadow, its fish-bladder eyes wide and menacing. Wisp-haired and painted mermaids sighed a circle around the front canvas, their forms barely visible against the painting's deep-sea backdrop in the dark of the closed midway. Charlie grimaced at the tableau and spat grime, splashed from the ground softened by the Georgia rain. The dog sat, tense, whining toward the tent.

Grit cracked between Charlie's teeth. These rednecks took too much of his money. They found him in every town, Sheriffs and councilmen, mayors and city fathers, thrusting their open hands and unzipped cocks, desperate to graft both. And this Committee — they thought they were better than the other locals, elevated by the power they held over their town. He knew they were just a bunch of marks. They all just wanted the magic of a dark ride. Absent wives, present women, a space to act out something hidden. Charlie did his job. He conjured highways of cocaine, prestidigitated wedges of cash, metamorphosed the men's badly drawn, inbred lives into something easier to face in the mirror. Something the memory of a mermaid would compliment in their fantasy.

The dog circled Charlie, complaining and agitated. Nearly eye level, the pair watched one another. The animal's sharp ears twitched independently before she pushed away from Charlie with her front paws, snapped a half circle, and ran into the kooch tent.

Charlie followed, past the ticket booth into the tent, steadying himself as he went. He reached with one hand to grip the tent's entrance flap, his body falling forward. He caught himself by the other claw against the sweating canvas, and pulled the flap aside.

The blue-lit tent had emptied. Moonlight shone through a hole surrounding the centerpole. Steam from the tank on stage rose and fell again to drift across the wet dirt floor. Down the center aisle, the dog paced a concentrated circle, her neck arced laterally, as though her body floated forward sideways, circling prey.

Charlie moved from the wall of cloth. A drop of moisture tapped his shoulder. The dog stilled, closing her eyes.

Her black smile turned, rounding at the end of her muzzle. A low tone rose from her throat. Charlie rubbed the two claw-like thumbs of his right hand together, his flesh wet from the canvas.

Sticky.

The dog sat back on her haunches, her nose reaching for the tent's peak. She started to howl.

Beneath the baying, Charlie heard the long, low despair of a rising police siren rush onto the lot. Up the midway. He held the fleshy claws he called hands up before his face, up into the light, and saw them blackened, sticky with blood gone dark in the glow of the moon.

Chapter 3

Melinda Barry watched around the edge of the shower curtain as the three men rifled her purse. One of them glanced toward the shower, unaware she had spotted them. Mel eased back into the cascading water, out of sight. She listened over the spray to hear them mumble, examining her possessions one at a time. Money. The car key. The driver's license that said she was Tacita Dean. She thought it would take fifteen seconds before they felt the hard outline of the Smith & Wesson Airweight in the handbag's concealed pocket — before they began to wonder who they were dealing with.

She'd pulled into the rundown truck stop as a luxury, weary of choosing between another creek bath or trying to balance on one foot while she washed the other in the sink of a gas station toilet. And she needed a break from her own constant vigilance — her paranoia that a military tracker might lie behind every doorway.

Motels were out of the question, unless she knew the place. Charlie had made contact. Worse, he'd called her from a police station, panicked, saying her name into the phone. "Melinda." He'd spoken the word in a hush, as though cupping the microphone against a listener over his shoulder, oblivious to listeners over the wire. "I'm in jail. I need your help." The man knew better. He was as watched as she was — watched *because* she was.

The men took their time digging through her bag. They hadn't seen her yet, but Mel thought they seemed confident they'd found easy prey. Alone. Stripped in a shower. Away from the crowd.

Silent, Mel reached up over the top edge of the shower stall tiles. She tested her grip against the wet ceramic, then pulled herself up until she could see over the grimy white shower wall. The men's heads were down, focussed on the purse, conspiring over her driver's license headshot and what might lie below her neckline. Two of the men were long-haired — short and paunchy, likely to feel the better part of a blow to the belly. The third towered over the others. Military tattoos raked his thick forearms. Shaved head. Combat scars. Another Oorah.

Despite that, Mel figured all three for citizens — probably bikers. A trucker wouldn't take the risk — not these days. And Mel was sure it wasn't an official visit. They weren't Military Police, just a gang of opportunists ready to take advantage of what life offered. Playtime. A little cash and a bit of pussy waiting in a truck stop shower.

Mel was sure she could take the tall one — take him first. But that might scare the fat boys. Make them run. Too much of a risk. All three had seen her photo — seen her face. They'd holler for help — probably rouse the truckers in the diner. Mel balanced it in her mind. The tall one wouldn't scare, and he looked quick. Knew how to handle himself. She was smaller, unarmed, no clothes for protection. If she took one of the others first, she'd lose her only advantage against the tall one — surprise. He had to go down first. She'd have to deal with the rest.

Mel toe-gripped the soap holder set in the shower wall and lifted herself, her hands wrapped tight over the top. She bounced twice and launched, pushed up from her wrists, vaulting her legs over the wall, levering them in an arc.

Toes pointed up as she swept down over the men, she drove both heels into the tall man's temple and ear. The blow came from above and the side, ripping cartilage. The others heard the crack, bone against bone beneath a thin layer of flesh. The man fell. His head split on the corner tiles of the shower wall.

Mel landed hard between the door and the fat men. She caught her upper body on fingertips, but slammed her knee into the tile floor. Pain shot up through her thighbone. She clenched her teeth, suppressing a wave of vertigo. No time for that. She faced the men.

One down. Maybe not out.

The fat ones looked shocked, but not shocked enough. Psychologically, her presence wasn't a surprise. Going through her wallet, they'd already imagined the interruption of getting caught. And fantasizing raping her in the shower, they'd visualized grappling with her body — the sight of her.

No. Not shocked enough.

The closest man made his move. Mel's brain kicked into *the zone*, a combat flow-state she'd picked up in Force Recon. She watched the man take two lumbering steps toward her. Mel waited, timing it through a kind of slow motion awareness. *Now.* Mel twisted her left fist straight out, in line with her navel, and buried it in the man's solar plexus. As he wheezed, she began a step around to his left. The man started to double over. Before he'd managed, Mel lifted her left leg, rocked forward on her extended right and fell back, her left heel smashing down into the side of the man's knee.

The joint snapped sideways beneath her bare arch. Mel planted the foot next to his, and grabbed the back of the man's shirt with both hands, swinging him through a downward arc as he began to pitch toward the floor.

Cantilevering on her left leg, she harnessed the man's weight to aim his fall and drive his head into the tall man's face. Two-hundred-fifty pounds of falling redneck smashed the bald vet's jaw. Mel released her hold and rolled the opposite direction, righting herself with her inertia.

Now they were shocked enough. Two down.

The third man screamed, throwing her own purse at her. *Pitiful.* Mel caught the bag with one hand and slipped her other into the hidden middle pocket holding the snubnose. She pulled the bag away from the gun, extending her left arm straight out at the man. He threw his hands up so quickly, Mel nearly laughed.

"Please, lady. You wouldn't shoot me, would you?"

Mel watched the man start to shake — his face blotched red and white. Ketchup stained the flannel shirt tucked into his too tight belt, his trousers riding low beneath his belly.

"You wouldn't rape me, would you?" she said.

Mel watched his eyes cut for the door, visualizing his escape. With her right hand she grabbed a roll of blue paper towels from the sink and slid it over the revolver's short barrel. She pulled back until the roll bent in the middle, her fingers clear of the bullet's path. Mel lowered the gun, aimed for his dick and fired.

Silencing the shot, the towel roll burst into flame from the heat. The man wailed, falling to the floor. Gun in one hand, fire in the other, Mel watched him writhe. She stomped the fat man's ribs with her heel before throwing the flaming towels at his hands clutched between his legs.

Mel found her jeans and t-shirt, dressed, slid the gun into her purse, slipped into a pair of plimsolls and ran.

Chapter 4

She rode the interstate for half an hour. She wanted to carry on, but either her instincts or her fear wouldn't let her continue. Mel usually tried to listen to both. Driving, she'd disassembled her cell, removed the SIM and snapped it before throwing the two halves out the driver's side window, ten miles apart. Now she drove deep into the Nantahala Forest, its curtains of pine open on North Carolina's cleaved mountains. Mel spotted an exit. She tossed the phone into the interstate's center lane and turned down the off-ramp.

She'd been AWOL two years. Running American roads, she'd learned a bit. Mel didn't know this part of the country, but intuition told her that short of a desert, she'd be hard-pressed to find a more abandoned stretch of land. Rock and trees lined both sides of the six-lane for fifty miles. Now on a state highway, she turned off and climbed the first scruffy two-lane she came across, hoping it led nowhere.

Rolling to a crossroads, she took the turn going up, further into the mountains. Before deserting, she'd given three years of her life to the military. First FORECON, then SpecOps. She'd finally landed in Marine Intelligence, trying to protect America and her enemies from XE, EODT and the other mercenary psychotics. That mission reeked from the start. She could have said no.

Should have.

Instead, she'd ended up a fugitive, underground the last two years. Hunted.

All together, that made five since she'd seen Charlie.

Once she'd gone over the wall, she'd longed to go back home. Back to Charlie and the carnies. They winterquartered in Gibtown, Florida just outside Tampa, traveling the rest of the year. It would have been easier that way — easier than this constant motion, one eye on the road, one on the rear view mirror. Alone. Carnivals were the last safe places to disappear in America and still have a community. Still have friends.

Charlie had closed that option for her, even before she'd enlisted. He'd adopted Mel as a child, but it was his best friend who'd looked after her. Calvin "Popeye" Woodruff. She and Charlie hadn't spoken face-to-face since Popeye's funeral. Angry and hurt, Charlie had used the ceremony to disown her, banishing her from the show. From Gibtown.

The first year AWOL Mel had been forced to contact him. She'd warned Charlie — she was on the run, and he'd be watched. She hadn't left quietly — the Marines weren't going to let this one go. There'd be MPs with questions. Armed trackers with warrants banging on his trailer door. Charlie couldn't know where she was; still, she needed his help. She needed her trust fund. Access meant a lifeline in a world where a tax return or a traffic ticket would see her locked down in Miramar Brig. She needed new accounts. New names.

Terse on the phone, he'd arranged it nonetheless. Charlie was expert at that — the forgery, the deception. Even when he couldn't do something, he knew people who would. He'd spent his life greasing the system for his carnies. Mel doubted anyone on Charlie's show traveled under their real name — everyone wanted for something, somewhere. Alimony, robbery, abandonment. Desertion.

They all owed him. Charlie collected their loyalty by putting together one of the few stable shows in America — a circus of reformed felons and misfits, with no turnover. Once you were in Charlie's circle of protection, you were safe. You'd never be found. That's what Mel had believed — Charlie believed it, too.

Now he'd called *her* for help. "I'm in jail, Mel."

The two lane she drove petered out into a dirt road, then nothing — brush and dust in an old-growth landscape, absent even the beer cans and used condoms that hallmarked adolescent hangouts.

A song she'd heard on a grunt radio station in Iraq played through the car's speakers:

The sweetest smelling tinder

I need you more than ever

She parked the car, took a breath, and leaving the radio playing, got to work.

Mel kept a Russian-made laser-sighted OTs-38 Stechkin in the glove compartment, along with a couple dozen clips, a pair of vice grips, and lipstick. A rare weapon — the left-handed, laser-sighted revolver featured a pivoting cylinder loaded with a full-moon clip of self-silenced SP-4 cartridges. She raked it all into her purse and gave the interior of the car a quick once-over before fishing a small backpack from the trunk.

She dropped both bags on the side of the road, uphill from the car. Mel palmed the vice grips, lay down and crawled under the car on her back. First she unbolted the plug at the bottom of the oil pan and drained it onto the road shoulder. She crawled away from the dark liquid toward the back of the car and did the same with the gas tank.

A hungry kiss

Starved of life

She lifted the hood and removed the spark plugs, radiator and crankcase caps and the car's smart chip. She wasn't sure what data it recorded, but she didn't want to find out.

Mel fetched the jack and a lug-wrench from the trunk and worked her way around the car. She removed the wheels one at a time, wiped them down and rolled them away, along with the spare. She put the jack back in the car and sat, ass in the dirt, twenty feet beyond the car, staring out into the valley clearing over the mountain's edge. She could see a town maybe five miles out. The twisting mountain road would be longer.

She double-checked the contents of her purse. Two pistols — the OTs and the Airweight — wallet and IDs, and one final letter from Popeye. His brother, EK, had delivered it at Popeye's funeral. Something Popeye had written before he died. She closed her eyes tight for a moment, then stripped her jeans and t-shirt, found fresh clothes in the backpack and dressed again.

My purple hands are worn

Sullied from the ashes

She left the bags and walked to the car, laid out her clothes on the passenger seat, slipped the Tacita Dean ID into the jeans pocket and pushed in the cigarette lighter. While it heated, she found a handful of dry leaves and set them in a pile at the edge of the gas stain spreading around the back of the car. She fetched the lighter and set fire to a single clutch of dry pine needles, then tossed it on the pile and walked back to her bags.

Baptise these sheets in gasoline

She felt the heat across her back as a rush of flame licked the car behind her. There'd be no explosion from the empty tank, no black smoke from burning tires — nothing to attract fast attention. By the time anyone checked, she'd be long gone, along with Tacita Dean.

Radio singed and silent, Mel's lips moved, the final lyric running through her head:

> *Baptise these sheets in gasoline*

> *Help me burn again*

She'd have to be someone else now.

Chapter 5

Charlie lay in an eight by four cell, an incessant tube light bleeding its way through his closed eyelids, impossible to escape. The hard cot hammered into the wall, and a square glass door panel criss-crossed with steel-blue ribbons of wire were the cell's only features.

Awake before dawn, his brain grinding, he'd paced the cell until his knees bled, the concrete floor brutal on his twisted limbs. The Sheriff had confiscated his kneepads when he'd brought him to the room. No one had seen him enter the cell, or even the police station. Now he lay sprawled on his back, willing himself to calm, hoping for the charity of sleep. Or at least focus.

He had to get out. Fight-or-flight wrapped itself around his heart, driving his pulse, pushing him toward panic. *Breathe.* He counted, shifting air past his raw throat.

He worried Mel wouldn't come. He'd called her, panicked, saying her name into the phone. Had he said her full name or just *Mel? Melinda?* He couldn't remember. It didn't matter. Anyone paying attention would know — Charlie, calling his adopted daughter, asking for help. 212. A New York number, but he suspected she'd gone to LA or some other place a combat blonde might blend into the scenery.

No one on the show had *it* the way Mel did. None of them could manage this. Jalinda he trusted, but she lacked experience. She was *1st of May* — a forty-miler trying to prove she'd last through winterquarter to the next season.

Monk, he may as well petition the Klan as turn up at the Sheriff's office, if there was a difference. And EK he trusted, but only to do the right thing — not to make a payoff, not in his own town.

He needed Mel — needed her to graft these bastards and get him out this cell. He couldn't think of one reason why she would. Charlie had run her out of Gibtown. He'd blamed Popeye's murder on the girl, lashing out at her when they should have grieved together.

And now there was this military thing — AWOL. Desertion. His own adopted daughter. Not that he cared about the crime, but desertion was the gift that kept on giving. She'd be underground the rest of her life.

Mel wouldn't come.

Charlie tried to quiet his mind, but the scene ran again.

Sliding into the kooch tent, he'd seen the dog first, whining, pacing a circle around something beyond the folding chairs. The lights out, he still caught the dog's outline, illuminated by the moon. The dog stopped, pushed at something with her nose, sniffed and whined and paced again. Hunting and wary.

The tent's entrance flap had fallen from Charlie's hands, sliding across his back. He'd felt the wet on the back of his neck as it seeped into his shirt. He'd ignored it and lurched forward. The aisles had gone muddy, grass burrowing back down into the Georgia dirt, escaping the tramp of hillbilly traffic.

A drop of warm liquid splashed the ground next to him. He'd rubbed the thumbs of one of his ill-shapen hands together. Slick and sticky. He looked down at his palms. Covered in dark liquid, they smelled of salt and iron.

The dog leaned back, howled at the blue moon beyond the opening of the tent top.

Charlie heard a siren, then turned back toward the entrance. The sound wasn't close — probably the other side of the lot.

He'd moved to the center of the tent, rounding the rows of chairs. The dog turned to him, her nose and mouth covered in slick. A body lay face down at the dog's feet. Torn meat dripped from her muzzle. Charlie screamed, half at the dog, half from the horror of what lay before him.

Adrenalin pulsed through the folds of his brain. Something threw time. He might have passed out — he didn't know. His next memory was of lying with his face in the mud, his head next to the body, the Sheriff struggling to cuff his hands behind him. He saw the dead man's face upside down, inches from his own. The gaping wet of the slit neck. Nearly decapitated, Charlie thought he could see the dead man's spine. His voice rose through his now-raw throat, the pain in his shoulders excruciating. He tried to tell the Sheriff his hands wouldn't touch behind his back, that his limbs were too short, but he was screaming.

The Sheriff yelled back, prying his arms, trying to gain leverage, his knee between Charlie's shoulder blades.

Remembering it, Charlie's back teeth ground together.

Freak.

The Sheriff had shouted the word, the same way Charlie was sure the man had shouted others.

Spic. Nigger. Faggot.

Freak.

When Charlie heard the word from his own mouth, it came out proud. Born not as others. Singularly unique, to the point that people shelled out good money just to stand in the same room. Just to gawk. From the Sheriff's mouth, the word ripped his identity. Piled injury on his impotence, powerless in the blanched cell.

Freak.

The grinding mental loop started again, and Charlie saw the dead man's face, covered in dirt and blood and glistening wet grass. Charlie'd seen him before, in Gibtown at winterquarters. With The Committee. The man had traveled down with the rest of the town fathers twice each year on hospitality visits, looking for coke and pussy. A hard-ass Marine gone soft. Thought he still had it. Charlie gave him what he wanted and then ignored him, happy to the see the ass end of the whole lot.

His mouth dry with panic, Charlie could hear the sound of his teeth grinding. *He had to get out of this cell.*

From the hall, Charlie heard the scrape of the sliding cell door.

"Freak Boy," the Sheriff shouted, walking in.

Charlie lay still, not reacting.

"Get up, Koontz. Visitor."

Charlie pushed down against the thin mattress, then the white brick walls, hand-walking his way into a sitting position. He smiled, game face on. The redneck's badge glinted against the room's flat fluorescence.

"Gimp for you, Koontz. I'd say he was family, if I didn't know he was a local."

Charlie felt blood rise at the back of his neck. He willed a smile, raising an eyebrow as a question.

"Says he's your counsel," the Sheriff said. "Looks more to me like a freak in a man suit."

Charlie waited, measuring the Sheriff's impatience at his silence.

"A lawyer, Koontz. Says you know him. Name's EK Woodruff."

Chapter 6

Mel waited in the Dairy Queen parking lot across from the Cuthbert, Georgia police station, watching.

She'd made her way from her burning car down the North Carolina mountain roads on foot, slipping into woods and thick brush when she heard passing trucks. At the first small town, she'd found a Greyhound pickup stop. She paid the driver cash to take her as far as Nashville, but slipped off an hour before while the driver was busy in the toilets of a Murfreesboro truck stop.

She hitched a ride the last thirty miles, got out at a diner at the edge of Nashville, and called a cab to the center of town. Once downtown, she walked 4th Ave through the banking district. One wire transfer at a time, Mel arranged a series of instant payments from offshore accounts, collecting each at different banks with different IDs, no transfer more than nine thousand dollars. She hailed a taxi across the Cumberland River to the Bordeaux Area and found a run-down used car lot manned by an overgrown adolescent who couldn't stop pulling at his crotch, a dough-faced country boy come to Nashville to sell overpriced junk cars to the urban poor.

Mel asked if he had anything special. The man walked her into a rusting metal garage where he kept a fleet of used SUVs, all with tinted windows.

All together, Mel figured they were worth more than the land under their tires.

Rides for drug dealers, confiscated from drug dealers, probably bought at police auction. Conspicuous enough to get anyone arrested. Sold back to knuckle-headed crews looking to do more time.

Mel passed and walked back outside. She found a resprayed P71 Crown Victoria Police Interceptor, the same car she'd driven before enlisting. V8. About 100,000 miles more than the odometer registered. She bought it anyway, paying cash, confident the man wouldn't file a Suspicious Activity Report.

Cruising Interstate 24, the old car felt like home in her hands. Like the rest of the carnies, Mel came alive when the road rushed beneath her feet. Cars, trucks, motorcycles — anything that carried her from the last town to the next. *Home.* A lifetime ago — someone else's life. But with the window down and her eyes closed for a moment, the suspension drifting over the worn Tennessee interstate, she could imagine herself in Florida again, cruising the interstate between Gibtown and Sarasota.

The thought of home blew through her. The idea of who she'd been.

She punched the accelerator, hoping the car might leave her memory in the dust.

Mel drove to Atlanta. Once in Midtown, she found a medical supply store in a strip shopping center and paid cash for a folding wheelchair. She parked the Interceptor away from the street, and checked into The Clermont, an aging hotel with a skin show in the bar.

Testament to its long-term trade, entry to The Clermont was via the back parking lot, the lobby no more than a hallway staffed by a caged and aging clerk.

Mel could hear the strip bar's bump and grind soundtrack umping its way through paper-thin walls as an elderly woman wrote out Mel's receipt for cash.

The woman's dull lids drooped low, reaching past her wet and yellow eyes for the sharp cheekbones of another age. She didn't ask about the wheelchair.

In her room, Mel worked out — push-ups, sit-ups, leg raises — four sets of each. Sweating, she checked herself in the mirror, pinching her sides. In the bathroom's chipped porcelain sink, she dyed her hair, something she'd done so many times she had trouble visualizing her original color. Black this time. She showered, then rehearsed with the wheelchair, learning to maneuver in the tight space between the thick painted bed frame and the old tube television. Learning to look confident with the thing.

This is how it would be. She'd use her Rose Selavy ID. She'd arrive at the Cuthbert police station. They'd take her for another freak from The Mermaid Parade.

She spent the night in The Clermont, savoring the shower and the clean if worn bed, then left before daylight. The drive to Cuthbert, Georgia took three hours.

Mel wondered why Charlie kept Cuthbert on The Mermaid Parade's annual route. Only the ghosts of a long-dead prosperity trafficked Cuthbert's lonesome streets. Driving into the little town, she'd counted no more than a dozen cars and trucks coasting the city's fractured roads. Where they were paved, dark seams held clumps of crumbling asphalt together to form narrow two-lanes. Most side streets lay unsurfaced, skinned in red Georgia clay, plowed by the wheels of aging pickups.

The only buildings she'd seen of any size were the courthouse, a red brick community college she mistook for a low-rent nursing home, and the Cuthbert police station.

Watching the station from her car, Mel ran the plan through her mind, reassessing the risk.

Charlie was in a cell in that station, she hoped. He needed her help. But he'd said her name on the phone.

Even without a trial, Charlie was a prisoner — wiretapping inmates' calls had become routine procedure. Mel knew forty-thousand Iraq War deserters' names were in the National Law Enforcement Telecommunications System database, including hers. The Sheriff's office would have a terminal. Any Barney Fife could tap "Melinda Barry" into NLETS, and they'd know every time she'd scratched her ass during the national anthem.

Black hair, a wheelchair and a fake ID weren't going to disguise her.

For a wild moment Mel considered a jailbreak, but she knew those movies were made before 9/11. Even a local jailhouse would probably be wired into some Homeland Security system. Not an option.

In a cell. In that station. She'd have to risk the disguise.

Mel took a deep breath, ready to get out of the Interceptor, but the sight of a 1971 blue El Camino stopped her. The driver pulled into the police station lot, parked diagonally across two spots and unfolded his tall body as he got out of the lowrider pickup. Mel watched the man walk toward the station's glass door.

Even with his face turned away, she recognized Ekphrasis "EK" Woodruff, impossible to miss in any setting. His goatee had grown longer than she remembered — its gray reached down past his bolo tie, touching the long-sleeved black shirt he wore in the July heat. Jeaned and booted, his pressed shirt tucked into his thick black belt, a mandorla of sweat gathered between his shoulder blades.

EK climbed the cement steps leading to the police station door. Mel's heart leapt when the man looked back over his shoulder, caught her eye from across the road and winked at her. EK removed his black hat, pulled the mirrored glass door open and disappeared inside.

Chapter 7

Mel checked her rearview mirrors, scanning the Dairy Queen parking lot on autopilot. She watched the door close behind EK.

She started the car, the Interceptor's big V8 roaring through the seat beneath her. Mel pulled across the parking lot, monitoring her emotions, resisting flight. She couldn't remember the last time she'd spent three consecutive days in the same town. Never more than a couple of weeks in the same state. That was her discipline, and because of it, she'd only been recognized once before in two years.

Eighteen months ago, crossing Delmar Blvd in St. Louis.

The vet had seen her first, before she'd even stepped into the street. Mel had panicked. She ran, which only made the man shout her name. Six hours later she checked into a Jackson Boulevard flophouse off Chicago's Circle Interchange three hundred miles north — the desk clerk suggested she not leave her room alone. She hadn't been to Missouri since.

Now she'd been spotted again. EK was Popeye's brother, yes. Almost family. But she didn't *know* the man. Mel gripped the steering wheel with both hands. *Change of plans.* She would *not* walk into the Cuthbert Police station — not today.

Pulling onto Court Street, Mel picked up the route to the carnival lot. Paper arrows stapled to telephone poles led the way through the city. Most people never noticed them, but carnies knew the arrows marked a route set up by a 24-hour advance man, moving the show down the highway from town to town.

The arrows led her through the town square and down the spoke of a residential road lined with box houses. Low-to-the-ground porches fronted each of the shabby worker's shacks. Mel passed a girl playing in a mud puddle, too old for the diapers she wore. She slapped a limp piece of asphalt shingling into the puddle, giggling and shouting as she splattered mud across her own bare chest. A wheelless Impala withered on cement blocks between the infant and a shotgun shack. The building's roof sloped like the spine of a worn field horse. Where children hadn't ripped them way, brown asphalt shingles covered the walls.

Mel checked herself for panic and found nothing, but she wasn't sure she trusted the situation.

She hadn't spent much time with EK, but growing up listening to Popeye's drunken stories, she'd learned plenty.

Born in Cuthbert, the brothers were raised by an Episcopalian Sunday School teacher and a lawman. Popeye had been seventeen and EK a year older when the boys arrived home from a school outing on Pataula Creek and found their parents hanging from the wrap-around porch of their antebellum house.

Popeye had told her the hours they'd spent grieving in visitation had been the longest he or EK had spent in a room, alone with their father.

EK stuck around and worked Cuthbert's tobacco fields long enough to see Popeye through high school.

After that, he left for two tours with the Marines, first as an MP stationed in Okinawa, then as a military prosecutor in DC. In between, he'd double-majored in law and art at Yale.

Mel never learned why EK had returned to Cuthbert, but here he was, the only towny Mel and Charlie could trust.

Mel had met the man as a child. Even before her real father had disappeared, he'd traveled to their winterquarters in Gibtown — a tall eccentric come to visit Popeye and escape what he called *the Georgia winter*. In her childhood, he'd reminded Mel of the gambling hall dandies she'd seen in old Westerns, all black and leather accented in silver and mother-of-pearl.

As a Cuthbert local, he'd introduced Charlie to the town fathers, putting Cuthbert on The Mermaid Parade's annual route. Mel remembered the first time they'd played the town. Her mother still alive, her real father still present. Just another family traveling on Charlie's show. Mel's mother was a sideshow fat lady, her father an outside talker working the bally, drawing town marks into the show. Mel didn't remember Cuthbert, but she could see the image of EK as he walked down the midway, lost in conversation with Popeye, two brothers oblivious to their surroundings.

Nearly family, Charlie would have called EK for help. And there it was again — *nearly* family. *Nearly* Popeye. Every time Mel saw EK, he reminded her of who he wasn't. Who she wanted him to be. That EK was also a retired military prosecutor — she was certain he'd sent deserters to the brig — was beside the point. Mel just didn't like her options.

She pulled onto the county highway leading to the carnival lot at the edge of town. Farm rigs rusted in the driveways of the better houses, waiting for the coming tobacco crop.

Mel noticed the photo of a red-faced crew-cut beaming out from four-color placards set on cheap wood stakes on most of the front lawns — *Reelect Milo Skinner, Mayor.* Mel didn't pick up the man's party.

From the road, Mel could see the spinning silver Ferris Wheel and the red, white and blue Rock-O-Plane, the tallest major rides on Charlie's show. She turned into the farm field that stood as a makeshift parking lot filled with cars for the Saturday matinee. She watched a pair of excited boys pile out of the back of a rusting pickup truck, their dusty parents locking the cab doors behind them. Dressed in straight leg boot jeans, the boy's father took off his sweaty, stained cowboy hat and hoisted the smallest boy onto his shoulders, bouncing him as they all walked toward the carnival entrance.

Mel thought she'd made the right decision. Charlie was in good hands with EK.

She breathed deep, knowing she wasn't panicked, but she wouldn't call it calm. It was EK's *recognition* of her that agitated. A man over the road who knew her. Recognized her and had communicated something other than — she didn't know. This knowledge that someone in this world might know who she was, and not call the police. That bothered her. Worried her because she wanted it.

Mel felt her chest tighten. She drove around the side of the carnival lot, steering the Interceptor through flattened grass behind a row of trailers and empty trucks parked between the midway and a local creek.

It hadn't been the right time for a reunion with Charlie. Not in jail. Not after all these years.

She told herself, she'd be more use on the carnival lot. She said the words aloud, "More use here."

Mel turned off the engine, got out of the car, and walked onto her stepfather's carnival lot for the first time in five years.

Chapter 8

A row of trailers surrounded the lot. She walked past the agnostic collection of silver Airstreams, white Mallard trailers and two-wheel jobs with foldout cloth tops, more tents-in-a-box than motor homes. Mel figured the tents belonged to the ride jocks.

The big top's red and yellow canvas loomed over the backlot. Three centerpoles rose above the midway, topped with red pendants slapping away the Georgia heat. Thick brown guy ropes reached down from the canvas, wrapping themselves around giant stakes driven into the grass. Three women worked their way around the guy wires on the backlot side, gathering freshly dried street clothes and costumes clothespinned to the ropes.

A hobo clown slumped across a pile of trunks, asleep in the shade of the makeshift clotheslines. Dressed in an outdated policeman's uniform, oversized tin star pinned to his lapel, his elbows slumped over the top of his thighs. Mel noticed his chin sunk into his chest. Black and white streaks of pancake makeup smeared from his chin across his costume.

One of the women whistled at him. The clown jumped, snorting. "Got-damn!" His big shoes flapped against the grass before he settled again, leaning back into the trunk.

Further along the tent, a man in his thirties leaned into one of the guy ropes. Dressed in red tights topped with a gold-sequined shirt, he gripped the cable with both hands, stretching stomach muscles and hamstrings, warming up. He pulled on the rope twice, checking, then jumped onto the guy wire, the angled rope slack under his weight. His legs wobbled back and forth beneath his center of gravity, his hips a pivot over the swaying line. He ran backward up the wire, then backflipped onto the ground before running through the backstage chute into the tent. Mel heard the towny audience roar inside the one-ring big top.

Mel rounded the tent, then walked between two canvas games, their agents shouting promises to the crowd of *a prize every time*, and a chance to *win the big one*. Stepping onto the midway, she heard one of the agents whistle loud behind her. Twenty feet away, the door of a ticket booth shaped like a clown's head swung open, hard.

A lithe woman wearing street makeup climbed out of the back of the booth. She closed the hinged ear flaps on each side of the huge wood box, locking them. Behind the booth, she found two almond-shaped pieces of plywood — giant flat painted eyes with metal handles on back. She secured the booth, fitting them in place, then locked the back door and marched toward Mel.

"That's ten dollars," the woman shouted, holding out an empty palm. "It costs ten dollars to enter The Mermaid Parade. And next time you come around here, the entrance is on the other side of the midway. You see all that work I had to do because of you? You owe me ten dollars." Mel thought she looked too good for the job — clean blonde dreadlocks, alabaster skin, nails too perfect for carny work. If she was eighteen, she was barely.

"I'm *with it*," Mel said.

The woman looked her over, her green eyes taking Mel in, assessing. "Oh, honey I'm *sorry*. Yeah, you ain't got to tell me. It's like you stepped off a picture on the wall and walked out on the midway."

"Excuse me?" Mel asked.

"You're Melinda Barry. You Charlie's step-daughter. Honey, he got pictures of you everywhere. In his wallet. All over his trailer. I'm surprised I ain't already seen your little baby ass."

Mel felt her heart clench again. *Damnit.*

"I'm Jalinda Destaine. I went down to see Charlie this morning, but they said it wasn't visiting hours. You been yet?"

"I tried. Didn't fancy meeting the Sheriff." Mel looked her in the eye, watched for her reaction.

Jalinda pulled her chin in, eyes wide. "Oh, it's like that?" she said, trying to sound more confident than her years.

"It's like that," Mel said.

"I'm one of Charlie's mermaids," Jalinda blinked, trying to shimmer.

Mel checked the woman's blond hair and clear heels. "I didn't take you for a ticket girl."

"I help where I can. When they busted Charlie, about half this show took off. Scared of *popo*, just like you. Charlie runs this show wide open. Flat stores, titty joint. And I know a couple of them ride jocks been faking business on the side." Flat stores were games the town marks couldn't win. Numbers joints. And Mel guessed the ride jocks sold shit coke — baking soda mixed with enough bleach to numb a mark's gums. "Ain't no Sunday school show. Police come around here, a lot of folks decided to hit the road."

"Have they?" Mel asked. "The police, I mean. They been around?"

Jalinda laughed. "I don't *think* so, baby. Except that Sheriff sticking his country-ass nose in our kooch tent, and that's only been like *once*, I ain't seen popo anywhere on this midway. Guess they made they mind up — who done it, that is."

Alarms in her head, Mel kept silent.

"You come around to help? Charlie said you was military intelligence, or something. Said you was good, too," Jalinda said. "If you here to help, we need it."

"I'm here to help Charlie," Mel said. "I need to walk the lot. You want to tell me what happened?"

Jalinda sucked an eyetooth, shooting Mel a look through squinted pale eyes. Her neck moved sideways across her shoulders. "You don't know?"

"That's right. I don't know. Charlie said he was in jail. He said someone died."

"Charlie's in jail, but they ain't no one died. Dying is all like, you don't feel good so you lay down and go to sleep, *forever*. This man was murdered. Sprayed blood and got stabbed all a million times until they can't even even tell if he a man or woman without checking his zipper. That ain't dying. That's someone getting they kill on. That's what got done to that man. Murdered, right there in the titty show."

"You were there?"

"No. It was after the show. Charlie told us to get. Cleared all us mermaids out. Said he had a meeting. Next thing I know, it's all like *whoop whoop*. Popo driving up the midway. That dog come running out the tent, dragging that man's liver behind her."

"Dog?"

"Charlie's dog. Got her face right in that man's guts and had a all-you-can-eat meat feast."

Mel wondered if the girl was smart enough to work kooch. Most strippers were sharp like carnies — they knew how to handle a stranger. Mel didn't know if she lacked the brains or the experience, but she doubted Jalinda would last long on the road.

"Listen, Jalinda. You might not want to say that to everyone who walks up."

"You Charlie's daughter, ain't you?" Jalinda asked, confused.

"*You* said I was, but I didn't. I could just be going along. You could be wrong."

"Well, I am *sorry*." She looked at her feet, an overgrown child, hurt and anger pulling at her bottom lip.

"Don't worry about it, honey." Mel put an arm around the girl. "It's a puzzle and we're all worried about Charlie. At some point, you got to talk it out. But right now, just keep it to yourself, okay?"

Jalinda nodded.

"You think you could point out the tent where it happened?"

"Other end of the lot. You won't miss it. That Sheriff put a yellow police tape around our tent. Where I work." Mel knew the color yellow was a bad omen for carnies. "It's like they strung a ring of bad luck and trouble all the way around us women."

Chapter 9

Jalinda walked Mel over the midway, describing it as they went. Saturday was Family Day — the lot heaved aggressive, exhausted women manhandling strollers across the uneven dirt and grass. Sugared-up toddlers made beelines for every bright color, careening toward snow cones and teddy bears. Tired moms chased screaming children, unaided by the fathers, most of whom took the opportunity to appreciate the two women walking the lot.

They passed the freak tent, a five-in-one show with a single admission price. Mel's eyes scanned the canvas showfronts — a display of clumsy paintings designed to pique towny imaginations. Giant spiders dragged the lifeless body of a white-bikinied blonde. A nurse dressed in green delivered a two-headed baby to a weeping new mother. Trapped in an iron rack, suspended over hot coals, a nude brunette endured the hellish abuse of a red-skinned, hairy-hooved devil. *Thrilling! Alive!* and *Was it THALIDOMIDE?* barked in italic black letters from deep red circles.

Mel noticed Charlie hadn't hired any fat acts. She hadn't known him to since her mother died, although the woman in the five-in-one ticket booth nearly qualified. She looked like she'd been poured into her red sweatsuit. She sat in the booth reading a magazine, eating a ketchup slathered corn dog. Mel thought with training she could probably go professional.

Through the long stretch from the gaming joints to the kooch tent, Jalinda talked non-stop. "And this here, this is the roller coaster just for children. When Charlie bought it, it was *ugly*. He had all of the artwork scraped off and repainted, so it matches the rest of the show — The Mermaid Parade."

Mel nodded and smiled and pretended to listen. In her mind she measured the distance they'd covered. According to Jalinda, Charlie walked from the cook wagon to the tent. One hundred yards. The Charlie Mel remembered could barely do it. He would have been exhausted before he got halfway.

Jalinda was still talking.

"Of course, children ain't allowed to go in and see the *actual* Mermaid Parade. But Charlie do let them go in the half-and-half — half-man-half-woman. I said to Charlie about Chesty — that's his name, Chesty the half-and-half. I said, 'Chesty ought to be in the kooch show, too, but maybe half-time, if he's only got half of one.' Charlie laughed at that. Do you think he's got half of one? How would having half of one work?"

At the kooch tent Jalinda made excuses, not wanting to go in. Mel tried to disguise her relief. She ducked under the yellow police tape sagging around the tent.

Painted in angels and mermaids, a twenty foot canvas front touted the show. Just above eye-level, an apron stage rose behind the ticket booth, a platform catwalk for the locals to taste a sample of the show inside.

Mel unthread the thick rope that held the entrance flap's brass eyelets closed. She pushed the canvas aside and stepped inside, her eyes adjusting to the dark.

Rows of wood chairs circled a diving tank the size of two semis.

Steam hung over the warm water, rising with the Georgia humidity. Jalinda had been right — a lot more than dying had gone on here.

Sprays of blood covered the inside of the tent, expressionist brushstrokes arcing across the canvas walls on both sides of the entrance. She lit a cigarette, the smell of souring blood overwhelming her — Mel hadn't walked a crime scene for years.

The grass under her feet was clotted red and black. A trail of it led down an aisle, rows of folding chairs scattered around the pathway. Blood smeared the grass. Mel imagined the body had been dragged across the ground, or the dying man pulled himself, clutching at clumps of grass and dirt. Every few feet, small pools gathered, surrounded by spatter. She guessed the man stopped as he dragged himself away. Someone beat and stabbed the victim, new wounds opened with each hesitation, forcing him to keep moving until he couldn't any longer.

The blood finally stopped at nothing, the body gone. No chalk outline. No record that a man once lay there, outside his lifeblood seeped into the earth.

Mel noticed tracks. She kneeled in the dirt to see closer. Shoes. Two sets. And dog prints.

Jalinda had struck out trying to visit Charlie, but she'd charmed the Sheriff, gathering information. The victim was Samuel "Sarge" Cooder, a local businessman. *Giant of a man*, the Sheriff had told Jalinda. *Ex-Marine*.

Maybe Jalinda wasn't as naive as she thought.

Mel knew enough to reconstruct the scene. She turned a circle, inspecting the space. The spray was arterial, probably from the neck. It projected into the tent from just inside the entrance, then circled and hit the canvas wall behind her, with one clean space in the middle — a void in the stain.

She walked it out in her mind. "Sarge" Cooder entered the tent. He was attacked from behind, his throat cut in a reach-around. The first blood stream soaked the grass in front of him. He spun to his right, spraying the walls.

Mel stepped up to the blank spot. She stopped and turned around, seeing the last thing the man saw before the attack. She took one step back, then turned at the waist and looked at the wall behind her. This was where the killer stood when he blocked the spray of Sarge's blood, arcing across the canvas.

His throat cut, the vic either fell to his knees, or was knocked down. What life he had left, he spent dragging himself across the tent. A surge of blood pumped from Sarge's neck, connecting small pools of blood where he stopped, now dried black and brown. He couldn't have put up much of a fight. But it also couldn't have been Charlie who'd *got their kill on.*

Mel repositioned herself halfway along the path and assessed the trail again. She walked back to where the vic first fell. Buried in a mud footprint, a flash of color caught her eye — shiny, bright blue. Mel used a pen to dig a patch of shining paper from the mud. A matchbook with a silver drawing of a woman in a martini glass. Lettered in black. *The Social.*

Mel put the matchbook in her pocket and left the tent, crossing the midway again. She found Jalinda outside the clown head ticket booth.

"You finished already?" the girl asked. "You find anything?"

"Enough," Mel said. "You said something about a dog."

"She's Charlie's."

"Black German Shepherd? Black tongue? About ten years old?"

"Shortie. How did you know?"

"She's not Charlie's dog — she's mine."

Chapter 10

Jalinda walked Mel across the midway to the cook wagon. A clutch of picnic tables laid out for the carnies circled the food trailer from the backlot side, separated from the midway by a see-through weave of cheap polyester fiber. The cook wagon churned out handheld food on the towny side of the cloth fence — corn dogs and burgers, cotton candy and popcorn. Mel felt her stomach turn at the smell of greasy corn meal mixed with the drift of burning sugar.

Carnies spread themselves around the backlot behind the cloth divider. A group of men drank beer and hovered over a picnic table, watching an aging white-faced clown challenge a shirtless acrobat at checkers. Mermaids and tumblers lounged on wood and canvas deck chairs, welcoming the break. Half a dozen men in white folding hats sat around a vat on the ground. Cigarettes hung from their mouths, they traded stories and worked at peeling the mountain of potatoes it would take to feed the show for a night.

Jalinda led Mel to a picnic table. On one table, two men sat either side, one with his back to them. The other nodded her direction, calling attention to Mel's approach. Shortie crouched beneath the table, the tip of her tail matching the white hair around her mouth. The dog seemed to wear a desperate smile across its nose-in-the-sugar-bowl muzzle, less happy than uncertain.

As Mel came closer, Shortie rose, but hesitated. Mel bent down and called her name. The dog overcame her disbelief and ran toward Mel, her back end curving forward, licking Mel's face. Mel felt a tic at the corner of her eye.

"If it ain't Melinda Barry." One of the men rose.

Mel was unsure if the man spoke her name as a hello, a tip-off to other carnies or as a warning to her. It seemed to work on all fronts. His greeting giving them permission, carnies at the other tables turned to watch. Mel noticed a bald black man in white and orange staring over his sandwich at the farthest table.

The man who called her name walked around the picnic table to face her. At first she couldn't place him, despite tattoos crawling from beneath his t-shirt, escaping over his neck and face.

"It's Blue," he said. "Blue from the Showman's Club." The man held out his hand.

Now Mel remembered him. She'd known Blue as a wanna-be — a tattooed surf punk bartender from Charlie's Gibtown Showman's Club, the carnies' winter drinking hole. He'd arrived with the right qualifications — no one knew his real name and he refused to say. That made him good in most people's books. They were *carny* credentials. Proof he knew how things worked. Mel and Charlie always figured he had a warrant across some state line, but Charlie took a liking to the kid. He'd hired him to tend bar while he saved money to needle his face, hoping to work the five-in-one as an illustrated man. Mel always wondered if Charlie had been seduced by Blue's ambition to become a freak.

"See you got your art done," Mel said, looking him over. "Nice work."

"It sure cost enough. Drove all to way to LA for the face work. Best pounder I could find."

He turned his head from side-to-side in a practiced display. Classic Maori, down to his neck. Mel was surprised how attractive she found the face-tattoo, but she couldn't say the same for what she could see of the rest. Tattoos spread up and down his biceps and forearms in an asymmetric pastiche of badges, dragons, nudes and slogans. Mel couldn't make sense of the design. She thought it would have worked fifty years ago, but every football player in the south had as many body tats as Blue. The face work had been necessary for Blue to go pro — she hoped it hadn't been a waste.

"She's here to pick up Shortie," Jalinda said.

The words sucked the air from the table, mooting Blue and Mel's greeting. Mel felt the bald man eyes, watching them from behind her.

"Why you want to do that? Take away Shortie." The man sitting with Blue rose. His voice sounded nasal and odd, like he had a cold. The dog moved around behind Mel, nervous. She tucked low to the ground, her front paws shivering.

"Mel is Charlie's daughter," Jalinda said.

"*Step*-daughter." Mel wasn't sure why she corrected the girl.

"You haven't been around for a while." Blue challenged Mel, but she still wasn't sure why. "Not since Popeye died."

"Been away. On the road."

"You still an Oorah?" he asked.

It felt like too much — first EK, then Jalinda. Now this punk. Mel wondered when she'd turned so sensitive. She'd just shot a man, beat his friends, burned her own car and walked away. Now a dog licked her face and a stripper said her name, and Mel let it throw her off-kilter.

Mad at herself, she looked the man in the eye. "You still a rube?"

"Hey, honest," Blue said, defiant. He shook his shoulders, jaunty. "No offense."

The other man looked ready to move, although Mel wasn't sure which direction.

"I didn't mean to say you wasn't *with it*," Blue said. "Just, you been gone a while. Now Charlie's in jail, and then you turn up. That's funny timing is all."

"When it's yours to say who's *with it*, I'll know who to ask." Mel leaned forward. This was a mistake, escalating the situation. She took a breath and tried to cover, rocking back on her heels. "I'm here *for* Charlie — and to get you people on the road. If you want to help, you can tell me what you know."

"What about the dog?" Blue's friend reached down to pat Shortie's head. The dog's paws shook hard, a shiver running down her shoulders.

"I don't think the dog's going to tell me anything."

"Her name's 'Shortie'," the man said, dumb and tense.

"I know that." Mel noticed the well-worn holes around the man's top and bottom lips. The stretched nostrils covered in scar tissue. Her eyes scanned his face. From the space between his eyes, his nose twisted left then right, ending in a mash at the tip. Mel figured him for Claude the Human Blockhead — she'd seen his marquee outside the five-in-one. The holes he'd made by hammering nails into his face three shows a day — the mashed nose happened every time he missed.

"I'm asking why you want to take her, because I'm looking after her while Charlie's gone. She's my friend."

Now Mel understood. She looked the man in the eye, trying to soften her expression, her words. "Before she belonged to Charlie, Shortie was my dog. I loved her the same as you."

Claude's mouth screwed, hurt and disappointment behind his expression. Jalinda broke in, reaching up to toss his hair. "Hey baby, why don't I get us all a couple of beers. Yeah? Then we can all talk."

Chapter 11

They sat around the picnic bench, draining a second round. Crowds of townies wandered the midway. The other carnies had disappeared, off to man joints and rides.

"Why'd they meet in the kooch tent, do you think? Why not Charlie's trailer?" Mel asked.

"Charlie keeps the pickled punks there. Maybe he didn't want anyone seeing them," Blue said.

Jalinda stared at her beer bottle, confused. "What's a pickled — "

"Pickled *punks*." Blue rolled his eyes. "*Bouncers*. Rubber freak babies. They're supposed to be fetuses in jars of formaldehyde, but they're just gaffs. Rubber dolls in water with food coloring."

Claude was unsure. "I've heard Charlie keeps some real ones. Gets them from a medical supply out in Arizona."

Mel caught Jalinda's surprise, but misunderstood. "They aren't real, Jalinda. They're rubber. Charlie orders them from the Acme truck, same as he stocks up on teddy bears and spoofers. You can buy them by the gross."

"I know that," Jalinda said. "Them babies is all over Charlie's trailer, but he never calls them — pickled — "

"Pickled punks," Blue said.

"He never says that. He just calls them *the kids*. He even got one without arms or legs or nothing — "

"He's not shy about the bouncers, anyway," Mel said.

"Well, I've never seen one," Blue said. Mel saw him give the girl a resentful look.

Mel turned back to Jalinda. "Are you sure he had everyone cleared out of the skin show? No one stayed behind?"

Jalinda spoke up. "Ask Blue. He come around and told us, 'Clear out. Charlie's got a meeting.' I didn't understand, but I come here to the cook wagon anyway."

"Did he say why?" Mel asked.

"Not to me," Blue said.

"Usually a meeting at the kooch tent means Charlie wants us around," Jalinda looked down at the beer cradled in her lap. "To look after his guests."

The table went silent, the men feeling Jalinda's embarrassment. It confirmed the girl's inexperience to Mel. A real forty-miler.

Blue tried to break the tension, his voice too upbeat for his words. "Someone looked after that bald bastard. His scalp was cut every which way when they carried him out."

"They find his hair?" Claude asked.

"None to find," Blue said. "I saw him earlier. Walked the midway straight up to the show front. Had a buzz cut. Marine-style."

"Uh uh," Claude said. "You're talking about someone else. I saw him, and he had hair down to his shoulder blades. Walked in through the chute, from the backlot."

"Hold it, hold it." Mel turned to Blue. "What time was this?"

"I don't know. Just come back from clearing the girls out." He looked at Jalinda. "Guess about eleven?"

Jalinda nodded.

Mel looked to the other man.

"Yeah, that's about right. Eleven o'clock," Claude said. "Looks like we got an extra towny ain't accounted for."

Mel and Jalinda walked back toward the Interceptor. Jalinda led Shortie while Mel tapped the flat face of her phone.

"Who you texting?" she asked.

"Not texting. Looking at a map. You know Cuthbert?" Mel said.

"No. This is my first season. First couple months."

"Really?" Mel said, faking surprise. "So what were you doing before?"

"I was in school," Jalinda said. "Well, for a while I was, then I dropped out last year."

"To do what?"

"Nothing. I wasn't doing nothing. I started dancing, you know, to make a little money."

Mel kept tapping. "We all got to eat."

"Can I ask you something?" Jalinda turned to face Mel. "How come you carry a cell around when the military's after you?"

Mel felt the urge to run again, to leave Georgia and never come back. "Bought it at a truck stop. No one knows it's mine. Who says someone's after me?"

"Charlie." Jalinda said it, as though everyone knew. "Don't worry. We all wanted for something, except me. Least on this show."

"That's no comfort."

"Should be," Jalinda said.

"Why's that?"

"Cause you know you safe. Cause no one going to turn you in. That's what Blue told me. He says that out there, they no one what will care for you. But here, he feels safe. Like he can quit running."

Chapter 12

Dylan Hide scanned the barroom through the porthole in the swinging leather door, chewing his teeth, he checked The Social's happy hour stragglers. Fidgety, he pulled at the bandage wrapped around his knuckles, cramming the hand in his pocket. He took a breath, blew the hair out of his face and pushed through the door. Before it had time to swing closed behind him, Dylan was pissed off.

Since when did he check the room before he walked into his own joint?

Dylan hated these happy hour motherfuckers — suits and secretaries, mingling between the buffet wagons and his bikini girls. The men acted like they didn't care about anything but the food, while the women tried to pretend they weren't standing in a room full of hookers.

Fucking mitigators. He wasn't sure mitigators was the right word, but he thought it fit. The Social was a strip joint. Dylan ran his den for bourbon-drinking men to slip downstairs and get their dicks wet, if they had the cash. Not for a bunch of mitigated fucking drumstick suckers.

Twenty-four hours a day for eighty years, The Social's neon sign had never went dark. Dylan knew how to run his joint.

His Momma had told him, *Keep your women clean, your jukebox country and your cooks niggers — everything'll be just fine.* Just like she learned it from his Granddaddy.

Maybe then. Today nothing was just fine. Dylan wondered if they even had juke boxes when the old man built his place in the middle of a county seat surrounded by fifty miles of tobacco field. Now sprawl pushed Columbus right to the edge of Cuthbert's county line, bringing mitigators and their fucking expectations. Corporate sons-of-bitches, with their loyalty cards and franchised hookers. Forcing things to change. He'd cleaned-up the name his Granddaddy gave the joint — *The White Way Social Club* — named specifically to keep the niggers out. He started doing happy hours and free buffets. He'd even put in a DJ booth and hired some loud-mouth with a microphone to keep the crowd coming in.

And this is what you get for it — a room full of tassel-shoed sons-of-bitches with their ties flicked over their shoulders, stuffing themselves on chicken wings and pink cocktails. If they wanted kooch shook over their supper, they should drive to one of those affiliated titty joints out on 185.

Dylan scanned the room. He knew what to expect. He'd watched the past two hours, sitting behind the two-way mirror separating his office from the The Social's barroom. Why would anything change just because he decided to stand up, cross the kitchen and walk through the swinging doors?

He pushed his way through the buffet crowd. He could feel the real source of his trouble bearing down on him, boring a hole in his back — the goddamned corner booth next to the two-way mirror, empty the whole night. The *reserved* sign still waiting in the middle of the table. A red rope crossed the booth, ready to drop. One day out of the week, that table belonged to The Committee, and barring Christian holidays and domestic anniversaries, The Committee always met at The Social.

The pain in his fist made him wince. He'd seen it coming. Why had he doubted himself?

He knew it even before Sarge come for him at the carnival. Goddamn ignorant grunt. People you know your whole life, turned into affiliated SOBs, over what? Greed and covetousness and more greed.

Dylan squeezed his fist and felt the bandage begin to slip, wet. A voice shouted over the club's sound system.

Ladies and gentlemen, welcome to The Social, your happy hour home for ladies and the men who love them. And now, here's the man himself, your proprietor, Dylan Hide!

Dylan scowled at the new man in the DJ booth, pulling a finger across his throat. Smart ass. He turned to walk back into the kitchen, but the silenced DJ put on some Jap-sounding plinky-plonk record. Six notes looped over a swooping kick drum. Dylan thought the music sounded like what you'd play in a movie when you were trying to show that someone was crazy. He was ready to ignore it, when a woman on the record yelled "Hollah!" Dylan caught sight of a white woman across the room waving her hand, cocking her chin and mouthing the word at the same time.

Hollah!

Dylan launched the eight steps into the booth and nearly dove behind the smoked glass dividing it from the room. He grabbed the DJ's collar, seething words. Blood oozed from his bandaged fist. Dylan flashed a spring loaded blade under the counter, out of sight of the customers, retracting it the moment he'd made his point.

Dylan kneed the DJ, dropping him to the floor. He turned to the laptop in the corner of the booth and tried to understand the odd app on the screen.

It looked like a picture of a tape deck surrounded by words and buttons. Dylan's mind ticked, his attention completely drawn, trying to make sense of the system of icons and album covers. He understood computers, but he didn't get any of this.

He pressed the stop button on the touchscreen. Silence cloaked the room like a heavy curtain, a high pitched ring hanging in the void of sound. He couldn't figure how to play another song. Dylan's breathing changed as he leaned into the screen. The DJ made a small noise at his feet, something to confirm his weakness. Dylan snapped to.

He left the booth and found the barman. "Bourbon, and put a tape on. If it's nigger music, it better be Charley fucking Pride."

The drink arrived. David Allan Coe sang from the speakers. Satisfied. Dylan walked to the buffet wagon and rolled it away from a man leaning over a tray of candy-red chicken wings drying under a heat-lamp. The man started to say something, but Dylan kept the wagon moving.

"Get the fuck out of my joint," he said over his shoulder. "And take all these mitigated motherfuckers with you."

Chapter 13

Dylan shoved the buffet through the swinging doors into the kitchen, crashing it into the stainless steel prep table. The cooks startled, running to catch the wagon before it did more damage. He walked past them and slammed his office door. He ran his good hand from his forehead to his chin, trying to wipe away tension.

Black and white flocked wallpaper covered the room, Bond girls in black felt columns repeating around the small office. Velvet curtains hung from the fourth wall, pulled back to frame a two-way mirror looking out over the barroom. The office revolved around a worn brown desk — his Grandaddy'd called it his *escritoire* — a weary foil to Dylan's velvet, mirrors and fuzzy women.

Arms out, Dylan shook his head, pulling his long black hair back and down his neck. He fell back, landing hard in his Grandaddy's brown leather chair.

He stared out his other office window at the traffic passing beyond The Social's parking lot. He flipped through the windows on his laptop. Checked his email. He picked up the black handle on his desk phone and called Sheriff Lewis Evans at the county jail. "Lew, it's Dylan. I'm flipping the switch."

Dylan had made Lew install scramblers on the desk phones of all The Committee members. Lew was a weekend geek. Useful most of the time, but Dylan didn't trust him the rest. The Sheriff had wanted access to all their cell phones, promising to install scrambler software on the handsets. Dylan let him know what he thought of that bullshit, and the man never mentioned it again. Their line squalled for a moment, then he heard Lew's voice.

"What can I do for you Dylan?"

"Don't fuck with me, Sheriff. What's this email you sent?"

"Just a picture, buddy. Something from the webcam on the station flagpole."

"No shit, Lew. What's it a picture of?"

"Dairy Queen parking lot across the road. Car sitting there a lot longer than it takes to eat a banana split."

"The Interceptor? How long?"

"Couple hours."

"You got a better shot?"

Dylan's computer pinged.

"You ask, you get."

Dylan punched the speaker button on the phone and cradled the handset. He opened the photo from his email and zoomed in on the black-haired woman in sunglasses sitting behind the steering wheel.

Lew's voice sounded tinny through the speaker. "I ran the plates. Belong to a 2003 VW registered in Huntsville. No reports yet, but I'd say she stole them."

"Gosh, Lew, do you think?" *Dumb asshole.*

"I'm just telling you, Dylan. She someone we know?"

"Hard to tell with the sunglasses. You think that's her, come for the freak?"

"Could be. Could be someone off the carnival, but I doubt it."

A flash through the window made Dylan turn. Light reflected off the windshield of a car pulling into the parking lot. The Interceptor.

"We're about to find out, Lew. Company pulling up at the club. I'll get back to you."

"You need backup?" the Sheriff asked.

"Do I ever fucking need backup?" Dylan paused, changed his mind. "You got any trackers over there?"

"I hear you. You keep her busy and I'll slip one under her bumper."

"Good man. And Lew?"

"What is it, boss?"

"Don't ever let me catch you putting one of them tracker things on me."

"How do you know I hadn't already?"

"You're alive." Dylan hung up.

He left the office and found the barman.

"Live one in the parking lot. Black hair. She comes in, alone or not, you sit her at The Committee table. Don't say anything. And don't come get me."

Dylan turned to walk away, nearly running into Stella, one of the dancers. Happy hour over, she'd dropped her yellow bikini.

Dylan watched her pick it up from the barroom floor —
he could see imprints from the absent straps across her
breasts. He imagined they hadn't moved an inch from the
lack of support. "Where'd I buy you those tits, Wal-Mart?
Get in here."

Dylan grabbed the woman by the arm and marched her
through the swinging kitchen doors, back to his office.

Chapter 14

Watching The Social's barroom through the mirror dominating his office, Dylan saw the barman meet Melinda Barry at the door.

He thought it was Melinda, but couldn't be certain. She was older than he imagined.

The bartender led Mel to the booth; she sat just feet from Dylan on the other side of the glass. He walked to the sealed interior window, watching close, her profile not more than a foot from his face.

The stripper sat on the couch behind him, feigning offense. "What do you want to watch her for?"

Dylan spun and backhanded her, knocking her off the couch, sprawling across the floor. "Shut up." The woman cowered, animal-like, nursing her bleeding mouth with the knuckles of her hand.

He looked back at this Melinda Barry. She'd aged, of course. He'd expected that. But the fresh image he'd had, there was something else — something powerful. She was too different. He didn't know if he liked it.

Dylan bent and lifted the stripper at his feet, struggling with her weight. "When I want your mouth open — "

He pushed her toward the glass, its double wall and the club's music covering the thump when her head hit the dark paneling beneath the window. Dylan grabbed the woman by the back of the neck and pushed her face against the glass, forcing her to look out into the barroom. Forced her to look at Melinda. Steam clung to the glass surface around her nostrils.

"I'm not fucking you." He ripped his zipper down and shoved his dick into the woman, feeling his own flesh tear against her dry skin's razor stubble. "I'm fucking her."

Not what he had imagined. She just sat there, comfortable in his joint. Not scared one little bit. Not bothered by the strippers. Just watching the room.

Dylan tried to focus on the old image he'd had of her. Younger. Shy. This woman was someone else.

The stripper struggled beneath him, vocalizing distress.

"Shut the fuck up."

Dylan reached around and grabbed her across the mouth, silencing her with his palm. His thumb worked its way up her face, pinching her nostrils. He could feel his dick bleed as she bucked against him, struggling for air. He let her breath, and with his right hand, snatched the back of the woman's head. Her hair was stiff, layers of hairspray making it crinkle and cling to his fingers. The bones and tendons in the back of his hand crackled against the sill around the mirror. He used his body weight to twist her, pumping faster. Dylan finished, growling. He pushed her away. She slumped at his feet, hurt and looking to him for approval.

Dylan ignored her, transfixed by Mel rubbing her fingers against the feathery hair at the back of her neck.

He watched like this, through the glass, quiet, as the stripper slunk her way out of his office, as the buffet wagons were cleared, as the crowd changed from redneck yuppies to the aged and divorced.

He watched her ask questions at the bar, chat to the working girls, flirt with the cooks. He watched her until her phone rang, her lips moved against its glass face, until she scowled and stood and walked out of The Social into the coming night.

Chapter 15

Mel crunched her way across The Social's crushed-shell parking lot. The dog waited in the Inceptor's passenger seat, wagging to see her again. She unlocked the door, sat behind the steering wheel, and smacked it with an open palm. She'd bought her pre-pay cellphone at a truck stop outside Atlanta, thinking she'd probably never use it. But back at the lot, she'd changed her mind and asked Jalinda to give Charlie the number. No one else.

Six hours later EK called.

He spoke her name over the line — *again* — then went on to set a meeting point at the carnival lot and give her a time. Now she was supposed to drive there and hope he'd be the only person waiting for her.

At the town's next intersection Mel turned an abrupt left, throwing the dog off balance. She drove slow to the city limits, then punched the engine as she rode out onto the desolate county highway. Outside a single car in her rearview mirror, there was no other traffic. Mel kept an eye on the car's lights until she crossed the county line and found herself driving alone.

Thirty minutes later she pulled into a convenience store outside Albany.

She got out of the car and gave the cashier two-hundred dollars plus change — gas, cigarettes, a handful of SIMs and a junky pre-pay smartphone with a small touchscreen.

She walked back to the gas pumps. As she unscrewed the car's gas cap, she dropped her old phone on the pavement near her feet. She pumped nineteen dollars in the tank, then splashed the last dollar's worth over the phone. She replaced the gas cap and nozzle, picked up the soaked handset, fetched Shortie from the car and walked to the women's room at the side of the building.

Inside, she locked the door behind them, removed the phone's battery, dropped the handset in the sink and lit it. Blue flame shot up to the mirror, the circuit board cooking in the porcelain sink. Mel chain-smoked three cigarettes to cover the stench as the phone melted. Watching the plastic bubble around the buckling glass face, she thought about the last letter from Popeye in her backpack.

Popeye had mentioned Cuthbert, and had spoken of EK, specifically. He'd said that EK would help her. But Popeye hadn't been writing about helping Charlie — he'd written about helping her find her missing father, and it that been more than five years ago.

Mel ran water, splashed her face, massaged a wet hand around the back of her neck, then washed as much of the phone down the sink as would go.

While she waited for the sink to drain, she fired up the new phone, navigated its browser to a familiar Russian website, downloaded a firmware hack for the model, and rebooted.

Now the new phone would change digital identities every time she turned it off. If she changed the SIM as well, tracing and tracking would be impossible.

Fifteen minutes after walking into the toilets, Mel dropped a paper towel full of wet ash and charred plastic into an oil-drum trash can before starting the county road drive back to Cuthbert.

Halfway to the city limits, two lights appeared in her rearview mirror, winking below the horizon as the vehicle passed through a foggy dip. She eased off the Interceptor's accelerator, dropping to ten below the speed limit.

EK will help, Popeye had written. Mel wondered how.

She'd met EK twice in Gibtown, the first time as a child, something she couldn't remember. EK was a legal "fixer", an attorney working in the background, cleaning messes too complex or unseemly for mainline lawyers to handle. He'd arrived in Gibtown for her mother's funeral, then took over Mel's legal arrangements. With her father gone, EK worked the system, arranging Mel's adoption paperwork as a favor to Popeye.

Mel couldn't remember EK from that time, but she carried an indelible image of him at Popeye's funeral five years ago. EK, Charlie and Mel had fallen into one another, a tripod of grief and loss. At the time, the old man seemed a bizarre impostor, a *surrogate-Popeye*, standing before her rather than lying in the grave. Older, gray-goateed, with the long hair and glasses of a neo-Victorian caricature, he still looked like Popeye beneath the disguise. The way he spoke reminded her of a diary she'd read from some Southern Civil War widow.

He'd arrived at the time with the letter from Popeye. Addressed to Mel, to be delivered should anything happen to him. One line burned itself in her vision.

If you decide it is ever worth looking for your father, Cuthbert, Georgia is a good place to start. EK will help.

Popeye had written the letter just before he died — just before he was murdered in Gibtown.

Mel ground her teeth, squeezing her eyes together hard. She refocussed on the road, trying to concentrate on the puzzle — EK, passing a letter to Mel, from the hand of Popeye, who knew something about her father and this town, where her stepfather now sat in jail.

Mel held her speed, waiting for the other car to catch up and pass. It didn't. She slowed the Interceptor again. The car behind came closer for a moment, then fell back, steady in the distance. Mel stretched her arm across Shortie in the passenger seat and reached into her purse's hidden pocket, retrieving the snubnose Smith & Wesson Airweight. She slipped it into the car door pocket to her left. Mel pressed her fingers into the turn signal switch without clicking it. *Wait. Decide.* She pushed the lever all the way up and slowed the car, pulling onto the gravel shoulder beside the county road.

The car behind didn't signal, nor did it come any closer. It seemed to have stopped. At this distance, Mel couldn't tell if the car had pulled over or parked in the highway. Her heart began to pound. Mel breathed through her nose and concentrated on slowing her pulse. The clicking turn signal created a tense polyrhythm against the pounding in her temple. Sensing her fear, Shortie started panting. Mel willed herself to focus, channeling her rising adrenaline.

She scanned the horizon around her. To her left and right, darkness and fields. Cuthbert's lights glowed beyond the horizon ahead. Behind her, the car's headlights sat steady, a shift of boggy mist drifting across their beams. Mel wrapped her hand around the gear shift and put the car in drive. She pushed the signal lever in the opposite direction, pulled onto the road and accelerated, finding a steady speed. The lights behind followed, constant. Mel kept one hand on the snubnose.

When she reached the city limits, the car's lights winked out, disappearing in the distant night.

Chapter 16

Mel drove the field behind the carnival guided by her running lights, the car juddering through each grassy pothole. She pulled behind the same row of backlot trailers and parked the car, the snubnose ready in her purse. EK wanted to meet backstage at The Mermaid Parade's big top — the main tent. Mel was an hour late.

With Shortie walking unleashed beside her, she made a circuit around the outside of the show. Deep bass thudded from each of the major rides' soundsystems, striking her ears in dull asynchronous rhythms. Here and there she heard shouts from bally talkers and agents calling townies into sideshows and five-in-ones, or the games the carnies called joints. On the Tilt-A-Whirl, the ride's DJ played Grinderman's *Worm Tamer*. She walked past listening to the man dip the music beneath his shouts — *Do you want to go faster?* — before gunning the big ride's diesel engine, conjuring screams from overexcited teens.

Mel passed the MurderDrome, a slat metal barrel six yards across, rising thirty feet above the ground. Townies climbed stairs snaking around the cylinder's outer wall.

They gathered on a circular balcony that looked down into the pit. Mel heard a bally talker inside the velodrome pitch the coming act.

Behind the MurderDrome, a white-haired man in a leather helmet straddled a mid-thirties American Indian motorcycle. The bally talker called his name, and a door in the wall lowered, transforming into a ramp at the back of the barrel. Mel watched the motorcyclist reach in his coat and pull on an antique flask before he revved his engine and launched up the ramp into the MurderDrome's wall of death.

At the main tent, Mel found the dressing top, a smaller tent attached at the back, set up as a dressing room. Beyond the guard at the entrance, performers dabbed at their make-up in mirrors and lights. Mel started to explain to the big guard that she was Charlie's daughter, but he waved her through before she could speak. *Had she met him before?* Mel doubted it.

Shortie following, she walked into the dressing room and spotted EK leaning against a tent pole at the end of the chute leading into the big top. The room was filled with sequins and feather boas. Even then, EK stood out.

"Stay," Mel told Shortie, unsure she would, but the dog sat, turning her gaze away, rejected. Mel walked up behind EK, suddenly wary.

The feeling swept over Mel that when EK turned to face her, she'd see Popeye again, his eyes soft and alive, his grin a cockeyed swoosh across his stubbled face.

Sensing Mel's presence, EK shifted her direction. "Melinda!"

Mel looked at the man's angular jaw. She couldn't repress her disappointment — her sadness at Popeye's absence.

EK pulled her into a hug. A line of female acrobats ran out of the big top. They danced past the pair, rolling their eyes in relief as they plopped into waiting chairs.

EK directed Mel's gaze into the big tent, pointing into the rigging at the top.

"Watch."

Through the darkness, three spotlights converged onto a high platform attached to the tent's centerpole. A melody from a lone wood pipe sluiced over the audience as a figure in orange and white stepped to the edge. He held his pose, silencing the crowd, then leapt into the darkness. A gasp rose from the townies — Mel couldn't help holding her breath.

As the man's arms spread out to his sides, his body plummeted head-first toward the one-ring floor below him. Mel recognized the bald black man from earlier in the day. He sank, plummeting past the high wire, then the trapeze, passing each point where he might have changed course. Hollow drums and asian cymbals clanged beneath the shakuhachi melody. Mel felt more than saw his path alter and angle, now halfway through his descent.

Only thirty feet from the ground, he flicked his hands. The instruments rose into a discordant cacophony of sound pumped through the tent. Somewhere in the audience, a woman screamed. Iridescent white cloth shot out from the man's wrists to his knees, snapping in the rush of air. He swooped a sharp arc, bending his path parallel to the floor.

His body passed so close to the sawdust, clouds of it rose in his wake as he shot out over the audience. The crowd screamed, the man buzzing their heads. Climbing higher above the bleachers, arms and legs extended, he flew a wide arc and turned to skim the bleachers again. He descended even nearer the ground before sweeping up over the other side of the tent, the crowd shrieking.

A quarter of the way around the ring, Mel noticed six Asian men pace as one, forward and back in the darkness, hands wrapped around a thick rope.

Each of them wore their own version of an "Asian" costume — tights and robes with thick cloth belts, hair knotted at the top of their heads or shaved completely. They pulled the rope and the flying man rose in the air, soaring until he nearly touched the tent top. As he swung back down, the men rushed forward, letting gravity drop him toward the ground, halting just in time to stop him crashing to the earth.

Not looking at Mel, EK whispered, "It feels like a dream."

"Who is he?" Mel asked.

"Someone I should have been." EK turned and looked at her, his eyes burning against her profile.

The man reached the peak of another arc, then turned. As he flew near the center of the ring, he threw his body back, shoulders first, and landed running on both feet. He twirled once and ran forward, taking off again. *Otherworldly.* Only the rope attached to his back belied the illusion that he might have been born with the gift of flight.

EK spoke, still watching the performance, "Charlie wants you to know he's sorry he pulled you into this."

The way EK spoke, turned away, his tone a formal whisper, Mel felt they were watched. "It's the exposure that's dangerous for me," she said, hushed. "And for him. The rest I can handle." Mel paused. "How bad is it?"

"For Charlie? As dire as is possible. Sounds like it might be the same for you."

"He told you?"

"Yes, but no one overheard. I can imagine your concern — " His voice trailed off.

Still watching the man as he ran again, his feet lifting from the ground, Mel exhaled a sharp snort through her nose.

"Let's walk, EK. I suspect we're safer in plain sight."

Chapter 17

They walked the midway, the dog following. Mel's hand draped the crook of EK's elbow. With his other arm, he swept his cane in arcs and points. He touched it to soft ground every other step, the dog distracted by the sweeping white tip. EK didn't appear to need it to get around. As they walked, he told her Charlie's version of the story.

A rural Saturday night crowd packed the lot. Teenage boys sporting wife-beaters and hoodies crowded the joints, their heads shaved beneath black baseball caps. Clutches of high-haired girls grouped behind them, too clever to put money on the games, but laden with stuffed bears nonetheless.

At the midway's main turn, a caged clown in wet overalls taunted the crowd from a hinged seat, dunk tank beneath him. A "Dunk Bozo" canvas sign flapped above the cage, just out of reach of the splashing water.

His makeup wet and distorted, the clown shouted insults at the crowd, working their anger, drawing them in. "*Hey fatty fatty fatty fatty. Hey fatty,*" he called, mimicking the rhythm of a baseball fan.

He honed in on a farmer, obvious for his jacket accented with a green and gold embroidered deer.

"Hey farm boy, you look like a stupid customer. Yeah you. What's your name? John?"

The farmer laughed self-consciously, chose a ball, lobbed it at the target beside the clown's cage, and started to walk away.

"Hey, John? Mr. Deere?" Bozo's voice lowered, growling melodic and wet, nearly a lover's whisper caught by the waterproof microphone hanging in front of him. "I hear your momma's so stupid, she had to study for the AIDs test."

The farmer's jaw set, the crowd around him laughing at the insult. He picked up another ball and let loose. It sailed from his hand too fast, missing the target.

"Hey John," the clown growled again. "I hate to tell you, Deere, but your momma's so ugly, I had to pay her to put her clothes back on."

The farmer threw another ball, wild. His ears burning red, he shouted at the clown. "You come out here and say that, you son-of-a-bitch." He grabbed two more balls and threw them at the cage.

"Save your breath, John," Bozo said. "You'll need it to blow up your date."

Raging, the farmer threw three more softballs straight at the clown before the agent moved him away from the joint, collecting two dollars for each angry ball thrown.

"Hey, fatso," the clown slurred sideways, close in the microphone. "Come back here, you left your momma tied to the tree."

Mel and EK turned the corner toward the kooch tent. Mel stopped.

Her expression held steady, but surprise rolled through her posture. At first she thought they'd walked the wrong direction before she recognized the north end of the midway. The tent was gone. In its place, yellow police tape surrounded an empty space.

EK nodded. "I've seen. It's like a shadow."

Together, they stared at the ground, feeling what was missing. Worn muddy paths alternated with plush tufts of grass. A mirrored swoosh of mud and packed dirt marked where the entrance had been, a deep rectangle of blue grass denoting the absent stage. Across the midway's central walk, Mel saw the husk of the kooch tent laid out like a deflated stadium, a single centerpole rising from the middle. Elephants surrounded the flattened tarp, their trunks swinging in protest as ride jocks coaxed them to pull the long cables attached to the six-foot center ring surrounding the pole. Blue shouted orders at the ride jocks, who walked the elephants in an expanding circle, away from the tent. The ring hovered around the pole, lifting the canvas like a crimson ghost risen from the midway.

EK pointed with his cane. "That young man, with the tattoos."

"Blue?" Mel asked.

"He said an inspector made them move the tent."

"It's a crime scene," Mel said.

"*Was* a crime scene. Now they've decided it's a public hazard. Blood-borne pathogens, according to the inspector. Blue said he claimed to be worried over barefoot children. These rednecks. The man made them bleach the walls. And look. Here." He pointed his cane at the ground. "They brought torches. Burned the blood from the grass."

They exchanged a look. "Evidence tampering," EK said.

Mel scanned the midway. "Let's keep moving."

Chapter 18

"You think it was the Sheriff?" Mel asked. They pair walked back, past the big top. Mel heard the growl of beasts menacing their trainers. Whipshot cracked through the canvas walls like pistol fire. Intoxicated with danger, the roar of a thousand townies drowned the big cat howls.

"Lewis Evans. You haven't met him, have you? This is hardly his style. Sheriff Lew would rather burn the whole lot. Blue said the man was a 'City Inspector'.

He didn't offer any ID, but Blue didn't put up a fight. I think they have enough trouble already."

Mel thought it through. Evans would be the only person authorized to order the crime scene cleared.

"I walked the tent this afternoon," Mel said. "What I saw would have cleared Charlie."

EK hesitated before speaking. "How?"

"Charlie's capable of more than you think — not just physically. But he couldn't reach around a man six feet tall and slice his throat. The arterial spray on the canvas walls was nearly eye level. Charlie's three foot six if he's anything."

EK nodded.

"Charlie couldn't have drug the man around, either. I saw signs of a ground struggle. It looked like the vic went down — "

"Sarge Cooder."

"Yes. After his throat was cut, someone either dragged him across the tent, or beat him while he crawled. Either way, it's beyond Charlie. Plus, there were two sets of shoe prints."

"What does that mean?"

"Charlie can't wear shoes. He walks on his knees. Uses kneepads. We may call him The Amazing Lobster Boy, but to a jury he's severely handicapped. Physically, he couldn't have done it. Anyway, it's all conjecture now. They've wiped the evidence."

Mel looked back over her shoulder at the scorched ground. Shortie sniffed the burnt grass, whined, then bounded after them.

"I was followed today," Mel said.

EK watched her, silent.

"Before I came here. I drove to the next town. Someone followed me both ways."

"Did you see the car?" EK asked.

"Just headlights."

"Where were you when I called? I heard music in the background," EK said.

"A bar," Mel said. She pulled the shiny blue matchbook from her pocket. "I found it in the tent."

EK's eyes narrowed.

"Do you suspect something?" she asked.

"Ill repute." He leaned back. His fingers wiggled at the tips of his upheld hands, tickling dark intent. "The Social is a strip joint."

"Is that important?" Mel asked, more keen than she intended.

EK paused. "You seem to think so."

"I'm grabbing straws, but yeah, it could be. There's something wrong with the way the meeting went down."

"How so?"

"Charlie's all theatre, you know."

"My brother said."

"Right." Mel paused at the thought. "Then Popeye probably told you it's always showtime with Charlie. These locals come around looking for graft, and Charlie resents it. That's normal. But he gets off on it, too. Gives them more of a show than they come asking for."

"How do you mean?"

"Charlie knows he horrifies the town marks. His deformity. So he makes a big show of his condition, how he can't move, how he struggles, then he shocks them with the power of what he *can* do. One of his tricks is to keep pickled punks in his trailer — rubber models of deformed babies. We call them *bouncers*. He keeps them in big jars, like they're specimen set in formaldehyde. Carnies usually build a *museum show* around them, a tent full of stuffed animals and bouncers in jars. But Charlie uses them as props to shock the townies looking for graft. Talks about how they're family members — *my poor lost sister, dead in the womb* kind of stuff. Then he walks the marks to the kooch tent and gets them laid. He freaks them out, then shows them his power."

"Subtle," EK said.

"Like a crowbar."

"No sarcasm intended, Melinda. It's horrifying, but subtle — a deformed child, an alien fetus. Now mix that with transgressive sex. Pure psychological theatre."

"I don't know that Charlie's thought it through at that level. I never know if he's working off instinct or design."

"You said it, Charlie's capable of more than you think. What does it have to do with The Social?"

"Sarge wasn't the only towny in the tent. The ride jocks saw two men go in. Separately. One in the front, the other from the back."

"Same time?"

"I don't know. But the dead Marine, or someone, called that meeting. Called it in the tent. And Charlie didn't want the women there. That breaks Charlie's pattern. Makes me think it might have been about the women. Then I find this matchbook cover. Anyone could have dropped it, sure, but if it's anything more than one hell of a coincidence, then maybe this whole thing is about the strippers."

"Local competition, wanting to shut Charlie down?" EK said.

"Exactly."

"A set up?"

"Or a payoff gone wrong. Either way, Charlie shows up and finds a dead man."

"Then you find your way to The Social."

"It was a place to start looking."

"A dangerous place," EK nodded. "Did you meet anyone?"

"No one who stood out."

"How would you know if they did?" EK stared at the dog. "Melinda, you're an outsider in Cuthbert, like me on this show. The Mermaid Parade has secrets I don't even know are secret. And there's people on this show who know those secrets, but they pretend like they don't. Even to themselves."

"And?"

"Cuthbert's just this show. Too much is hidden. And there's no way for an outsider to know whether they've stumbled on a secret or a disavowal. Who'd you talk to at The Social?"

"Staff. Some dancers."

"Assume some of them know you — "

"How?" Mel asked.

"Your town has been in the local papers."

"Because of your brother's murder — "

"Yes." EK looked offended. He gave an odd smile. "You say it like I might have forgotten."

"Sorry."

"But you're right. We're from Cuthbert — Popeye and I. We introduced Charlie to this town, and we brought the city fathers to his winterquarter parties."

"I don't remember them," Mel said.

"You were too young." He stopped, looking off. "But later, when Popeye was murdered, they splashed it across the local paper. People remember him. And when they think about his death, they associate it with Gibtown and the carnies. Believe me, they know. And you and Charlie are guilty by association."

"I can handle myself. And I've got protection." She leaned down and pet Shortie.

"I'm afraid you're going to need more than an old dog." Shortie watched him, unoffended. A silence hung in the moment. "Do you still have Popeye's letter?"

"Yes. Did you read it?" Mel asked.

"I didn't need to."

They stopped walking, watching one another, each waiting in the silence. Mel went first. "I'm not here for my father. I'm here for Charlie. And if Charlie were in jail in Timbuktu, I'd be there instead."

"But you'd have come here eventually."

"Eventually, yes. Popeye told me to start here. To start by asking you."

"That man in jail for murder, in my opinion *that's* your father."

Mel flashed anger. "Don't fuck with me, EK."

"Yes, well," EK said. "You're in danger here. And Charlie's in jail. I think you should stay with me, back at the house. I have a beautiful antebellum home, just outside of town. And it would be graced by your presence. Come on, we'll swing by your motel for your things."

"Thanks, but I think I'll stay put."

Their eyes met. Mel could feel the prosecutor in EK, trying to read her.

"Suit yourself," EK said. "But I've said it — *you're in danger.* The house isn't going anywhere. It'll still be there when you change your mind." He leaned over, pet the dog and walked away.

Chapter 19

The four men made a loose circle at the foot of the embalming table, trying to look at anything in the room other than Sarge Cooder's body. Hopkins Funeral Home doubled as the morgue. The funeral home's stark white cellar held an odd mix of bleach clean metal instruments and valueless antique furniture worn and frayed around the edges. Everything stank of embalming fluid and decay — that's how Milo Skinner put it to himself, but he wasn't for sure about *decay*. He knew that smell, or something like it from dressing deer. That moment after you got one strung up by the hind legs, blood dripping from its nostrils.

The stench that rose from the entrails when you split her belly, steam pouring with the reek and blood and yellow mucous or whatever it was. That's what the room smelled like, that yellow mucous.

It embarrassed Milo to think that one day some sand doctor named Ravi or Bishnu would split him open after he'd died — probably at home in his bed or sitting at his desk in the little office he'd built out back of the mansion — and then he'd stink like old Cooder; like him and all the others that got laid out on that steel table with the little gutters running down each side, dripping blood in a bucket on the floor.

The other men started to argue and weep, claustrophobic from the smell and the cramped cellar, lined with thick hollow needles and stainless steel hooks.

"I don't see why we're meeting here." Max Marshall — the son-of-a-bitch was always complaining about something. Milo didn't blame him. The good Lord hadn't give him more than about five foot of height. Just to add to the insult, he'd planted Max on a dirt farm with an asshole for an old man — the kind that made his boy drive a tractor to high school every day, saying it'd help him build character.

Max was chewing on Dave Fields' ear, getting in the man's face without standing anywhere near him. Milo didn't think much of Dave, but Max hated him. For going on twenty years, Dave had been under the impression he was a rock star, just because his old man had died and left him the newspaper and the radio station. And since Dave believed it, so did every decent piece of ass in Cuthbert. All of it'd be water off a duck's butt if Dave didn't have a foot-and-a-half on Max. And if he wasn't fucking Max's ex-wife.

"Why call a meeting in a funeral home?" Max wasn't letting it go.

"Because we're in charge, and he's our friend," Dave said. "It's *what we'd do*. Check things out down at the morgue."

"The *morgue*. It's a funeral home — "

"Where you think we should be, then? The Social? Dumb fucker."

"You can't talk like that with Cooder laid out." Now Max barked in Dave's face. "Say it again and I'll — "

"Shut up, both of you," Milo hissed. "Shut up." He had to stop them — to get this mess under control.

He dug in his leather satchel for his flask and lifted it to his nose, hoping the smell of bourbon would relieve him for just a moment. Instead it mixed with the room's festering sweet air, bringing on a nausea that made him tired and woozy.

"To Cooder." Milo pulled on the flask before he passed it, wishing for something cheaper, something to bite the back of his throat and dampen the rebellion in his gut.

The men took turns at the flask. No one spoke more than a mumbled toast. The eldest man, Willy O., sat in the corner, weeping. Dave and Max waited for Milo's lead — they always did when Dylan wasn't around. Like a clutch of turkeys. Together, if you counted in Dylan and poor old Cooder, there wasn't one bit of Cuthbert County they didn't have their teeth in, but sometimes they were the dumbest sons-of-bitches Milo ever saw. How he'd kept their company almost fifty years, he didn't pretend to understand.

Willy O. leaned over in his chair, plugged one nostril with the print of his thumb and blew snot on the floor beside him. He swiped his nose with the inside of his wrist, snorting. Still crying, he asked, "You think he's going to come for us, next?"

"Of course he's coming," Max said. "What would you do? Middle of the night I sent someone to kill you?"

"Will you *please* shut the fuck up?" Milo said. "Sweet Jesus, he is *not* coming for us."

"How do you know?"

"Because — " Milo hesitated. He didn't know. "Because what's he going to do after that? Where's he going to go? Us here, we're it. Us and Cooder and Dylan. We *are* Cuthbert. He going to come kill us all in our beds, then disappear up to Atlanta and start a new whorehouse? Start fighting nigger wars over street corners? He ain't got no choice."

"But he killed Cooder — "

"Well no shit. So would you if you thought you was about to die. Just because he slit Cooder's throat don't mean he's going to come after all of us. Cooder went to do some killing and must of fucked it up. So Dylan done some killing instead. Now it's over. We're all even. Dylan ain't coming for us, and we ain't going for him. Killing's done. That make sense to y'all?"

Milo waited for an answer. The others were silent.

"Well does it? Does he even know we done it? Cooder could have decided to kill him all by his self. Dylan don't even know why — if he knew why, we wouldn't have had to do it, would we? If he don't know why, he ain't going to know who."

"What about the carnies?" Dave asked.

Milo took the flask passed back to him, hitting it again. "What about them? I thought that was the plan. Cooder kills Dylan, and the Lobster Boy gets done for it."

Willy O. tried to speak through his sobs. "We didn't plan on Cooder dying —"

"No, goddamn it, we *did not* plan on Cooder dying, but he's dead. And we'll figure out about Dylan. But the rest of it — it's what we planned. Isn't it?"

"Just the part about the freak. And he don't really matter," Max said.

Milo spun a frustrated half circle, fists coiled, knees bent. "That was half the plan, and at least that half got done. If that ain't the plan, say it. Right now. If one of y'all's changed his mind, he goddamned better say it."

The men mumbled again, closer to assent, until Willy O., no longer crying, spoke up. "That's the way it is, Milo. That's the plan."

"Well all right then, that's the plan. Dylan can wait, but for now, there's no more killing. Lobster Boy's going to prison. And every last one of us is staying the fucking course."

Chapter 20

Mel sat in the orange and brown armchair staring at the motel's green-water pool through the room's one window. She'd driven an hour across the Alabama border until she found the empty motel north of Eufala. In the time she'd paid attention, only a handful of cars had passed the winking motel sign.

Stripped to shorts and a t-shirt, she drank from a long neck, empties soldiering the table beside her. The dog was in the room with her, but unsettled. Shortie would sit at Mel's feet, then stand and walk the room before returning to her side, curling at a different angle.

It pissed her off, EK thinking it was his to tell her how she should think about her father. She loved Charlie. More than you could say for most step-children. But William and Christina Barry were her real parents, even if both had been gone twenty-five years.

By every reckoning Mel had heard, her mother died of natural causes. Mel didn't know if she had always been obese, but she remembered watching her father in the trailer, pouring bags of sugar into giant Ball jars — three each day — topping them with water from a hose attached to the trailer's tiny sink. Her daddy called it *professional training*.

Mel remembered the last time she had seen her mother try to stand, maybe two years before she died.

Her father had bought them a new trailer — a surprise for her mother. Mel and her daddy had to help the woman mount the trailer's single fold-out step and make her way to the big bed stretching wall-to-wall in the trailer's scaled down living room. Her father had cut a panel out of one of the walls, reworking it to flip out like an awning. He built a step-up walkway the length of the trailer, made to run beside the open wall space.

When they went on the road that year, Mel sat for hours watching townies ogle her mother in the shade of the awning's shelter. Sneezing at the cheap powder her mother used to cover the odor trapped between the folds of her skin.

Mel didn't understand why her mother went along with it. It felt like the woman spent the last few years of her life imprisoned.

Mel thought her father had worked during winterquarter, but she wasn't certain. He disappeared during the day, so he must have.

Long days in the trailer, alone with her mother, Mel took care of Christina Barry — bathing her and tending her needs. Together, they'd created a routine. Every morning, Mel helped her mother roll into a fetal mound. Prostrate across the sheets, waves of her flaccid skin spilled over the side of the bed like the creeping flow of congealing flesh. Mel gathered the rolls of fat and skin, pushing them over her mother's frame, trying to make them fall on the opposite side of the bed.

With a bucket and sponge, Mel wiped and massaged her mother's back, beneath her arms, between her legs and buttocks.

She checked for bed sores and irritations between the folds.

Mel rolled the fitted sheet up to her mother's body. With rubbing alcohol as an antiseptic, she wiped down one half of the plastic sheet covering the mattress, spread a new fitted sheet and helped her mother roll onto her back again. Mel would pull her mother back toward her, the woman flailing, trying to help Mel roll her onto her other side so Mel could bathe her breasts and belly.

Aware of the burden on the girl, her mother tried to help make light of the work, telling Mel yo-momma-so-fat jokes. Mel never knew whether she heard them on television or spent her long days making up new ones, but the woman told her a new joke every day.

Mel hated it.

The smell of her mother's body reminded Mel of the hot fat and sugar pumping out of the carnival lot cook wagon. After chores, Mel took long walks. Tearing herself away from the world, Mel trekked to a creek running through the woods behind their trailer park down to the Alafia River. Mel would gather clean leaves to protect her trousers, then kneel down and stick her middle finger down her throat. Like she'd seen her father do after too much booze. Nights she lay awake in her tiny room at the back of the trailer, dreading the morning.

Mel did everything for her mother but bring food — she refused without understanding why, leaving meals to her father. During the long hours of her mother's feedings, Mel fled to the back of the trailer, reading in her bunk, writing in her diaries.

She wished she still had those diaries, or some other record of her family's life together.

94

She remembered so little about her father. The sugar water. Drinking beer outside the trailer.

Watching his taillights from her bedroom window the last time he drove away.

Mel drained the last beer bottle, watching the dog pace the room. "You want out?" She dropped her feet from the chair, slipped into the plimsolls resting on the dirty green carpet, and opened the door. Shortie wouldn't leave the room. The dog stuck her head through the door, paws behind the threshold, then slow-walked a circle back into the motel room. Mel tried again, giving her rump a gentle push, but the dog pivoted on her hand and walked another circle. Mel gave up. She dug in her purse for change then stepped through the door, closing it behind her.

The sky was a void, starless, the moon invisible behind a bank of cloud, wind calling over the field across the highway. Mel scanned the parking lot. The Interceptor sat parked, a lone horse tethered in the night. Green light hummed around the fluorescent-trimmed sidewalk leading from empty room to empty room. Mel counted her change as she walked toward the Coke machine refrigerating at the end of the pavement.

Cracks split the machine's big plastic front, the light behind it flickering, desperate, trying to ignite. An ice machine chugged beside it, spewing heat. Between them, a rusting red box held a fire extinguisher behind glass.

A woman stepped out of the ice machine's shadow. Mel looked up from her fistful of change and stopped. The woman didn't move either.

She stared at Mel, dazed. Heavy eyes pressed dark circles into her wan skin.

She wore jeans and a halter, a yellow scarf wrapped around her neck, incongruous in the July heat. She tried to speak, but her pupils slid to the outer corners of her eyes, her jaw an angular projection. She managed *Hiya*.

"Hi," Mel answered.

The woman spun a clumsy circle, then came back to face Mel without looking at her. A smile crossed her lips. She pointed at Mel's chest with a drooping hand. "You're her, ain't you?"

"Her who?" Mel asked. "Where's your car? Are you staying here?"

The woman shook her head. Her hands clasped one another, angled and folding like an embarrassed child's. "You're her. He said you'd come."

Her jaw gurned beneath her huge pupils. She looked too spangled to be dangerous, but whoever brought her might be a different story. Mel checked over her shoulder, then backed away from the machine, moving toward the walk's edge. "*Who* said?"

"Don't go," the woman whined. "I need to talk." She looked over her own shoulder, anticipating. "Before he gets here."

Mel edged farther away, remembering EK's warning. "*He* who? The man who said I was coming?"

"No — " Fear crossed the woman's eyes. She stopped talking, looking past Mel. Following her gaze, a flood of light hit Mel's eyes from across the road, blinding her. She heard a big engine's four-barrel roar. A car tore onto the parking lot. Mel thought of the dog, her Airweight, the OTs-38 with five silent bullets in the loading clip — all useless in the room.

The car screamed her direction.

She needed a weapon. Down the walk, deep and violent, Shortie growled and barked through the door. Mel turned, ready to run. The woman shouted. "It wasn't him. It was *Billy*." The woman's voice was sing-song. "It was your daddy."

Whipping rocks, the car slid into a stopped turn in front of them. The passenger door of the black sixties Lincoln swung open. The woman ran for the car.

Mel leapt straight up, kicking out at the fire extinguisher with her left foot. Glass shattered around her heel. She leaned forward against the red canister and gripped it. With a single motion she pushed herself off the wall, turning mid-step. As the Lincoln's door closed, Mel ran toward the car.

On her fourth step, she leapt, swinging the extinguisher up over her right shoulder. She landed on the hood and caught the top edge in her left hand, bringing the red metal canister down into the windshield. Mel pulled back and stabbed again. The blunt metal bottom left spider webs across the cracked windshield. She cocked the extinguisher for a third blow, but the car launched, throwing her off balance. Reaching for the base of the old car's antenna, trying to regain her footing, she lost the canister. Mel righted herself and snapped the antenna. She whipped it down through the open window, lashing the driver's face. The car lurched right. Mel flew sideways off the hood. She pushed off at the last moment, taking control of her fall. Midair, she tucked her shoulder down and drifted forward into a flip. Barely landing on her feet, she rolled out across the sharp gravel lot.

Rocks showered her from the car's spinning wheels. Crouching, she heard shouts as the Lincoln tore onto the highway, the woman's face pressed against her window, laughing at Mel as they drove away.

Chapter 21

Dylan pushed Stella tumbling across the funeral home parking lot. She laughed and kicked her legs forward, catching herself. She took a deep breath, smiled with eyes wide, then fell back into him, pressing her nose into his neck.

"I did good?" she asked.

"You're a star, baby. A bright, shining fucking star." He smacked her ass. "Now get off me." He pushed her away again, his voice a whisper. "I need to conduct some business with *these* motherfuckers."

At the back door, Dylan leaned into her ear and whispered — *no offense* — before he pushed her down the stairs, tumbling into the embalming room. At the stairs' turn, she thudded against the stairwell, catching her fall. Startled, the men in the basement jerked their heads toward her.

"Gentlemen, you know Stella." Dylan descended into the room. He took the last step and flicked his knife open with one hand, holding it with two fingers over his head. "Cooder cooder cooder." The men parted as he walked toward Cooder's body.

"Cooder cooder cooder."

Dylan leaned one arm down on the table, elbow to wrist, the knife in the other hand. He raked the blade's edge across Cooder's face. In the silence, stubble bristled against steel, the sound metallic and dull. "You look uptight, Cooder." Dylan whispered into the dead man's ear. "A little tense." He raked the knife again. Scabbed blood pinged the walls. Dylan turned to the men, laughing.

"Cooder's a bit tight, isn't it boys?" He slapped Max's arm. The short man almost flinched. "Tight Cooder," Dylan shouted, braying. Milo smiled, nervous, and laughed with him. Tension rolled around the room.

Dylan turned fast and plunged the knife into one of Cooder's eye sockets. Stabbing through the eyeball, he set the blade deep in Cooder's brain. The men froze. "That's what you get when you fuck with a tight Cooder," he laughed again. Dylan worked the knife in a slow circle, slicing brain until he wrenched it free. Milo worried the eyeball might come with it.

Stella whimpered and moved to the corner of the basement.

"Now which one of you fucked with me?" He paced around the table, grabbing Cooder's body with heavy smacks, shaking first a heavy arm then a leg. "Which one?"

The men backed away. "Don't go anywhere. Don't go." Dylan spoke quiet now, affecting friendliness.

He walked up to Milo. "Tell me who fucked me, *Miles*. It's okay, I like a good fuck. Or should I tell you? Tell you who fucked old Dylan? This one here." He lifted the knife and plunged it into Cooder's chest. "This one fucked with Dylan. This one fucked with Dylan."

He stabbed Cooder so many times, Milo lost count. Yellow liquid oozed from the body's new wounds. The men covered their mouths and backed away, pushing down bile.

"This is one hell of a situation, isn't it?" Dylan said.

Willy O. wretched. Dylan looked offended. "Here, here, take that shit over in the corner with the cunt. Hey, cunt," he shouted at Stella. She flinched at his voice. "Calm this man. Suck his prick or something." He pushed the offender into her and turned back to the men. "Now we got another problem — another *issue* on the table."

He pulled the knife from the body and folded it, wet.

"I got a little town and everything's quiet." He turned and punched Cooder's body. Liquid gushed with the blow. "It don't need to fucking change."

Willy O. threw up.

Dylan pulled a handkerchief from his back pocket and patted at the blood and embalming fluid dripping from his hands. He snapped the cloth in the air, then wiped Willy O.'s face before giving him the handkerchief. Dylan turned back to the others again, his voice calm. He held his hands out in front of him, palms up.

"Y'all sent Cooder to kill me — "

Milo blinked, preparing to lie. "It wasn't like that — "

"Jesus, someone take the credit. You set me up good. Why deny it? You think of this one, Willy?"

Willy O.'s lids pulled back around his eyes, fear crisscrossing the whites surrounding his irises.

"I didn't think so — too much initiative." Dylan turned to Milo. He couldn't help himself — Milo took a step backward. "Sent me on a drop with the carnies, sent in Cooder to kill me first, blamed it on the Lobster Boy. Sweet. Can't have any loose cannons when you're going for the prize, can you *Miles*?"

"Dylan — "

"Tell me Cooder didn't volunteer. Go on, *Mi-low*," Dylan tasted the man's name, bouncing each syllable. "Tell me how you had to talk Cooder into it — "

"No one — "

"You can't, can you? That rat-fuck son-of-a-bitch. He didn't need convincing. Well, if old Cooder offered to fuck me, old Cooder must have wanted to die." Dylan gestured at the body. "I try to accommodate. Now I got something *I* want. And I'm going to tell y'all what happens next."

He held up a hand, pinched his thumb and middle finger together. Dylan smiled again. Dave and Max tried to smile with him. "You still get to send Lobster Boy to prison. Our prison. For his own safety. With medical facilities. Protected from the other inmates."

Milo nodded.

"Straight out of jail and straight into prison, for killing old Cooder here. You hear me Milo?"

"I hear you."

Dylan slapped the dead man's leg. "Good. You get it done. Then we'll move on to the rest."

Chapter 22

Shortie growled, clawing at the car window, shocking Mel awake. Adrenalin rushing, she lay across the front seat of the Interceptor, not moving. Dew covered the windows, the night obscured beyond them. Shortie tried to launch at the passenger-side window. Her paws scrabbled across Mel's body. Shortie's dripping muzzle hovered over her face. Mel felt the blunt end of a fist pound the car window. Shortie barked twice, sharp, then growled from her chest.

Through the window, Mel could just make out Jalinda, the girl's blonde dreads backlit by the moon. Carnival lights starred through the window's mist. The sounds of midnight bally talkers and the midway sound systems thudded against the Interceptor's sealed windows.

Shortie snapped at Jalinda's outline. The girl leapt back.

Mel had abandoned her motel. She'd almost made it back to her room before the owner ran onto the parking lot, his shotgun pointing at the sky.

"You know them people?" he'd shouted, accusing.

"I do now," Mel said. She'd grimaced at her bare legs, brushing away dirt and gravel. "You're a little late to the party."

"We don't have no partying at this motel." The man's eyes traced Mel's outline. "And no dogs. You going to have to pay for that, you know."

"Pay for what?"

"Fire extinguisher. Cost me fifty dollars. Only one I got."

Mel looked the man in the eye. "Well, Mr. — "

"Baldwin."

"I'll give you a hundred."

"No need to get uppity — "

"That's fifty for the fire extinguisher and twenty-five for the dog. That sound fair?"

The man had lowered the barrel of the gun and pointed it at the ground.

"What's the other twenty-five for?"

"For you to stand there with that shotgun while I crawl under my car."

The man had agreed, turning nervously, eyes on the road. Mel scooted under the Interceptor on her back. She found a GPS tracker attached to the gas tank.

She crawled back out and held the tracker up for the man to see. Baldwin had fetched tools from his garage. He met her back in the motel office, watching while she disassembled the rig on a table in the tiny, wood-paneled check-in lobby.

The device was an off-the-shelf espionage unit. The transmitter looked like a matte black walkie-talkie with a battery pack the size of a Maglite — more of a hobbled together corporate rig than a sealed military unit.

She'd disabled the battery and dropped the kit in her backpack.

Before she left, Mel tore the top sheet from the guest register, wiping any record of her stay. She handed the vexed man an extra fifty dollars. She'd driven the hour-long ride back to the carnival lot, rolling the scene in her mind. As much as she feared company, she needed sleep, and that wouldn't happen unless she was relatively safe. She'd parked behind Charlie's office trailer.

Now Jalinda's voice muffled through the window. "*Wake up, Mel. What you doing out here?*" She pounded again.

Mel jackknifed her body in a reach for the door handle, holding Shortie back as she popped it open.

Jalinda stuck her head in the car. "You awake, Mel?"

"What do you think?"

Shortie calmed at the sight of the girl, licking Jalinda's face. Wagging for forgiveness, her tail slapped Mel's cheek.

"What you doing here? I thought you had a hotel."

Mel rubbed her eyes. "It's overrated."

"Christ, girl. Get your ass in here. We done got one dead body — "

Chapter 23

Jalinda dug between her breasts, fishing for Charlie's trailer key. Double-wide, the long aluminum box trailer was a drop-deck lowboy conversion. Big panels had been cut from the trailer walls, replaced by double glazed smoked plexiglas and a doorway as wide as the trailer itself. Mel climbed the metal stairway and stepped into Charlie's den.

Wood paneling and dark mahogany shrouded an L-shaped black leather couch. Only the velvet Wilton carpet and the long rows of jars lining the walls told her she hadn't stumbled into the salon of a new-money yacht.

Halogens up-lit a pair of circus posters, framed on the wall. Mel had seen them before. On the left, Charlie's father glared wildly from a lithographed poster advertising the Al G. Barnes Circus sideshow. Shock-headed and hovering above a hand-lettered *Amazing Lobster Man* logo, an idealized drawing of the elder Koontz waved four claws at the viewer, his wild hair an electric halo around an unsettling expression.

The second poster featured Charlie's mother, *The Woman Who Married a Monster*. Raphaela Koontz smiled beatifically from the center of the frame, cuddling her claw-laden infant — *The Amazing Lobster Boy*. Charlie's father hovered in the background, an omen ignored.

Between the posters, backlit shelves held rows of pickled punks, the outer edges of their silhouettes glowing against their dense cores.

The largest of the glass vials suspended a two-headed calf in amber-tinted liquid. The fetus' eyes lay closed, the expressions on its slowly balding faces somewhere between suffering and sleep. The smaller jars to each side held babies. Mel was certain they were real. Too degraded for bouncers, bits of real skin flecked away from their fleshy bodies, waving like amphibious gills with each vibration of the trailer.

The jar to the right held a three-legged girl, her odd limb thrusting from the top of one normal thigh. What looked like a bulbous extra stomach ballooned from her side. The other glass vial preserved a human frog baby, its heart-shaped skull split down the center. The crest of the forehead reached down into the fetus' nose cavity, a void in the middle of its face.

Mel dropped her backpack in front of the shelves and fell into the couch. Jalinda shivered, quick-walking away from the jars toward a brass-plated wet bar dividing the den from Charlie's office. Mel looked around for Shortie, the dog already curled on its bed by the door.

"Let me fix you a drink," Jalinda called.

Mel watched her move around Charlie's display. "You look like you're at home."

"I been here a little," Jalinda said. She clinked ice into two short glasses.

Mel sank into the leather cushions around her, feeling her spine ease out of its car-seat-shaped curve. Jalinda handed her a silvered glass. Mel watched the woman's mood vibrate.

"Did you and that man have some trouble?" Jalinda asked.

Mel blinked for a moment, not understanding who Jalinda meant. "*EK?* No. He's fine." She sipped at her glass. Single malt — something soft and northern.

"I think he's strange," Jalinda said.

Mel raised her eyebrows. "Like we're not?"

"I mean for a towny. Walking around with that cane, like he's all Queen Somebody."

"I imagine it takes a lot of attitude for him to get by in this town."

"I imagine," Jalinda said. "Don't trust him though."

"I don't think we have much choice. He offered me his place." Mel sipped her drink again. "Probably might have listened to him."

"You didn't like your motel?"

Mel didn't answer.

Jalinda tried to sound casual. "I don't think Charlie would mind you staying here, if you want."

Mel's eyebrows rose. It had come out wrong, as though Jalinda were granting permission. "You don't think so?"

"He's talked about you time to time."

"Talked how?" Mel asked.

"Real nice. He's always bigging you up, saying *Mel done this* and *Mel done that. You should see Mel —* "

"He knows what I've been doing?"

"Sometimes. I guess." Jalinda's voice drifted off.

Mel knit her eyebrows together. The room's carpet muffled the silence between the women. The lot was silent, the woods around it a buffer against the distant interstate's traffic.

"He said you was some kind of badass in the military. Says you was good at it."

Mel grimaced. "It was a little different than how he describes it."

They went quiet again, the room a vacuum.

"We all just hoping you come to help."

"Yeah, well I'm trying," Mel said.

"You talked to anyone yet? Like, interviewed people and all? That's what you do, ain't it?"

"Sometimes." Mel sat up on her elbows. "You uncomfortable with my work?"

"No, I wasn't saying that."

"You got a problem with me?"

"I just worry about Charlie. Maybe you should go see him — "

Mel shot the girl a look.

"Except you can't." Jalinda stared at her feet.

"That's right, Jalinda. I can't."

Hurt crossed the girl's face.

"Look — " Mel started to say more, then stopped, exasperated.

"If you can't ask Charlie what happened, what about Monk?"

The girl brightened at her own thought. "He see everything out on that lot. Charlie says he's like a walking life support system for a pair of eyes."

Mel chuckled under her breath. "Who's Monk?"

"I don't know his name. But he *is* a monk — he used to be — got his own troupe. They call them *The Shallying Monks*."

"Shaolin?"

"That's it. *Shaolin Monks*." She nodded, excited now. "Charlie say some of them's for real. Monk be that flying man."

Mel sat up again. "Do you think he saw the murder?"

"I don't know. He wanted to go to that meeting — Charlie wouldn't let him. But Monk, he was all acting like he ain't going, then he followed Charlie anyway. Around behind the rides, where Charlie wouldn't see him. But by the time he got there, police was already coming down the lot."

"You saw that? Monk following Charlie?"

"Some. Saw him go around behind some tent joints, too. And I could tell what he was trying to do — following Charlie. But then it was all like he disappeared or something. Charlie says they do that."

"What?"

"Disappear. Them monks. Like them invisible movie ninjas."

Mel lay back down. "I think he's pulling your leg, Jalinda."

Silence — the vacuum again. Mel could hear her head ringing. She stared out the window.

Jalinda watched her, wary. "You all right?" she asked.

Mel didn't turn back to her. "Not really."

"It can get complicated, when it's your parents. *I* know." Jalinda watched the ice cubes melt in her glass. "All kind of complicated."

Mel nodded, frowning out the window.

Jalinda got up and walked toward Charlie's bedroom, giving up. "I'm going to bed. You should talk to Monk anyhow. That man, he see everything."

Chapter 24

Mel turned off the county highway down the long dirt lane leading to EK's house. Giant magnolia lined both sides of the drive — Mel imagined them planted early in another century. She'd set her car radio on the local station — a lone newscaster, nasal and resonant, read copy with the artificial urgency of AM. Local crime suspects were young, drunk and dark-skinned. Victims aged and undeserving. Accidents involved motorcycles on dark country bends. The newscast ended without mention of Sarge Cooder's murder. When the newsman segued to a Red Neckerson rerun, Mel flicked the station off. Shortie sat beside her in the front seat.

At the end of the road, she spotted EK sitting at an easel on the antebellum mansion's crumbling wraparound porch. He rose as she walked from the car to the steps, brown magnolia leaves and pecan shells crunching beneath her heels. Kudzu shrouded the trees around the old house, their sweet blossom smell pulling her across the lawn. Mel noticed brown tufts from the year before blown into the corners of EK's porch, the wood slat floor a patchwork of grey paint, dust and dry crumbling weed.

A sweating pitcher and glass, both filled with crushed ice and dusky liquid, sat next to a palette and brushes on the wicker table beside EK. The scent of oils and turpentine mixed with the sweet, wet breeze circling the house. He rose to greet her. "*A pretty woman is a welcome guest.*"

EK smiled and stepped forward to hug her. Mel stole a look over his shoulder at the easel. Pulled by gravity, paint seemed to flow down EK's canvas, obscuring a central figure she couldn't make out. Beyond the easel, slabs of raw meat draped over a kitchen stool covered in wax paper, flies buzzing the meat's glistening fat.

"Come," EK said. "Let's find you a glass."

Mel waited in the big dining hall. An old oak table big enough to seat a dozen guests took up most of the room. Covered in dust, eleven of the seats looked like they hadn't been moved in months. Newspapers and leftovers from a morning breakfast scattered in front of the twelfth chair. A fifties Hammond organ sat in the corner, its keys yellowed, the gold weave across its speaker torn and unravelled. Glass in hand, EK returned from the kitchen and stepped into the dark room.

Through half-opened sliding oak doors, Mel watched Shortie sniff at a dog lying motionless in the living room corner.

Its brown and white coat led from its tail to a split neck, where the creature became a three-headed chimera. The center head's mouth hung open, its tongue lolling between lower fangs. The dry flesh of its lips emphasized the stuffed monstrosity's lifelessness.

Mel turned to stare at the odd man. Shortie walked up beside her.

Almost imperceptibly, EK raised his eyebrows and shrugged. "I make art."

"From dead animals?"

"None that I kill myself. I have an arrangement with a medical school in Atlanta." EK smiled and stared into the distance. "That dog almost saw me thrown out of Yale."

"I can't imagine how."

"You say that as I joke, but I'll bet you can't," EK said. "My time in New Haven — let's just say I was a bit *much* for the Patrician temperament. But Yale Art was very forward thinking. They never objected to my work. But one night I'm cruising the local bars, and who do I meet but one of my law professors. An older man, of course. No surprise. A couple drinks, a little talk, and I walk the man back to my place."

EK reminded Mel of Popeye, amused at himself, settling into his story.

"I lived in a fourth floor walkup — a loft over Wooster Square. And when I say an older man, I mean an *older* man. By the time we climbed those stairs, that man was sweating. Red in the face. All I could think was to get that man a glass of water. I ran into my studio — it was dark — and without thinking I just flipped on the lights. And right there, he fell over, dead from a heart attack."

EK looked at the stuffed animal. "It was the dog. Frightened that poor man to death." EK gave Mel a wicked grin.

"I'm not surprised." Mel smiled back.

"Well he certainly was. Yale suggested I might take a little *sabbatical* after, in the interest of discretion. And the widow's feelings. So I called Popeye and off I went."

"Back to Cuthbert?"

"No. Apalachicola, Florida. The most beautiful little fishing village. Popeye was Chief of Police at the time. He'd long since left this sad place."

"Was this your parents home?" Mel asked.

"It was. I suppose it still *is*." EK gave her a wistful smile. He pulled a framed photograph from a drawer, handing it to Mel. "The dead can be so much more powerful than the living. It is a question of ghosts."

Mel looked at the photograph — a man and woman stood on the porch of a shotgun shack. Half a dozen black children huddled between the pair, some without shoes. Together they held a carved wood sign — *Roosevelt School for Children.*

Mel put her hand over her mouth, surprised. "Is that Eleanor Roosevelt?"

"And Papa. He was Sheriff of Cuthbert County. One of the first civil rights lawmen in the state — that's not an official title, of course. It's just what he did. He and Mrs. Roosevelt built the first migratory labor camp in Georgia. Food and housing. Education for the children — black, white, Mexican. Whoever needed a home and was willing to work."

Mel met the eyes of the man staring out from the grainy photo. He wore a Sam Browne belt, its thin shoulder strap crossing the loaded Bandolier he wore over the opposite shoulder, making an odd X over his heart. Hanging from his hip belt, he wore a Colt — Mel recognized the grip. A bullwhip hung from the other side.

"He looks fierce," Mel said. "That whip."

"He had to be. The tobacco farmers here — they weren't taking reform lightly. Those weapons were warnings to the Ku Klux Klan."

"Is that — "

"Then you know — "

"Popeye told me. He didn't say who."

"The Klan lynched my parents." EK cleared his throat. "We never had proof. The deputy — he made Sheriff one day later — that bastard declared it double-suicide, but — "

"I'm sorry."

"Don't be," EK said. "I'm sure my father died the way he lived — defying the sons-of-bitches."

"It's a terrible thing, losing both your parents at the same time."

"If anyone understands, Mel, I know it is you." The moment hung thick in the air. Mel heard a fly buzz the half-eaten sausages on the dining table. "Come. We have more important things to worry about."

Chapter 25

"At this motel," EK said. "Who was the girl?"

"I thought you'd know."

"I might." He walked around Mel. A hovering arm steered her back toward the porch, Shortie following. "Did you see the driver?"

"Not enough for an ID. I whipped his face — assuming it was a man — whipped him with his car antenna. Pretty sure I scarred him."

EK smiled and opened the front door for her. "Remind me to not run you down." They sat at the wicker table beside the painting. EK pushed the canvas away. Mel could smell the meat begin to turn.

"Did you know my father?" she asked.

"Melinda, you know the answer." EK leaned back. "I knew both of your parents."

"And how did you meet?"

"Charlie's winterquarters." EK filled her glass. "Is this an interrogation?"

"I need to know. That woman said my father told her I'd come."

EK's eyebrows lifted. Mel couldn't read his expression. "I'm sure she meant Charlie."

"She called him *Billy*. Said his name, specifically. Called him my *daddy*."

"Coincidence. You said yourself she was lubricated."

"Not drunk, EK. *Off her face*, plus we were two hours from Cuthbert — over the state line. It was a challenge. They came to spook me or something. You can see that."

"And what did I tell you? The last time we spoke." He sipped his drink. "Do you think you were followed?"

"I found a tracker on the car."

"Sheriff Lew." EK sat back and folded his fingers across his chest. "He's handy with the electronics. And he's a cop, so it's legal. Supreme Court decision — leave your vehicle outside a private garage, police have the right to plant a tracking device."

"For no reason?"

"If you're a suspect, and you *are* a fugitive, Melinda. I'm surprised they don't force you into custody."

"Why is my father in Cuthbert?"

EK sipped his drink, meeting her stare over the edge of his glass. "You have no idea if that is true."

"Then why would she — "

"Melinda. Please. She was wasted. It's a game. You said it yourself. You're a toy for them. I mean no offense, but you're out of your depth — "

"Really? Try me." Mel gulped her drink. She choked, jerking her palm across her lips, falling into a coughing spasm.

Hard Kentucky Bourbon bit her throat, mint rising up into her nostrils from the back of her mouth.

EK smiled, apologetic. He handed her a napkin. "You expected tea." He moved his chair closer, patting her back until she could breath.

Mel wiped away tears. She sat back, eyes cast at the porch's high ceiling. Mel couldn't keep the thought of his parents from flashing through her mind, wondering where they'd been hung on the wide porch. She let her shoulders fall, sighing. "EK, please. Tell me what you know."

"Almost nothing. But as a lawyer — and Melinda, I have prosecuted many cases like yours — I have to say it again. You are a fugitive. I am not your council, and I can't be. Even if you turn yourself in. Every conversation we have puts me in jeopardy, and worse, can be used against Charlie. Your crime was not an event — it is ongoing. A happening. Every day of desertion adds to the duration of the act."

"EK, we're not talking about me. We're talking about my father — "

"No, we *are* talking about you." He wagged a finger. "And after last night, there is only one thing *to* know. You have been *found out*. The police know you're here. If Sheriff Lew hasn't arrested you, he has a reason that likely involves sticking it to Charlie. And if you plan on staying around, you will likely spend some of that time in custody."

"Are you telling me to surrender?"

"I have to. By law."

"But you won't tell me about my father."

"I haven't seen William Barry. But I've seen Charlie Koontz, and he is the man I'm concerned with. I *will* tell you this — when you do turn yourself in, and you can do it anywhere in the world, Melinda. I suggest you find somewhere offering better treatment than you'll receive from Sheriff Lew."

Chapter 26

Mel searched the big top for Monk. Sunlight filtered through the marquee's red and yellow canvas, soaking the centre ring in a bloody orange glow. Blue and luminous, a spotlight cut through the tent, silver light reflected in a shard from the high wire and buckles above. An old wood tool box hung from a pair of claws hooked around the wire.

Bleachers raked up around her. The top rows grazed the canvas ceiling near the walls. Three other spotlights nodded at the floor, unattended on risers squaring the round tent. Mel turned a half circle. She counted the exits in the empty tent, plus the two chutes leading from the back lot dressing rooms.

A chaotic spiral rose like an assemblage memorial from the center ring. Looming twenty feet over the tent's sawdust floor, a ramp spiraled toward the canvas top, looping through unlit gas hoops, surrounded by sharp razor wire. Soft tennis shoes sat beside a knee-high wood globe at the ramp's base, ready for the next performance.

Spinning a circle in the centre of the spiral, Mel felt a shiver grip the back of her neck. "What can I do for you?" A deep voice behind her. Mel turned around.

The man walked toward her from behind the burning spotlight — at first a silhouette, as the figure came closer Mel could see it was Monk, out of costume in jeans and a loose white t-shirt. He walked a straight line, relaxed, his eyes locked on hers as he took each step. He gave her an easy smile. Mel's pulse flickered. She wanted to step backward as he came close. He stopped two feet away.

"You must be Melinda." He held his hand out.

Mel felt her fingers enclosed in his palm, the pads of his big hands warm.

"Matt Clay," he said. "But you can call me Monk. You here to fly?" He smiled again, held her grip for a moment, then let go.

"Do you — " Mel cocked her head, pulling back in. "Can we talk?"

"Sure. But showtime's in a couple hours. I need to prep the rig. Do you mind talking while I work?"

"I'll tag along," Mel said. "Where to?"

Monk smiled at her again, then pointed to the tool box hanging from the high wire.

Strapped in a carabiner rig, canvas loops wrapped around his ass and buckled in front, he hung from the metal wire stretched between the tent's main poles. Monk pulled himself along the cable, stopping every couple of feet, inspecting. He worked the thick wire with a butane hand torch and hard-wire brush. He'd scrub away dirt and jellied residue before dipping his hands into the bag hanging from his belt, chalking the cable before moving on.

Even at this distance she could feel his wood brown irises when he glanced over at her.

Mel sat on a small deck on the opposite pole. He'd walked her to its base, showing her the rope ladder leading up to the platform.

"I think I'd rather stay down here, if you don't mind."

"*The show must go on*," he'd said. "If you want to talk — "

She'd grabbed the strap of her purse and pushed it up over her head and across her chest. Her jaw set. "You don't make it easy."

"You're Charlie's daughter — I'm sure you can fly."

The ladder was made of two thick ropes held apart by rubber-coated wood dowels every twelve inches. Monk reached out to steady the ladder, but Mel stopped him. "I've got it," she said, then gripped two of the dowels at eye level. She put a tentative foot on the bottom rung. The ladder twisted, throwing her balance. She slipped her forearm through the ropes and hung from an elbow.

Mel could hear Monk almost laugh. "You might try — "

"I've *got* it." Mel had cut him off. She'd dropped from the ladder, assessed it, then twisted it a quarter turn, the dowels pointing straight at her. With an arm and leg on each side, she'd started again.

She scrabbled up the rope hanging backwards, the ladder bent at sharp angles between her hands and feet. At the platform she'd stopped and looked down — the drop was fifty feet, maybe more. She swung her weight around, landing ass first on the small metal deck.

Monk had already climbed the other pole. He slapped his thick palms together, applauding. "You *do* fly."

"Not for a long time."

She'd tried to catch her breath, her legs dangling over the platform's edge.

Monk kept one eye one her while he stepped into his harness. He'd snapped a carabiner to the high wire and swung out, dangling his legs over the center ring.

Mel watched the man work. Meticulous, but not obsessed. Dangling by a carabiner and canvas fifty feet from the ground, surrounded by calm. He had the kind of voice Mel liked to hear from an airline pilot. She reached her arms back and wrapped her wrists around the pole behind her, getting used to the height. "I saw your act last night. You're good."

Monk smiled again, almost blushing. "All thanks to Charlie."

"You been with him long?"

"Not long enough. I have a lot to learn."

Mel smiled sideways. "You don't look like you need to learn anything."

"*Not looking like* and *not needing to* — very different things. Charlie's a capital-S Showman. I just look like one."

"You look more priestly."

He turned toward her, and Mel caught the glint of light. "As I said, *looking like* isn't the same as *being*." He pulled himself back onto the platform, then sat and unbuckled the carabiner. He leaned back.

She shifted on the platform and looked down. "What next?"

He smiled. "Rest is a part of preparation."

Mel shifted again. "You think maybe we could rest on the ground?"

Monk laughed. "I think we could do better. Come on."

Mel watched Monk put his hands on each side of the platform and push himself off. Out in the air his body rolled backward, his legs angled straight above him. He landed on his back in the catch net fifty feet down.

"You expect me to follow? Just like that?" she called.

"Just like that." Monk watched her from the ground. "Time it right. You won't miss. I promise."

Mel took a breath, then heard herself yelp as she pushed her body out into the air, high above the ring.

Chapter 27

Every table in Shun Lee Palace stood empty. Guided by an Asian woman in a worn denim dress, Mel and Monk chose a back corner table without a word. They turned their chairs to keep an eye out the big front window, shoving their motorcycle helmets under their seats. They'd ridden Monk's '79 Honda CB750, now standing guard outside in the parking lot.

The restaurant's name had ambition — Shun Lee occupied a converted gas station at the edge of town, the closest restaurant to the carnival lot. The Asian woman — Mel put her mid-thirties — looked after all of the red plastic-covered tables. As they sat down, Mel felt her stomach churn, the kitchen's hot fat odors riding a wave of MSG and deep-fried egg-dipped batter. The sounds from the kitchen told Mel there might be only one other person in the building.

The waitress brought water, handing them two laminated menus she'd tucked under her arm.

She told them the specials, asked what they would drink — Mel sensed the woman directed the questions to her, her body angled away from Monk.

After she spoke, Monk handed back his menu. The woman accepted it, ignoring him. Monk began speaking another language. His words low and melodic, his voice moved through a string of soft consonants.

The woman turned Monk's direction, her attitude changing as Mel watched. Speaking her language clearly trumped the sin of his blackness. She answered Monk — Mel *thought* she was answering — but the language fell so sing-song on Mel's ears, she couldn't distinguish questions from statements. The waitress gathered both menus and walked back to the kitchen.

"What was that?" Mel asked.

"She's from Sanmenxia. She speaks Jin dialect," Monk said. "But softer."

The waitress appeared again with a paper menu in what looked to Mel like Chinese. After a discrete bow toward Monk, she disappeared again.

"What did you say?" Mel asked.

"I more or less told her she speaks beautiful Mandarin. That she has a sophisticated accent for a country girl. And I said that in a restaurant with such cultured staff, surely they must offer a more authentic menu. Something for her own people."

"In a town this size? I'd think she'd be about it," Mel said.

Monk held up the menu. "Apparently not."

The woman brought green tea — *Xin Yang Mao Jian*, Monk told her. Mel watched while he ordered for them both. He caught Mel staring. Her mouth didn't quite hang open, but she realized she must have looked astonished.

Monk smiled. "What's the matter, Barbie? You never seen a brother speak Mandarin?"

Mel laughed, embarrassed. "I just don't think I've met a monk before."

"We've had this conversation." He smiled through his eyelashes.

"And you keep denying the cloth. Good. You didn't strike me as chaste."

"That would be a challenging position, running with Charlie's tribe."

The waitress brought two bowls of pungent soup filled with strips of meat. Mel felt the ginger rise off the liquid. Over the pork liver soup, Monk explained his time at the temple. The YouTube video. Charlie finding him in the Boston walk-up.

"I went to China to be a warrior priest," he said. "At first, I'd look at the Abbott and see a man who could engage the material world, but also rise above it. Then one day I'm packing up after another tourist show. I looked at him and all I saw was a fat bastard in a Cadillac, yelling into a phone. I left the next week." He shook his head. "If I'd known I was going to spend five years as an underpaid dancer, I'd have gone to New York. At least I'd have had running water."

Mel laughed, touched by his honesty — that he hadn't succumbed to believing his own PR.

"What about family?" Mel asked.

"Not much to tell. Nuns mostly. The odd priest. There's two ways for a black kid to end up in South Boston. One's on a bus. The other's at the Home for Destitute Children. We all called it Destie."

"An orphanage?" Mel wasn't sure she wanted to know. "That must have been — "

"Hey, not everyone can be an orphan." He smiled at her. Mel wanted to smile back, but held it in, a loosening in the corner of her eye. Something wanting to escape.

Monk touched the back of her hand, reassuring her. "I had good people around me. The religion didn't take, but I *did* go for the cloth myself. Even if it was an orange one." He smiled again, his eyes flashing. "Destie's gone now. I've tried a little, but never found a single one of the sisters. Honey, you *know* you can't go home when they tear down your orphanage."

Mel nodded. "So the thing with Charlie — "

"Maybe." Monk explained how Charlie had taken him on, given him a home and taught him what a show was about. "I was so traditional — I tried to do things the Temple way. We put on shows there — exhibitions, more like — but we didn't understand the audience, or each other. Always trying to make them understand us."

"Now you do things the circus way — "

"I do things *my* way, and my way is the Temple way, the circus way, plus the black-orphan-growing-up-in-Southie way. That's what Charlie taught me — when you have people, all you have to do is be like the old folks. But when you're alone, you're unlike anyone in the world. An outlaw. *That's* who I bring to the stage. It's how I become part of the show."

Mel watched the man settle into the topic like a friend he hadn't seen for ages.

"Late in my training at Shao-lin Ssu, the Temple, I would hike up Mount Song to an abandoned courtyard I found. A kind of cobblestone garden.

I'd never seen anything like it. The walls were made from broken stones, no two alike. Each fit perfectly with the ones around it. I thought they'd been carved, one-by-one, each made to fit a particular space. Then after a year I realized the stones weren't carved. They'd been *chosen*. It must have taken decades to build.

"To be part of that, out there," Monk pointed beyond the window to Cuthbert, lying silent in the night. "You have to be a brick. Individual, yes, even handmade, but shaped more like the others than not. You, me, Charlie — we live outside that world. We're broken stones. Find enough of us, fit us in the right place, and you build a home." He paused, slurped his soup and smiled. "Or you can roll solo."

Mel smiled with him, feeling her guard drop along with Monk's. Liking it.

"What about you?" he asked. "You do things like a carny, or like Special Ops?"

"Where makes you say that?"

"You were SpecOps. I can see it in the way you move. And you have some acrobat in you. You wear them both all over your body. That rope ladder. I live with acrobats — I know them. And the kind you served beside, the mercenaries, I've met."

"Where?"

"They used to come to the Temple, thinking we had some ancient Chinese secret."

"And do you?"

"Maybe." Monk smiled. "We were talking about you. Charlie said you've been *with it* your whole life."

"My parents were circus." She paused, unused to speaking about herself. She sighed, yielding to it. "Mom was a sideshow fat lady. Dad was an acrobat, but he had an accident before I was born. I never saw him perform. I don't know if they met before the accident or what, but Dad trained me — low wire, trapeze. Some floor work — teeterboard, acrobatics. My Mom died when I was eight. Dad disappeared. After that, Charlie and a friend of his looked after me."

"Is that the Popeye I keep hearing about?"

"Yeah. We called him that because he had one glass eye. He was like my uncle, but — I don't know. He was my best friend." Mel felt agitated, talking about Popeye. She realized she hadn't for years.

"How'd you end up military?"

"You're assuming."

"Assuming what?"

"The military. *SpecOps*, as you put it. You said those things. Not me."

"I see." Monk nodded, smiling at her.

Mel wasn't sure if he was passing judgement or just refusing to push. She decided to change the conversation. "Jalinda said you followed Charlie. The night of the murder."

"Yes, that was on purpose. I made sure she saw me. I didn't want to walk into the unknown without anyone knowing about it."

"See anything?"

"Too much. And not enough. Halfway there I heard Charlie scream. By the time I got to the back of the tent, that Sheriff was coming in the front."

"And you didn't see anyone else?"

"No. I saw them cuff Charlie — it was horrific."

"And you just walked away?"

"No. *I ran.*" Monk gave her a stern look. "If the police were in the process, there wasn't anything I could do. I'm Southie — I know that."

"But — "

"What would you have done? Rescue Charlie? Kill the Sheriff? This isn't Fallujah. Charlie's whole show is here. All his people. He's not a man who runs."

"True," Mel said.

"Neither am I. Don't make that mistake. But I'm more use to him outside than locked down. So are you."

Chapter 28

Mel had excused herself, hoping to take their tension with her. Returning, she stopped before making it through the restroom door. In her chair, the waitress sat with her back toward Mel. She leaned over the table, her arms turned into themselves, her back heaving a sobbed and silent rhythm. Without moving his eyes, his hand on his knee, Monk lifted one finger.

Mel shifted backward into the toilets, watching the scene through a crack in the door.

Monk comforted the woman, her words pouring out between quiet gasps. After a while she stopped crying. Mel thought she looked more exhausted than relieved. Monk grimaced.

He held the woman's hands between his own. When she retreated through the swinging kitchen door, Monk picked up their helmets and nodded for Mel to follow.

Outside they stood around the bike, strapping on helmets in silence. Mel waited for Monk to back out before she threw her leg over the Honda's flat black seat, gently holding on to each side of the man's waist.

"She's not really a country girl," Monk said once they pulled onto the county road.

His eyes on the highway, he spoke loud over his shoulder, his voice competing with wind and the old engine's roar. "She's from a city, but it's in the back end of nowhere. One of the oldest cities in the world, almost pre-historic. I asked how she ended up in Cuthbert."

"And?"

"I don't think she ever met an American who speaks her language — who understood where she's from. She told me things."

"Like?" Mel pulled herself forward. Her hands gripped either side of Monk's abdomen, pushing her chin over his shoulder to hear better.

"Like she was brought here by a civic club — the Lions. They flew in a group of what they called *refugees* — mostly women and children."

"That's not unusual."

"The refugees didn't come together. Some came ahead — some later. A lot of them, she never saw again."

Logistics. Mel didn't see the problem.

Monk thought before speaking again. "She said she knew the dead man."

Mel leaned close. Wind forced its way into the few gaps in her helmet. The road moaned beneath them.

"He was here that night, in the restaurant."

"Alone?" Mel asked.

"Yeah. He just sat in the window. Staring at the carnival lot. She says he didn't speak a word to her. But that isn't how she knows him. She said he's the one who arranged her immigration. Eight years ago. That he took care of her, until he got tired of her. She was ashamed, Mel."

"Then why would she tell you that? Because you speak Mandarin?"

"Yes. And because she knew I'm from the show. Because I know the man people think killed her lover. She wanted me to thank him — to thank Charlie for killing him."

Chapter 29

Mel eased off the throttle and let the motorcycle fall back, hoping she wasn't visible in EK's rearview mirror. She rode Monk's Honda — for an old bike, it handled well, but she preferred the open-throat power of a Harley.

She'd told Monk about the motel — that she'd been rumbled. Whoever followed her knew the Interceptor. She needed a new ride. Monk offered his Honda, but he had conditions. He'd wanted to see her ride.

They'd met on the backlot before the show opened. Carnies milled between the trailers, drilling routines and gearing up for the day's performances.

Three ride jocks in jeans and t-shirts hosed down a row of elephants, scrubbing their hides with long-handled brushes. A fourth man filled water buckets for the show. Next to him, a baby sat in a borrowed pail of water, his mother washing his gossamer hair.

Monk had expected to give her a training session — Motorcycle Orientation 101. He'd started by explaining the machine, pointing out each of the controls. Mel tried to indulge him, but after a couple minutes she held up one hand to silence Monk. She held out the other hand for the keys.

Three mermaids stopped their work in the wardrobe trailer, and climbed on top of a circus wagon to take in the scene. All whispers and lewd smiles, they watched the pair hover around the bike. The group of ride jocks left their elephants and pails and joined the mermaids, giving Mel and Monk an audience.

Mel had mounted the bike, feeling its weight, even heavier than the over-specced Harley dirt she'd driven along the sandy highways connecting Basra, Samarra and Kirkuk. She bypassed the Honda's electric ignition and kick-started the old engine, just for the thrill. She revved it, still holding the front brake. Mel revved, clutched, tapped the break, rev, clutch, tap, making the bike buck and stop to get a sense of its balance.

Confused, Monk had started to walk over and take control of the feral machine, but Mel leaned forward across the tank and took off in a scream. In third gear, she raised the front wheel and rode a wheelie the length of a football field.

At the other end of the midway, she let the heavy front wheel hit the ground, the tank banging against her chest. She sat up and turned two-and-a-half 360s, one foot on the ground, spinning circles around the front wheel. Mel gunned the ride back across the lot, braking hard the moment she hit fifth, reining the bike to a controlled stop at Monk's feet.

The exhaust smelled hot as a two-stroke. Still straddling the bike, Mel lifted her helmet and shook her hair out. Monk tried not to smile but failed. "You'll need leathers then," he said. He turned and walked toward the wardrobe trailer.

Mel followed, giving the man his due. The mermaids smiled down at her, flashing rude winks as she followed Monk into the trailer. One of the women sucked the end of her Coke bottle. The others cracked up.

The big rolling wardrobe seemed packed with spangles and feathers in the bright hues of flags and clowns. All of it too conspicuous for the job Mel had in mind. They finally settled on a black leather jacket that belonged to the human cannonball and a pair of worn jackboots from one of the show's old cat acts.

Now she followed EK's blue El Camino through Cuthbert's desolate streets. Mel caught a whiff of the jacket's flash powder residue, making her wonder what life might be like as a human bullet.

Chapter 30

She followed EK the whole of morning. There was more than one way to learn what he knew. She'd picked up his trail as he pulled out of his long driveway onto the county highway.

At first, it felt like a pointless journey through a hopeless Southern county seat — a meandering tour of the worst of the Southern rural wasteland. With less than ten-thousand people, Cuthbert seemed like a futile attempt at a town.

EK made a twenty minute circuit of the downtown's gratuitous one way streets — a needless fifties nod toward the fashion of traffic management. He drove from Wal-Mart on one side of town, past closed and shuttered mom-and-pops, out to the "restaurant district" — a Dairy Queen sat between Pizza Hut and Wendy's — before turning back again and parking downtown.

Mel noticed the number of boarded-up buildings — nearly a third of the town's businesses had closed doors. Where the lights were still on, handfuls of frayed men idled outside, chewing and reading papers.

Mel pulled the Honda into the courthouse lot, following on foot. EK made rounds; now a dry cleaners (dropping off, not picking up), now a florist (chrysanthemums in paper).

At the newsstand (magazines and *The New York Times*) Mel noticed the over-sized Lion's Club decal on the front door. Golden beasts roared from each side of a blue circle, teeth bared, their eyes forever opened. Walking back to the Honda, she caught the shield in most business windows, displayed like an amulet warding off the impression of civic irresponsibility.

EK dropped his pickings in the well of the coupé pickup and drove back to Wal-Mart. Mel held her distance, worried at following too close or for too long. She kept an eye on the parking lot exits, watching the parade of work-worn Americans pull onto the highway, the drivers weary-eyed, their children slapped and baying over the backs of passenger seats.

Mel watched a group of men in the parking lot, gathering around the back of a pickup. One man in coveralls and a gimme cap stood in the bed. The man read from a clipboard and scanned the crowd of dusty men hovering around the tailgate. Like victims of a robbery, the men raised their hands in the air. The man with the clipboard took his pick. Anglos, Mexicans and Black men climbed into the well of the truck. The man looked back at the clipboard, reading again. More hands reached for the sky.

After a half hour, the El Camino pulled out at the furthest exit, back toward town center. She'd followed the man past the courthouse, wondering how much time to waste on the exercise. Mel changed her mind when EK pulled into the police station. Wary of Sheriff Lew, she parked behind the Dairy Queen across the road. She walked to the side entrance in front of the drive-thru, bought a local paper from a blue box attached to the building with a rusting lock and chain, and ordered fries and a hot fudge sundae from a chubby girl with asymmetric hair. She found a window seat and unfolded the paper, ignoring the food.

Mel watched EK unpack the flowers, newspapers and magazines, a frozen cake and bags of corn chips before carrying the gifts into the station's front entrance. *Visiting Charlie.*

Mel waited nearly two hours.

Waves of high school kids, emancipated after a day's captivity, passed through the parking lot. Bypassing the drive-through window, they used the fast food joint as a turnaround point, making laps around the town's main drag. In an hour, Mel noticed the same rustbucket pickup loop Dairy Queen three times, carrying a new group of kids with each circuit. Supersized families hogged the restaurant's big windows, wolfing early dinners from the bleached wax paper boxes they scattered across the table before leaving.

Mel picked at her fries and the melted sundae, fantasizing walking into the station, sitting in the cell and talking with Charlie. Seeing him again. Everything would be understood. Charlie would have missed her. He'd have wished for their time together, relieved that moment had come. He would be contrite. He'd know she'd needed to get away. He'd ask his *daughter* to come back into the fold.

She felt herself edging into despair — an emotion that she didn't allow herself out of self-preservation. EK walked out the door.

He hovered around the entrance, smoking, watching the road, speaking into his phone. When he walked toward his car, Mel left the paper and exited through the Dairy Queen's back entrance, donned her helmet and started the Honda from the red ignition button, gliding out onto the two-lane once his car passed.

Mel followed him to the Commerce Bank, a high-ceilinged thin-brick drive-through construction jutting out over its own sidewalk in a sixties architectonic lean.

Carrying a backpack in his hand, he walked in, looking over his shoulder as the automatic doors closed behind him. Ten minutes later, he emerged with the bag over his shoulder. EK threw it onto the lone seat of the El Camino, Mel noticing a new weight in the bag's arc.

From the bank they drove through a part of town Mel thought she recognized. She found her bearings when EK pulled onto a crushed-shell parking lot standing between the road and a worn cinder block building. Next to the road the outline of a pink and yellow dancer ran across an animated neon sign before pouring the business' blue name into a fluorescent martini glass.

The Social — we never close.

Chapter 31

Mel gunned the 750cc engine, furious. She made the block around The Social and parked near the club in the empty driveway of an abandoned shack, waiting around the building's corner like a policeman setting a speed trap. The unlikely badge of a Lion's Club decal called out from The Social's smoked-glass door. EK wasn't inside five minutes before he left again.

Mel felt manipulated, stunned at what EK had done. First he bought Charlie gifts, then visited with the man for two hours. Now he'd driven to the very club he warned her away from. Mel wondered what had happened inside; why he'd gone to The Social and who he'd seen.

EK drove past Mel, back toward his property, taking the county road's dips and turns in top gear. As they approached his house, the car picked up speed, blowing past the mile-long tree-lined driveway, headed toward the county line. Mel lost sight of the El Camino when the road dipped through a trough between two hills. Scanning as she topped the first hill, Mel spotted a brown cloud rising off to her right, EK's car plowing a dirt road over a flattened, scorched crop field. She drove down into the trough, pulled onto the highway shoulder and stopped, wary of exposing herself if she followed him across the plain.

Waiting there, Mel ran projections, trying to figure out EK's game — except for Wal-Mart, the Lion's Club decal marked every business he'd visited, even the bank and the strip joint. Was he reporting to someone? When he left the bank his shoulder-bag looked heavier than when he walked in. He could have picked up anything — bonds, deeds, cash. Was he making a break for it? She wanted to talk to Charlie, to get the man's history. Something to help her unpack this.

Mel watched the dust cloud melt away in the distance, judging it safe. She turned onto the dirt road. Deep gullies ran down either side of the road, mud crackling in the dry heat. There were no crossroads, just scorched tobacco row. She rode slow at first, hoping to keep the dust down, certain she'd catch up further along the field. After a quarter mile, still unable to see anything, she picked up speed, pushing forty. If she couldn't see EK, he probably wouldn't see her either.

The road loped a slow rise before cutting into an island of pine. As she hit the top of the knoll, Mel caught a flash of light up ahead. She felt her front wheel judder. An unmistakable pop left her ears ringing — a mini sonic-boom followed by a rifle shot, its sound slower than the lead now in her front tire. A second bullet zipped past the bike, a fast hornet in the July heat tearing at the shoulder of her leather jacket.

The bike lurched. The front tire exploded off its rim, the wheel nearly collapsing the instant before the Honda launched out over the gully's ledge. Mid-air, Mel pushed the motorcycle away, frantic to avoid a tangle of heat and metal. She slammed the ground hard, rolling. As her body spun out, she heard the bike crack into the side of the ditch. Her helmet slammed a boulder at the edge of a crop row, twisting her neck sideways. Her arms flopped, her rolling body coming to a stop. Mel sank into the dark of unconsciousness.

Chapter 32

She woke to the stab of a fracturing rib, the pain muted by the haze in her skull.

Grup. Girrup.

A voice shouted at her through amber. Mel tried to open her eyes, but couldn't will herself to — the sharp possibility of searing daylight sealing them shut. She groaned, trying to move as the ache seeped down her side. One of her arms waved out to her left, beyond her control.

Gittup!

The second boot in her ribs brought Mel upright, eyes wide, gasping behind the smoked visor of her black helmet. Her breath fogged the dark plastic covering her eyes and face.

Get up. Who are you? Get that helmet off.

Deep in the back of her right shoulder Mel felt the cold jab of a rifle barrel. She leaned away from the pain, the steel hard against the tendons around her shoulder.

Go on. Get it off.

He poked again. Mel waited, knowing a third prod would come.

She tried to focus, to quiet the pain. Through the helmet she listened to the man's breathing. She waited. *Out. A breath in. Out again. Now a deep intake.* A determined bite and exhalation through his nostrils. The shifting of one foot. She sensed the steel driving from behind, aimed for her shoulder. She dodged the blow and leaned away from the barrel. Mel grabbed the rifle with one hand, pulling the weapon past her body. With her right hand, she gripped the stock near the hammer. The man held tight. A deafening percussion ripped the air, followed by the mute silence of her stunned eardrums — a high-pitched ring hung in the vacuum around Mel's ears, following the gunshot into the ground. The barrel seared in her hands. Mel held tight, rolling forward, using the man's grip around the gunstock to throw him forward, face-first in the dirt. Splaying his hands to catch his fall, he let go. In a single motion Mel rose, flipped the rifle and pressed it deep into his neck, crushing the soft tissue around the atlas of the his spine, pinning his chin to the ground. With her thumb, she pulled the hammer back.

"Move and it goes off," she said.

The man grunted.

"Shut up, EK." With one hand Mel unfastened the helmet's strap. Grabbing the chin guard, she pulled the helmet off, dropping it onto EK's bony ass. The pain made him throw his arms out. Mel backed up three feet, out of reach.

"Hands over your head." Mel watched EK stretch his arms out across the dirt. "Now roll over. Fold your hands behind your head."

Silent, EK did as he was told.

"Way I read it, you just did yourself a drive-by and came back to pick through the pieces," Mel said. "I've got about five questions for you. You don't answer the way I like, I'm exercising my right to self-defense. We understand one another?"

"Melinda, I assure you — "

She fired the gun between his legs, missing each knee by a hands-width. EK flinched, pulling his elbows over his face, screwing his eyes tight. The rest of his body trembled.

"That one was yes-or-no, fucker. True-false. Don't do it again. Understand me?"

"Yes."

"Good. Why did you shoot my fucking bike?"

"I thought you were a thief."

"I'd rob you?"

"Not you. Someone else."

"Who?"

"Anyone, Melinda. You've been following me all day. In this town, I have reason to be paranoid. I saw you this morning as soon as I pulled onto the highway."

Shit. Mel kicked the dirt. "What would I steal? What have you got?"

"Cash. Fifteen-thousand in the backpack. You saw me at the bank."

Mel thought through the sense of what he said. He'd spotted her, but behind the helmet, EK couldn't tell who she was. The man had been protecting himself — a reverse ambush. She'd have done the same. Still, it didn't explain much.

"Where you headed? What's the money for?"

"To do what Charlie asked — "

Mel cocked the gun and shot at the ground again, this time past his head, a good few feet.

"Jesus Christ, woman. Stop. I get the point."

She looked at the rifle, an antique seven-shot Spencer. The first she'd seen in the flesh. She might have one shot left. "Answer the question. What's the money for?"

"A bribe. A pay-off to get Charlie out."

"A pay-off at a strip-joint. To get a man out of jail?"

"If you want Charlie out, there is hell to pay at The Social. *If* they'll even accept."

"What happened?"

"Nothing. The man I went to see wasn't in. I was told to come back."

"Who's the man?"

"I'm not saying. Charlie was very specific about that — "

"Charlie what?" Mel balked.

"He *forbids* it, Melinda. He doesn't want you there, and neither do I. You have no idea of the danger — this goddamned town."

"I'll find out on my own — "

"Then do it. Go. I thought this was about Charlie. But go on. Go against him. All he wants is for you to stay away from the jail. And from that club."

"How do I stay away from people I don't know?"

"You're smarter than you're pretending to be," EK said.

"What else did Charlie say?"

"That if you want to help, you will leave Cuthbert."

"Like that's going to happen. He asked me to come here in the first place."

"He wants you to go to Gibtown."

"Why?"

"He says you'll know when you know."

Mel cocked the rifle. Pressed it just below EK's Adam's apple.

"You rednecks. Fuck sake." EK struggled to breath, his voice a rasp.

"Last I checked, you shot me." Mel pulled the gun away.

EK sighed, exasperated.

"What difference would going to Gibtown make?" Mel asked. "Give me your opinion."

"I have no idea."

Mel watched as EK stared at the sky, avoiding her eyes. She wasn't sure he was telling the truth, but they both knew she wouldn't hurt him. Mel uncocked the hammer and threw the Spencer down beside the man. "Get up."

"You've decided not to shoot me." A statement.

"I can shoot you any time. Right now I need you."

"As I've been saying — "

"I need you to load that motorcycle on your car and take it back to the lot."

"Nice thought, but I can't lift a motorcycle alone."

"Then you'll have to find a board or something. Roll it up. I'm not helping."

EK sat up. He brushed his hands, staring at her. "Why not?"

Stiff now, Mel turned and walked toward EK's car. "Because you cracked my fucking ribs."

Chapter 33

Dylan climbed the back stairs at the police station, stepping up to a blue steel door at the top of the concrete steps. He swiped his card-key across the door's reader, a digital lock displaying a name before clicking open — *Robert Dundee*. Dylan wasn't sure who that was, but if anyone showed an interest, Dundee usually visited the station every other Thursday, and in emergencies. Today was Monday.

Dylan said hello to Sheriff Lewis Evan's girl and walked into the man's office. On cue, Sheriff Lew turned in his chair. Behind him, a bank of televisions flashed images from odd angles, covering every corner of the building's surroundings, cells and hallways.

"Not like you to pay a visit," Lew said, standing up.

"Not like you to take prisoners," Dylan said. "You're looking tired, Lew. Sit down." Dylan leaned over Lew's desk with both hands and peered into the monitors. Lew'd bought the outfit with a grant from the Georgia Homeland Security twinks, paying Milo and a couple of the boys one thousand percent markup. Seven figures of government money, just so Lew didn't have to get off his fat ass to check if someone was on the toilet.

On the monitors, they could see Charlie in his cell. He sat on the floor hunched over the side of the steel bed, using it like a desk. "What's a man like that do all day?" Dylan wondered out loud.

"Sit, mostly," Lew said. "He paced around for a while, but I think that concrete done wore out his flippers. Old queer-boy brought him some pen and paper this morning. Ain't moved since. Maybe he's writing his autobiography."

"He can write his will and testament, all I care. Long's it don't get outside these walls," Dylan said.

"Ain't no thing, boss. No one's been in except EK, plus a little piece from the carnival lot. Didn't check the homo too good, but I was real thorough with the missus. Give her the TSA treatment — from her twins right down to the camel toe."

Dylan stared at the screen, spellbound.

"You hear me, boss?" Lew asked.

"I saw him in Florida once — you been there? To Gibtown?"

"I hear y'all have a good time down there, but it's pretty far down on my wish list. Got to say." Lew put his feet on his desk, leaning back.

"The carnies own that whole town. Nine months a year, there's hardly no one there. It's a ghost town. Winter comes, place is like Five Points. Carnies and freaks everywhere. Got their trailers parked up in their back yards. Painting rides. Fixing tents. And this one — he owns more than the rest of them put together. Restaurants and bars. Even got his own strip joint."

"The hell you say. I thought he just run that show."

"*And* he's the mayor. I shit you not. Lobster Boy. Mayor of motherfucking Gibtown, Florida. And more money than Jesus. One winter, I'm down there — hospitality tour with The Committee. And this sumbitch, he's got a big-titty blonde under each of his flippers. And they love him. Had their hands all over him. Now explain that shit, would you?"

"'Pussy Money Weed', boss. You know that."

"No, Lew. I don't know." Dylan's mood splintered. "I'm not even sure what language you're talking. Get your fucking feet off the desk." He shoved at Lew's boots.

Lew sat up.

Dylan turned back to the screens. "Now look at him. He's like a baby." Dylan cocked his head, as though trying to find a view. Something to lend sense to the image of the twisted little man sitting at a school notebook, scrawling with a deformed claw.

Dylan snapped out of it, turning his attention back to the Sheriff. "You said you got something."

"Deed I do, but you might not like it."

"Try me."

"It's about your sweetheart — "

"Keep it up, Lew."

"That carny woman. Lobster Boy's step-daughter. She's come back to the station."

"When?"

"Yesterday. Sat in the Dairy Queen while the queer come in for a conjugal with flippers. First, I thought she was watching his back, keeping lookout, but when he left, she took off on a motorbike, sneaking behind. Tailing him."

"You follow?"

"No need. Had me a tracker on that El Camino since he come in the first time."

"Where'd he go?"

"Commerce Bank, then he come by your place."

"My man told him come back later."

"That's what I thought you'd do."

"You got something new?"

"Yep. After, he goes flying out to the county line, then drove across old Carter's field. That woman following, I imagine. Hour later, he's back in town with the missus in the passenger seat, motorcycle in back. Looked like she wrapped it round a tree."

"She hurt?"

"That's what I'm getting to."

"Goddamnit, Lew." Dylan paced, impatient.

"So they drive out to the carnival, unload the bike. Miss Thing sets up out back, gets her some tools and a welder and starts fixing the bike. She's good, too. Got a talent. But she's moving funny. Stiff, like she had a accident. After the show's over, this big one comes out — that *flying* nigger. And he sees she's hurting. Makes her stop messing with the bike. He starts looking to her injuries. All gentle, like. Wrapping her ribs. Well you know, you wrap a woman's ribcage, you got to get to it first."

"How do you know this?"

"I seen it. Set myself up in the grove, out to the side of the field. Watched the whole thing with night vision binoculars."

"With one hand."

"That's what I'm saying. Cause next thing, that flying nigger's all up in that woman. Fucking her — "

"Lew."

" — right there in the field — "

"Shut up, Lew."

" — but all sweet, like, cause she's hurting — "

Dylan slammed the desk. "Lew. Shut. Fucking. Up." He turned a circle, walked to the wall and slammed it with a fist. Breathing hard, Dylan rushed the desk and put his face in Lew's.

"Where are they?"

"He's out to the lot, I imagine. You always keep saying, *One nigger, one problem. No niggers, no problems.* I can see to that, boss. Old school."

Dylan leaned his head back, eyes closed, arms down, breathing deep. He slapped one hand over his mouth, opening his eyes again. "Later, Lew. Where's the girl?"

"See, while they was fucking, I slipped in and put a tracker on that bike, too. Good, ain't it?"

Dylan bent down and grabbed the man by his collar. "Where is the goddamn girl?"

"She's gone, boss. Hour ago. Last I looked, she was near about Ochlocknee. Looked to be making for Tallahassee."

Chapter 34

The Honda slipped over the I-275 bridge between St. Petersburg and Tampa Bay's eastern shore. For the past seven hours, Mel had wound a route south along Florida's two-lanes, driving through forests, then groves, until she reached the Gulf's coastal roads, wary of the interstate highways. The big six-lanes made her feel like a sitting target, waiting for a State Trooper to pop her with a radar gun, run her ID and take her home — the big prize from a lucky day's asphalt trawl.

The bike rode fine, except for a front end wobble that kicked in between fifty and seventy miles an hour — the front forks twisted from the crash, just above the shocks. Mel only managed to bend them back into shape with a crowbar and a good deal of torque from Monk. Riding, she had to keep her speed down, or go over the limit, no in-between.

Monk had done his best dressing her wounds — the crash left her gashed and bruised, rough enough to look like she'd had a fight with the business end of a baseball bat. EK's silver-toe cowboy boots finished the job.

Mel figured she had three fractured ribs and one possible break.

The pain spread across her torso, making it difficult to locate the damage.

She felt every stop and start along the highway. Each shift of the Honda's gearbox. But this I-275 bridge was a particular kind of torture — like having her fingernails pulled after an all-day ass kicking. Most of the highway's asphalt had been rough but even. I-275's Sunshine Skyway Bridge had been built from enormous concrete slabs shot through by steel rods bolted every thirty feet. The *thuck-a-thuck, thuck-a-thuck* of her tires crossing each slab's join vibrated the bike into an asymmetric bounce, each bump lifting her hips a fraction of an inch closer to her shoulders. The movement rocked her ribcage with painful oscillations.

Mel hated the fucker who'd built the bridge.

Monk had taped her ribs. His hands on each side of her torso, feeling muscle and ligament, checking damage. He'd just finished his show. Mel could smell the man's body. Feel the strength in his hands. The third time his face passed close to hers, she leaned into him despite the pain, closing her eyes. She could still feel the night in her body. Naked, his head shaved, he'd seemed all flesh, his big hands leaving electric prints across her skin, muting the pain cinching her ribcage.

Halfway to Tampa, Mel had stopped at a service station toilet. She'd washed the road away from her face, then gently unwound the tape, throwing it away. She'd seen too many soldiers start with a rib fracture and end up with pneumonia from a taped chest.

Mel finally reached the end of the bridge, grateful. Over the bay now, she doubled back and drove north on Highway 41, riding past the Manatee Airport through Ruskin and Apollo Beach to the south side of Gibtown.

Crossing town, south to north, took less than two minutes — Gibtown was a suburb, Tampa Bay separating the poor step-child from its wealthy metropolitan parent. Just over Gibtown's watery sunset horizon, the superrich took the air in Kompressor two-seaters along the Western Shore.

The aspirational and the retired, with their small craft airport and seaside bungalows, lived to the south. The Alafia River marked Gibtown's northern city limit, dividing the suburb from a gentrified Cuban playground filled with college students and bachelor parties, clamoring for pitchers of Disney-tinted liquor and limed Mexican beer. Orange groves lay to the east, leaving a two-mile strip of no man's land in the center. Odd carny bars and fast food drive-throughs lined Gibtown's one main road. Patches of tall grass surrounded cinder block houses, broken-down rides and rusting trailers parked on their overgrown lawns.

Mel pulled into the empty parking lot of the Gibtown Bar & Grill, one of Charlie's joints. Five-in-one style murals of freaks and oddities covered the outside walls, turning the nondescript building into a showman's hideaway. Practically boarded up, the B&G always closed for the nine-month carny summer. She parked the motorcycle, shedding her helmet. Mel tried to stretch but winced instead, her ribcage popping in odd ways. She unzipped her jacket and walked around the building toward the trailer park she knew was out back.

The town would be nearly abandoned. Local carnies had checked out for the season, traveling routes from New York to Minnesota, Louisiana to the Atlantic Coast.

The empty trailer park behind the B&G stretched over fifteen acres of abandoned concrete palettes, their gaping waste fittings rusting around open PVC mouths.

The lot would pack four months from now, carnies gathering at Charlie's bar to party into the night over grilled steak and buckets of longneck. Now the only rigs in the trailer park were Charlie's mammoth, triple-wide mobile home, and Popeye's camper, set high on blocks behind the B&G — still there after his death, empty nearly five years.

Mel climbed metal stairs to Charlie's trailer door. She found her key pressed flat in her wallet's coin purse, the leather flap deformed into a key-shaped frieze. The key stuck in the doorknob, corroded by weather. For a moment Mel felt a grieved panic. *Charlie had changed the locks, barring her.* She tried again. The key turned. The rubber lined door opened like a vacuum lock, sealed by the Spring's mildew. Without going in, Mel dropped her backpack and helmet over the threshold and pulled the door closed, locking it again.

One memory at a time. Mel decided to start with Popeye's camper.

Chapter 35

On breeze blocks and jack legs, alone on the empty lot, the camper looked like a mausoleum in a vast and desolate graveyard. A blue milk crate decomposed beneath the door, its crackling plastic an unsteady step into a quilt of memory. Mel tried the door. Her key worked there, too.

She opened it and stepped inside the single tiny room. Light poured through the windows, everything still as she remembered. Smaller than a cell, the room offered just enough space for one person to spin in place. A worn acoustic guitar rested in one small corner, the headstock propped against a portable tube television's small screen. Photos covered the miniature refrigerator. Charlie as a young man, touting mermaids from a makeshift stage outside a small tent. Popeye painting the canvas front of a five-in-one show. A photograph of Mel as a child, practicing trapeze on The Mermaid Parade.

The three of them gathered around the clown-head ticket booth, Mel older. The trio toasted for the camera, Popeye's one glass eye drifting at an odd angle, his head hanging over his beer bottle.

On the unused stovetop, a flat piece of plywood covered the burners. A new cardboard gift box sat in the middle.

Mel noticed the layer of dust covering the box, thinner than on the board. *An addition.* An envelope tucked beneath the string wrapped around the box's six sides.

She read the inscription, written in Charlie's two-fingered scrawl — *For Mel.*

She picked up the box and sat on the knit blanket covering Popeye's bed. Her hair brushed the ceiling as she shifted back and leaned against the tiny window over the old mattress. Mel checked the envelope — unsealed and empty — then untied the box.

A stack of papers.

Charlie's simple will lay on top — Mel would administer his estate, distributing his possessions as she saw fit. A dodge. In effect, he'd leave her everything, including the guilt and responsibility. Mel found contact details for five lawyers in three states. A couple of deeds. Keys. Bank books recording nearly grotesque sums. Appropriate to Charlie's style, a zippered green leather bank satchel held an insane stack of cash.

An 8x10 envelope lay at the bottom of the box containing two pieces of paper — an old Polaroid and a letter.

Mel smiled out from the photo. She couldn't remember having seen it. She thought she must have been four when it was taken. She wore tights and a bodice beneath a Karinska tutu, the acrobat costume she remembered from her childhood. On a patio behind one of Gibtown's party houses, she sat on her father's knee. Far in the background, men gathered around a barbecue, drinking beer. A man she didn't know posed with them, hands on her father's shoulders, leering at the camera. Mel flipped the photo over. Charlie's scrawl — *Melinda and Billy Barry.*

Mel didn't have any pictures of her father.

She read the letter.

My dear Melinda

I hope I am with you when you read this.

You are my daughter, have been since the day you came into my care, and will be beyond the limit of my life.

I love you.

Charlie

Mel lay back on the bed, the photo and note pressed against her chest.

Chapter 36

She lay like that for hours. The sun set. Darkness cloaked the empty lot. Mel's tears long since dry, salt caked her cheeks.

She felt thirsty. She needed to pee.

Mel sat up. Her head bumped the low ceiling. She rubbed the spot and tried to rouse herself from the small bed. She found the note and photograph and slipped them into her jacket pocket.

She tried to turn on the lamp beside the television, but there was no electricity.

Her ribs ached.

Mel reached for the door, opened it and stepped outside. She balanced for a moment on the wobbly blue milk crate, worried she might fall through. She stepped down.

Mel heard a hiss and a thunk. Pain spread through her right shoulder down into the upper part of her arm. She swatted at the sting, jerking, making it worse. Looking down, she saw an odd dart sunk hilt-deep in her jacket, piercing her skin to the bone.

Mel snatched the dart out of her coat and threw it across the lot.

Her head swooned. She fell forward onto her knees. She tried to get up again, but fell on all fours before rolling onto her back.

She wanted to move but couldn't. A trickle of piss ran down her leg, its warmth seeping out around her thigh as it soaked her jeans.

Chapter 37

Mel came to, naked from the waist down. A dirty towel covered her hips. She struggled to breath — her heart pounding, her mouth covered in duct tape. Mel's hands were tied behind her. Maybe with duct tape. She couldn't be sure. She hadn't been raped. She knew that much.

She was sitting in the back of a Cadillac, its smoked windows impenetrable to anyone trying to look inside. Four other people in the car. Two men sat in front. One person each side of her in the back. Without looking, she guessed they were men. They both sat turned toward their windows, hands folded high across their chests as though stubbornly trying to ignore her. The smell of stale sweat and fried food covered the back seat.

At first Mel tried not to move, pretending she was still unconscious. She noticed the man in the front passenger seat watching her in his visor mirror. He turned his head, hair loose on his shoulders, smiling wide. A jackal in black.

"Melinda Barry." He stretched the word, tasting it. The men laughed as though he'd cracked a dirty joke.

Mel remembered the photo in Popeye's trailer, the strange man leering at the camera.

She moved her head, trying her neck, flexing her wrists. Assessing. Her knees felt bruised. Beyond her ribs, she didn't feel seriously injured, just groggy. Slow. Her shoulder throbbed — a dull ache reminded her of the dart. Probably an animal tranquilizer.

Waves of vertigo clamped her head, promising worse. Closing her eyes brought hallucinations — the car's footwell opened beneath her feet. Outside her body, she watched herself fall into the darkness. Lights around her like tracer bullets, phosphorescent trails whizzed past. She tried to keep her eyes open. To not even blink. Mel guessed they'd dosed her with ketamine, likely mixed with a sedative to knock her out.

Panic dissipated any euphoria the drug might have offered. *Good.* She couldn't afford to trip like this. She had to *do* something to bring her mind back. To stay out of the K-hole.

The more she moved, the more the tape bound Mel's wrists. Her legs felt trapped. Pinned against the ashtray between the front seats, immovable and thick in the treacle of her haze.

The car was old. The roof liner sagged, blocking her view of the rear view mirror. The rotted foam backing spattered around the floorboards. Air conditioning mildewed the air, the car's dark windows sealed in the night heat.

The man on her right held a Davis P380 Saturday night special, his arms folded. The barrel tapped the window with each road bump.

Mel looked from one man to the other. She noticed a fresh scar on the cheek of the man from the photo. Something shouted at her from the bottom of her consciousness, but she didn't understand the words.

Mel shifted her bare skin against the car's rotting leather seats. The man with the gun grabbed her knee. "Be still, missy." Gravel-voiced. He clamped her thigh with one hand, holding her down. The man with the scar turned around fast in the seat in front of her. He cocked his arm and punched the gunman in the nose.

The gunman's head whiplashed into the seat back. He grunted with the shock. He dropped the pistol in his lap. His hands flew to his face. "Jesus."

"Jimmy, I have told you. *Keep your fucking hands* — " the man with the scar hit him again " — *off the fucking merchandise*." Jimmy started to protest, but the man with the scar stared him into silence. Jimmy picked up the Saturday night special, crossed his arms and turned back toward the window. One hand explored his nostrils for blood.

The man with the scar turned his attention to Mel. "You sit the fuck still. This is my party."

He twisted forward in his seat, watching the night sky pass outside the windshield. The Allman Brothers' "Midnight Rider" jangled the speakers behind Mel's head, making her woozy. "Turn that shit up," the man said.

The driver reached for the volume, twisting the chromed knob. Throbbing bass threatened to pull Mel into hallucinations. She fought it, silently counting backward from one hundred. Her eyes drifted around the car.

The man with the scar emptied a tall can of Budweiser, crushing it. He pressed a button on the passenger-side door, rolling the window down. He threw the can out. In a haze, Mel saw an ocean blue sign through the open window — *Tamiami Trail*. It whipped by leaving a stream of blue and orange tracers across her vision. The man with the scar rolled the window up again.

He opened another beer. Jimmy noticed. "Can I get one of them?" The man with the scar turned, looking offended.

"Being as it's your party," Jimmy said.

The man reconsidered, smiling again. He pulled another can off his six-pack, throwing it in Jimmy's lap. Jimmy flustered the catch, his gun flailing in all directions.

"Hey. Hey," the man with the scar yelled. "Watch that shit."

"Sorry, boss."

He tore off two more cans, throwing one in the lap on Mel's left, handing the other to the driver. The men opened them, their beers spraying. Mel decided to use the distraction, but couldn't make her body move. The car was so fast. Her hands were tied. She started falling into the footwell again.

The men settled into their beers, Mel's opportunity lost.

The car slowed, turned off the dark Tamiami, switched to running lights and drove a sandy two-lane toward the Gulf of Mexico.

Chapter 38

The man with the scar pulled Mel out of the Cadillac. Her towel fell around her knees, dropping into the sand. "Come on. Time to walk."

He pushed her toward the water, up over a grassy sand dune, hauling her up by her arm when she stumbled, a Czech CZ-75 *Chubby* pressed into her ribs.

Jimmy walked behind them, his Saturday night special trained on her back.

They stopped at the water's edge. Mel's eyes cut toward the waves and back to the car, now out of sight over the dune.

"What's the matter, Melinda?" the man with the scar asked. "You nervous? I'm not going to hurt you. Are you going hurt Melinda, Jimmy?"

Jimmy shook his head. "Nope."

"See? No one's getting hurt. So what's your fucking problem?" the man with the scar said. "Jimmy, get your pants off."

Rape. Mel couldn't hold the thought in her head. She tried to pull away. The man pushed the Chubby deep in her ribs.

"What? Melinda?" he said. "What did you think? We'd rape you?" He held his arms out wide. "Now what did I just fucking say, honey? I ain't going to hurt you. Jimmy, here. He ain't going to hurt you, neither. Is that what you thought in that druggy brain of yours? That I'd make this man rape you?"

Mel shook her head, the motion nauseous and dizzying.

"What *are* we going to do?" Jimmy asked.

"Jimmy, get your fucking pants off and shut the fuck up." He backhanded the man. "Jesus *fucking* Christ."

Jimmy cowered, his pistol pointed away from Mel. He unbuckled his belt and let his trousers drop while the other man held Mel's arm.

"Now," he said. "Give them to Melinda."

Jimmy started to hand the jeans to Mel, but realized she couldn't hold them with her hands tied behind her back. He lay them in the damp surf at her feet.

"We're going to do a little maneuver here. You understand?" The man with the scar pressed the gun into Mel's side again. She nodded. "I'm going push you over. And Jimmy's going to keep pointing that cheap piece of shit at your forehead. You just can't tell when that thing might go off. Get it?" Mel didn't answer. He dug the pistol in her kidney. She gasped behind the duct tape, nodding.

"You're going to close your eyes, I'm going to push you over, and you're going to fall. But only if you trust me. You ever play that game? You close your eyes, someone you trust pushes you over, and then you fall. Do you trust me, Melinda?

Mel nodded her head.

"Come on then. Close your eyes."

Mel closed her eyes. The tracers came back. She felt herself falling before the man pushed her backwards. She landed in the sand on her back, a rock jolting her kidney, tender from the ketamine. Air leapt from her chest. She gasped behind the tape. A shock of adrenalin rushed her brain, erasing the hallucinations. Mel pushed away from the men with her feet, scrambling. The sharp rock scraped a line down her back until it was safe in her palm.

"Quit moving," the man with the scar shouted.

Mel stopped. She had the rock.

"Good. So, Jimmy here. He drew the short straw. Jimmy's going to have to put your pants on. It's real simple. We're putting your pants *on*. Because I take care of you. Because you trust me. I'll make you presentable. Nod and tell me you understand."

Mel didn't move. She held the rock in her hand, feeling its edges with her fingers. The man walked over to her, bent at the waist, pressed the gun into her cheek and shouted. "Tell me you fucking understand, you fuck."

Mel nodded, eyes wide.

"Jimmy, put her pants on. Don't touch the merchandise. And you, fuck, I'm trying to give you a fucking gift. A present. But if you move, I'll blow that beautiful cunt of yours all over the fucking beach."

The man with the scar backed away, the gun trained on her chest. He nodded. Jimmy gave him his pistol, then worked the jeans over Mel's legs, lifting them one at a time. When he got to her ass, Mel thrust her hips so Jimmy could get the pants over her ass. She stared the man in the eye as he pulled her jeans up past her pelvic bone, fastening the buttons.

"Good girl. Now get her up."

Jimmy hauled Mel up by the arm until she was standing. He put his belt around her waist, taking his time with the loops around her ass before he fastened the belt in front.

Both men stood back, appraising. The man with the scar handed Jimmy's pistol back.

"She's got a attitude," Jimmy said.

"Fuck it. Let's party," the man with the scar hollered. Mel tried to scream underneath the tape, shaking her head. The man raised the gun and brought it down hard across her forehead. Mel stumbled back, her hands still behind her. The rock fell to the sand, lost. Blood seeped from her eye, running down her face to the corner of her mouth, thick and metallic.

"Stop bleeding." The man with the scar grabbed her by the elbow. He pushed her back toward the car. "Stop her fucking bleeding, Jimmy. Time to play."

Jimmy reached for his pocket, then remembered he was in his boxer shorts. He dug in Mel's back pocket, found his handkerchief and wiped her eye down.

"Come on," the man with the scar said. He climbed the dune. "Time for company."

Chapter 39

They topped the sandy knoll. Jimmy dabbed at Mel's face again and wiped his hands on the bloody handkerchief. He tried to shove it back in Mel's pocket. He flubbed the first try, the pocket blocked by a can of Skoal. Jimmy moved closer, tucked his Saturday night special under his armpit, pulled the pocket out with one hand and pushed the cloth in with the other. Close now, the man with the scar ahead of them, Jimmy copped a reach-under, feeling up Mel from behind.

Through clenched teeth, he spoke in a whisper. "You got a attitude." He ran his hand between her ass cheeks.

A shiver pierced the back of Mel's neck. She stood at the top of the hill and willed her concentration. Tried to pretend it wasn't happening without falling into a pit of disassociation.

She focused on the scene around her. A second car drove toward them, a few hundred yards down the road, navigating the two-lane by running lights.

A light plane flew low overhead, its landing gear retracting. She felt a sharp light of focus in her mind. *Manatee Airport.* Her location. Mel knew Manatee lay two miles from Tampa Bay.

Dazed, she tried to remember what the man with the scar said. *Time for company*. She had to get out of here before they turned up.

Jimmy moved forward to get a better look at the approaching car, his gun pointed back at her. Mel shifted her bound hands and dug both into the pocket of Jimmy's jeans. Her fingers found the can of Skoal. She pried away the metal lid, careful not to drop tobacco on the sand around her feet. With the disc between her palms, she got her hands out of the pocket before Jimmy turned around again. Behind her back, she folded the lid in half and worked both sides, weakening the metal until it split with a dull, silent snap.

The second car — a black Escalade, rental plates — pulled onto the roadside sand patch beside the old Cadillac. She heard the engine shut down. The running lights dimmed. The man with the scar leaned into the driver's window on the opposite side of the car.

Twisting one wrist, Mel worked the lid's sharp edge across the tape around her wrists. Duct tape. She could tell by the way each thread gave in to the dull aluminum blade. The man with the scar moved away from the window of the Escalade, motioning their direction. Jimmy grabbed Mel's arm. She stopped working at the tape, clutching the lid so tight it cut into her palm. She couldn't afford to lose it.

Jimmy pulled her down the sandy hill, pressing the gun into her ribs. He jerked at her arm again, more for his own pleasure than to move her. She felt her hands shift away from one another. The tape tore, ready to snap. Mel worked her wrists. The tape gave way. She clasped her palms behind her back, hoping Jimmy wouldn't notice.

At the bottom of the dune, he pushed her out into a clearing between the beachgrass and the two cars. The other men made a thirty foot circle surrounding her. The man with the scar walked into the center.

He wrapped his hand around her face and squeezed her cheeks together, shaking her head too hard. "You're looking pretty, Melinda. My pretty baby." He leaned in and kissed each of her eyelids, his breath hot with coffee and booze. "The kind of baby a daddy could love."

He moved back, looked her up and down, then lifted his hands over his head and clapped them together. "Show time."

Two women climbed out of the dark Escalade's back seat. Heels and short skirts, aged and muffin-topped. They swung their hips, walking toward the man with the scar. He spread his arms until his elbows crooked the back of each woman's neck. Pulling the two close, knocking them off balance. He clapped his hands again.

"Meet baby girl."

For a moment nothing happened — Mel ready to use the hesitation, ready to turn and run through the man behind her. The passenger door opened.

Mel's father stepped out of the Escalade onto the edge of the sandy asphalt road.

Chapter 40

Mel felt herself float above her body, watching Billy Barry walk toward his daughter. The blood loss — half her face covered in drying red mush. Ketamine. *Her father.*

He had grown old. Grayer than her image of him. Gaunt. White hair hung down past his neck, greasy and thin. His rumpled clothes were clean, but his belt cinched around a waist shrunk smaller than his trousers. His eyes sunk deep behind their sockets, in retreat from the world.

"My baby."

His voice sounded sedated and flat.

Mel thought she should cry.

Her father wrapped his arms around her. He kissed the open wound above her eye, his whiskers stinging the wide gash.

When he pulled back, her blood traced across his lips. She could smell tobacco and booze and the rot of age — the sharp black hairs in his nose, the mildewed stubble of his unshaven cheeks.

Mel tried to speak but couldn't — her mangled voice a puppy's yelp behind the tape.

He leaned back to take her in, then hugged her again. His arms still wrapped around hers, his hands ran down the hard muscles of her lower back.

The top two buttons of his shirt hung on threads, undone. Mel saw the wizened red skin around his Adam's apple, the speckles of black and white stubble drifting down his sweaty neck, the hairs laying long and sideways, ready to crawl back into his skin.

He stared into her eyes, vacant behind his own. His black breath felt wet. Her father's hands drifted further. Grazed the insides of her elbows, her forearms. Down past her waist. His fingers reached her own, still clasped together, the nails of each hand digging into the flesh of its opposite, the Skoal lid biting.

Her fathers hands stopped. His eyes widened, the moon reflected in their pink and yellow mucous. She felt a silent plea pass from her own eyes to his.

Eyes locked on her, moving slow, he turned his head toward the man with the scar.

"She's loose."

Everyone moved except Mel.

Her father tightened his arms around her. He bound them close to her body, gripping each of her elbows with his opposite hand — a fleshy octopus restraining her with a straightjacket grip.

The two men in Mel's line of sight tightened the circle. From behind, hard metal prodded her spine.

"On your knees." Jimmy's voice.

Her father's body pressed deep into her own, she couldn't move.

"On your fucking knees." Jimmy's voice rose with his anger, the illogic of her motionlessness lost on him. He jabbed her with the Saturday night special again. Mel didn't move.

Through his next words, Mel felt the gun ready to lunge a third time. "I said — "

Mel snapped forward at the waist — threw one leg out behind her. Her father tumbled backward, his grip lost. Jimmy's gun hand lunged past her shoulder. Mel grabbed his arm and drove her heel into Jimmy's shin — a lucky shot.

Mel snatched the Saturday night special with one hand. The other bent the man's thumb into itself. Jimmy wailed. She threw her weight backward into Jimmy. They hit the ground hard. Mel drove her elbow into his groin.

Her father ran for the car, already three paces away. The man with the scar leapt for the driver's side and climbed into the Escalade, the women abandoned in the sand. Mel jumped back to her feet. She extended her shooting arm, turned a fast circle and fired wild at each of the men positioned around her. The third bullet found home. Her target fell at the bottom of the dune lying between Mel and the sea. She ran that direction, stomping a foot in the man's bleeding gut before she scrabbled up the grassy hill and launched over the side. She tumbled down the back of the dune and ran down the beach. Twenty yards south, Mel risked a look back. Headlights seared the knoll. The backlit silhouette of a man in shorts clambered over the grassy top.

Mel turned and ran for the dune. Jimmy ran toward her. She weighed the outcome in her mind — arrest, prison, lethal injection — and shot Jimmy in the face, point blank. She ran back down the beach, scanning the horizon for planes and airport beacons.

Chapter 41

Billy Barry fell again. His blood spattered the sandy brush between the long rows of orange trees. He scrambled forward through the dirty sand on all fours. Tried to get away.

Blood seeped down both sides of his face. Dripped from his long hair, tangled, sticky in his eyes. Twenty, thirty yards back, closer to the road, he'd fallen the first time. Dylan shot the sand around him before the pistol whipping started.

Billy had to get up. He wanted to live.

He sensed the sun rise behind him. Light began to wash the grove, but there were no signs of pickers or ladders or trucks. Not the season.

He was going to die out here, surrounded by bramble and trees and hard green fruits waiting to mature. His skull split by a bullet.

He tried to crawl faster but fell shoulder-first into the sand, exhausted and dizzy, unable to even stand, even on hands and knees.

"Dylan," he said. "Please, God. Please." The last word stretched, a yowled plea from the back of his throat.

Dylan pointed the pistol at his forehead. He moved it an inch, then fired into the ground close to Billy's head. Sand spit across his eyes.

Billy let out a hoarse and animal wail. "Your friend, Dylan. You know I'm your friend, Dylan."

"Stop saying my name." Dylan kicked him hard in the ass. His toe drove into Billy's coccyx. Billy covered his face. Didn't fight back.

"You were never my fucking friend," Dylan said, calm and flat. "We just had a deal. That's all." He shot the ground.

"My God, Jesus." Billy's mind raced, looking for a way out.

"You can't fucking deliver." Dylan fired the Chubby again.

"I tried. My God, you know I did. Don't kill me. Please, please not now. Not here." Billy clasped his hands. He started to weep.

Dylan kicked him again, hard. "You don't get to die yet."

Billy stopped. Unsure. He crawled toward the man, grabbed his legs with both hands, clutched for Dylan's reprieve. "Really? Thank you. Thank you, Dylan. You'll be happy, I swear. I'll do anything."

"Stop saying my *fucking* name." Dylan kicked him away, screaming. "Get off or I'll change my mind."

"I'm off. Oh, God, thank you." He broke down, kneeled before the man, rocking and crying.

"Get back in the car."

Billy's eyes went worried.

"Back in the fucking car."

Billy jumped, scrambling toward the Escalade. Dylan shot near his feet. "Run."

He pumped sand.

"Run, fucker," Dylan said under his breath. "You got business to tend to."

Chapter 42

Three miles down the Gulf, Manatee Airport's beacons winked over the Florida horizon. Mel followed them to the Tamiami Trail. The two-lane ran south from Tampa, hugging the Gulf Coast until it crossed the Everglades to Miami in a straight shot. Mel stumbled across the highway into an irrigation ditch outside the tiny airport's chain-link fence. She washed the blood from her face, tamping at the head wound with Jimmy's handkerchief.

No money. No car. No ID. Jimmy's shit gun in her pocket for protection.

Mel dodged every set of passing headlights, ducking behind Tamiami's dark roadside scrub. She reached Gibtown six hours later.

Dawn broke. Mel watched Popeye's camper for an hour, wary of a second ambush. Convincing herself it was safe, she ran across the empty trailer park and prized the door with Jimmy's belt buckle.

Mel found her backpack and stuffed it with the cash and papers from Charlie's box. Back outside, she pushed Monk's Honda around behind Charlie's trailer.

She found a nickel-thin GPS tracker tucked beneath the rear fender. She opened the casing, removed the flat battery and dropped the tracker in her bag. Walking back streets to Gibtown's Alafia River Truck Stop, passing broken down carnival rides and concession trailers abandoned for the season, Mel fished her phone out of the backpack and called a taxi.

She booked into a suite at one of Tampa's mega-lobby hotels along the Riverwalk. Handing the desk clerk one-hundred dollars, she flashed the Rose Selavy passport and let the man scan her prepaid Channel Islands credit card. He glanced at the black plastic, met her eyes for less than a moment, then turned to his computer. Discreet, he didn't repeat her name aloud. Mel felt he hadn't even ignored her — the clothes, the slash across her eyebrow, the ketamine comedown etched beneath her eyes.

In the room, she double-locked the door, pushed a chair against the handle and stripped. With two vodka shorts from the mini-bar, she carried the backpack to the bathroom. Her guns laid out on the toilet seat, she sat in the dry bath, turning the taps.

Warm water poured over her feet. She threw her head back and emptied each of the small bottles in one shot.

Chapter 43

She slept thirty-five hours, waking on the second day. She lay for an hour, eyes shut, her sleep a wound she tried not to disturb.

When Mel rose, she caught a taxi to the city's Harley dealership. Without haggling she paid cash for the most subdued used bike on the lot — a mid-noughties Night Train. Matte black exhausts and softail shocks.

The ketamine now out of her system, the pain in her ribs felt crippling — the temporary narcotic reprieve made her notice even more.

While the salesman set up her paperwork, Mel stole the license plate off the motorcycle least likely to sell, a black Harley trike. She switched it for the Night Train's.

The dealer returned with a set of worn leathers and a black full-face helmet. Mel used the dealership toilets to change out of the sundress she'd bought in the hotel lobby, savoring the stiff leather against her legs. She rode the bike off the lot.

Mel drove Dale Mabry Highway north, feeling the Harley's weight, measuring its power.

Forty hours since she'd shot two men on the beach.

She turned off Dale Mabry onto Waters, a desolate North Tampa highway lined with the kind of anonymous strip shopping that turns kids to Goth. At the back of a long parking lot Mel found an unmarked door between a shooting range and a shuttered bowling alley. She parked the bike and rang the bell.

Between an intercom and a small lens in the wall, an LED pulsed. Mel looked into the camera. She waited thirty seconds before the lock buzzed open. She walked through the door and was met by another. The first door closed behind her. Its automatic lock sealed before the second door buzzed open.

Mel walked into a thirty by thirty room, empty save an expensive desk and chair, a door at the back, and a noisy fan oscillating in the corner. A chubby man with short white hair and a brown tan sat behind the computer. He tore a sheet from an ancient tractor-drive printer and read it out loud.

"Melinda Barry. Also known as Rose Selavy. AKA Kiki Smith. AKA Fiona Banner. *Nach a mool.*" The man got up, still reading. "Suspected alias — Tacita Dean, wanted for vehicular destruction and assault with a deadly weapon, five days ago in North Carolina." He looked up at her before carrying on. "Former Marine Sergeant First Class, wanted for desertion, flight to avoid prosecution, and larceny of government property."

He stopped in front of her, meeting her eyes over his reading glasses.

"I forgot to return the canteen," Mel said.

The man's face broke into a sad smile. "*Bubbala*, how the hell are y'all?" He threw his arms out and pulled her into a gentle hug.

In the big silent room, Mel stood and wept.

Chapter 44

"The man told you right. In the eyes of the law, you're just a *deserter*. And you don't stop being one until you turn yourself in."

"Bubba" Aschheim bit into his sandwich. A mayonnaise drip spattered down his shirt. Mel wiped at it with her paper towel. Bubba held his arms out at his sides, lettuce drooping onto the floor.

The room's back door led to a kitchen and storeroom. She'd found a confused menu of white bread, lettuce, kosher bologna and condiments on the countertop.

The milk in the curdling refrigerator had turned to water and clot. They drank instant black coffee without sugar.

She licked the scrunched end of her paper towel, then swiped at his shirt again.

"Here, stop that." He batted at her hands. "It's fine. Who would see?"

Bubba slurped at his styrofoam cup, black residue from a thousand coffees seeped between the spongy pebbles.

Since childhood, Mel had looked to Bubba as a carny elder, one of a circle of men who'd godfathered her following her mother's death.

Now forger-in-Chief for her underground life, Bubba acquired Mel's passports, helped Charlie shift her funds between accounts and ran digital recon for Mel when she needed information.

He spoke with a deep Southern drawl, littered with memories of his father's Yiddish. "Bubba" was the only name she'd heard anyone call him. The son of an immigrant rabbi, he'd grown up motherless in Biloxi, his father attached to Temple Beth El, Mississippi's last Orthodox synagogue.

After his father died, Bubba and the synagogue's last four members closed the temple. A grown orphan, he joined the first carnival passing through, going anywhere. Since childhood Mel had known the man as a charismatic grey-haired agent, running flat stores for Mississippi Valley Shows.

"I like Charlie. He's good business," Bubba said. "And I got friends, but this is a big ask. To call in the Feds because a deserter claims the wrong man's in jail? Ain't going to fly. Anyone — lawyers, cops, Feds — *anyone* who helps you in any way, if they know you're AWOL, they're implicated. Aiding and abetting."

Mel nodded.

"Same with the press," Bubba said. "Plus, if they pick up on this, you won't get Charlie out. You'll make things worse. Folks want their monsters in cages, not on the street."

"I'm surprised it's not in the papers already."

"Probably nothing to print. Look." Bubba logged into a website. "NLETS. That's the law's network. It ties up all the police, military, feds. Everything all together. You know. But, Charlie don't show up. Not even a traffic ticket."

"So they haven't — "

"Hadn't logged the arrest. If he's sitting in jail and he ain't in this system, he's got more trouble than a squirrel on a six-lane."

Mel hung her head. "I suppose I'm still in there."

"Still? I type your name, this thing smokes like a bacon-loaded Bar-B-Q."

Mel snickered through her nose. She smiled at Bubba, and they laughed. His barrel chest bounced on the chair, making her laugh more. Tears streamed down her cheeks into the corners of her mouth. She cried and laughed until it was finally out — the attack, her father, the hopelessness of her freak stepfather jailed by a gang of unreformed rednecks.

Bubba put his hand on Mel's cheek. He leaned close, pointing with two fingers, first at her eyes then his own. He spoke, his voice low. "It ain't hopeless. See? Some folks know he's in there. You. Monk. That local lawyer. The Sheriff can't do him no harm in the jailhouse or it'll come back on him. But you get to the bottom of this, fast. The most dangerous time is if they move him. Y'all got to get Charlie out, before he gets moved and has an accident. Or worse."

Mel hung her head. With closed eyes, she acknowledged the words he spoke. She put her hand on his.

"Come on." He patted her hand. "Let me see y'all's *tchotchka*."

Mel found the tracker at the bottom of the backpack.

Bubba cocked his glasses over his forehead. He held the GPS unit up to the light. The size of two stacked quarters. Bubba shook his head.

"What do you think?" Mel asked.

"It ain't *schlock*. Looks Israeli, but what ain't?"

Mel watched the man unscrew the two halves. He examined the insides with a magnifying glass, grunting. "And this is the second time? I got something. Y'all stay here." He walked into the kitchen, placed his hand, palm open, on the wall beside the fridge. A door Mel hadn't seen opened.

While he was gone, Mel dug the feeds from Bubba's trashcan, each printed on broad sheets of tractor-fed paper. She read the dot-matrix letters spaced evenly across green and white rows fit for accountants and engineers. At first, Mel thought the situation wasn't as bad as Bubba made out. She found the desertion listed along with her details and what she thought of as a poor physical description. The system hadn't tied together her aliases, or associated any of them with her real name. That was Bubba teasing.

But a stack of three and four-page printouts worried her more. Each on normal paper with a cover page, the sheets lay just under the crumpled NLETS feeds. Typical of Bubba, he'd collated and stapled the documents separately, more meticulous with his research than his environment. Mel scanned their covers.

Most were diplomatic communiques — Mel couldn't tell if they were Wikileaks, original hacks or a combination of both. Long upper-case alphanumeric sequences headed each page, followed by dates and times, security authorizations and centered titles in quotes. A narrative of Mel's service history, or the end of it, at least.

Reading the first pages, Mel became aware of the fan moving air around the room, pushing it against the back of her neck. She'd seen the cables before — reports from inside the Green Zone, documenting Command's suspicions over contract personnel. Mel remembered the incident, a random event that threatened to erupt into an international crisis, all started by an American MP detaining a drunk contractor.

Asked for documents and unable to speak English, the contractor ranted in Nepali. That would have been the end of it if the MP hadn't grown up with hippy parents who ran a Freak Street hotel in Kathmandu.

The contractor explained in Nepali that he'd signed up for an eighteen month contract to cook in Dubai. As soon as his plane left Nepalese airspace, his passport had been confiscated. When the transport ferrying new workers touched ground, he and a couple dozen of his countrymen were told they had landed in Baghdad, and wouldn't get their passports back until they'd worked out the term of their contract.

The man told the MP he didn't know how many of the others were still alive. Half had disappeared.

Two days later, Mel found herself on a Special Operation under civilian cover in Baghdad.

The communiques laid out everything — the incident, Mel's investigation, her cover and how it had been blown. The detentions and the rapes. Sergeant First Class Melinda Barry — AWOL.

Someone, somewhere knew everything. Now Bubba did, too. Whether that was good, Mel wasn't sure. None of it changed reality — Mel seeking shelter in a Tampa strip-mall, dodging cops and psychos.

Bubba walked back to the desk carrying a paper shopping bag. He handed Mel what looked like an old cell phone without a screen.

"GSM jammer. Shock-proof. Water-proof. Keep it near you — in your pocket, not the bag. One switch — it shuts down every cell in a hundred yards."

"Handy at the movies," Mel said.

"Or after, *alivay.*" He pulled a sleeveless t-shirt from the bag. "Put this on. I'll turn my head."

Mel looked suspicious. He smiled and turned his back to her, whistling at the ceiling. Mel took off her blouse.

"That's a Miguel Caballero — the Armani of body armor," he said. "It'll stop a bullet. Or a dart."

Mel slipped the thick t-shirt over her head. "I need something else, Bubba. Turn around."

"Thought y'all'd never ask."

"Too soon, Bubba."

He grimaced an apologetic smile. "I'm sorry."

Mel smiled back, letting him know it was okay. She buttoned her blouse over the t-shirt. "I need a check on my father."

"Billy Barry? That son-of-a-bitch? No need."

"You've looked?"

"Time to time."

"And?"

"Nothing. No bills. Phone. Bank. License. Criminal record. I mean *bubkes*. Trail stops when your mother dies — an angel, that woman. *Aleha Ha-Sholem*. She brought out the best in people. Everyone who knew her was a better person for it. Except your father."

"You'd tell me if you knew something."

"You and only you, honey."

"Thanks."

"It's nothing. That'll be $15,000."

"Fifteen thousand? For nothing?"

"Fifteen-thousand for the shirt. *Bubkes* y'all get for free."

Chapter 45

Dylan watched Willy O.'s pickup turn into the lodge and drive around back with the rest. *Willy O.* He'd never had any use for that prissy son-of-a-bitch.

Dylan popped the door on the Lincoln's glove compartment and pulled out a handheld TV. He clicked the "On" switch and flicked through a set of grainy color channels until he found the one he was looking for. On the screen, Dylan watched a group of men lurch around a long table, clumsy in their skin. All glad-handing one another.

A meeting of The Committee. Dylan didn't remember calling a meeting. *Must be an emergency.*

Max and Dave chose their seats, pouring drinks, Milo at the head of the table. Willy O. came in and sat in the last empty chair, opposite.

Dylan smoked and watched while an argument broke out on the little screen. He couldn't hear what they were saying, but it wasn't hard to see everyone was agitated. Once in a while Max would put his hands up over his face and shake his head, like he needed to hide his eyes from something.

Willy O.'d bang the table. Milo'd put a hand out and talk him down. They did it two or three times.

Dylan knew what they were saying. He watched Willy O.'s face. Imagined Willy's voice behind Willy's blubbering lips. *Time's up*, he'd say. *Time for Dylan to go.*

Milo stayed calm. Dylan liked that about him. He watched the man stand up and walk over to Max, who looked like he was about to cry. Milo put his hand on the man's shoulder. Patted his back. Leaned down and talked close in his ear. He soothed Max and got him to look Milo in the eye. They shook hands and Milo sat down again.

Then he said something and all the men raised one hand.

Dylan looked at himself in the rearview mirror. He smiled before putting on a serious look like Milo's. He tried it again. Satisfied, he tried the other — the nearly crying look. It was hard, because Max had had his eyes scrunched together, and when Dylan scrunched his eyes, he couldn't tell what his face looked like. He put his hand to his eyebrows, trying to feel if he had the right expression. Hell, he couldn't tell.

Dylan looked back at the screen. The men were starting to leave. Milo met each one of them at the door before they walked out, shaking each hand. Probably thanking them for dropping by. Dave's pickup pulled out from behind the lodge, the driver looking both ways before turning onto the country road. Dylan sat parked on the other side, a good fifty yards back from the pavement behind a clutch of trees. Out of sight.

The pickup drove away.

Dylan watched the others come out one-by-one, every couple of minutes, timed perfect like they was having some secret parade. Milo wasn't the last. The last was Willy O., and Dylan thought that was just Willy's bad luck.

Dylan jammed the Lincoln into drive, tearing down the little dirt path to the asphalt road. His car lurched onto the two-lane, a cloud of rocks and dirt rising behind. Fishtailing. He could see Willy's face in his big wing mirrors. His eyes bugged out, mouth hanging open. Dumb son-of-a-bitch.

Dylan put his foot to the floor. He loved it when the four-barrel kicked in, its roar throaty and hollow at the center. He ran the Lincoln right up behind Willy's pickup before he let off the gas, falling back a few feet. He eased the pedal down again, moved in closer, playing.

The pickup drifted right, Willy's attention on the rearview. His right side tires slipped off the asphalt. Willy snapped the steering wheel, pulling back on the road. The truck jerked left then right. The wobble slowed the pickup. Its rear bumper kissed the Lincoln's hood, bending the silver crosshair ornament.

Dylan tapped his brakes and fell back. The ornament lay on the hood, hanging by a cable.

Goddamnit. His Momma'd give him this car.

Dylan hit the gas, slamming the Lincoln's front end into the pickup. Willy swerved again and Dylan backed off. They were doing seventy, easy. Maddox Lake Bridge just up ahead. Dylan dropped back a few car lengths, giving Willy space. He eyed Dylan in the mirror. The truck steadied. Willy wiped his forehead. Dylan kept falling back, distracted. Staring at the crumpled hood.

Goddamn car was fucked.

Dylan hit the steering wheel with the palm of his hand.

Fucking Willy.

Dylan put on his seatbelt, slammed the heel of his palm into the car horn and jammed the accelerator into the floor.

The horn startled Willy, already on the bridge. Losing control. Dylan heard his headlights shatter when the Lincoln hit the pickup doing sixty. The truck jacked to the right, dipped for a second, then launched off the railless bridge.

It felt like a moment of silence before Dylan heard the splash. He slammed his brakes and got the Lincoln stopped before it reached the end of the bridge. The pickup floated behind him, nose down, windows up. Dylan could see Willy struggle with the door, wailing at the windows like the pussy that he was.

Dumb fucker.

All he had to do was to calm down and shoot out the fucking window.

Dylan put the Lincoln in reverse, backing up slow. A raft of bubbles blew up from the pickup's engine. The front sank another few feet. Old Willy looked panicked. Dylan kept backing up, taking his time, until he was even with the truck. He rolled the passenger side windows down one at a time. Willy wasn't far off. Not more than twenty-five, thirty feet.

Dylan didn't think he'd need his rifle. Hell, at this distance, he could kill Willy with the Chubby.

Chapter 46

Mel found EK on the merry-go-round, eating a corn dog and reading the paper. He sat in one of the ride's big winged seats, gliding behind four abreast rows of wooden animals.

The carousel looked older than any Mel had seen. Green-framed mirrors surrounded the centerpole, accented in flake gold paint and warm carnival incandescents. Carved and lacquered horses vied with giant geese and quarter-sized giraffe, running clockwise circles around a mechanical calliope.

EK looked enchanted, riding the circuit alone, his expression too bright for Mel's mood.

He'd agreed to meet her at Tallahassee's North Florida Fairgrounds. Southland Million Dollar Midway played Tallahassee County Fair every year. Mel knew the owner, Iřene Husová, from Gibtown. A Prague Spring immigrant, Iřene wore a fierce outer core over a heart as stout as her body. A woman who understood loyalties and the power of the state, Mel thought of her as one of the few people she could ask for help.

Mel explained on the phone what she needed — a meeting place away from prying ears. A sentry with a firearm.

Mel tacked an extra half day onto EK's short journey south from Cuthbert. She insisted he drive west to Dothan, Alabama and switch cars. She'd sent word from Bubba's through a PGP-encrypted email, concerned his phone might be hacked.

Bugged by a nagging instinct she couldn't put her finger on, and worried as much for Monk's safety as for her own exposure, she'd designed an even more circuitous route for the man. He drove a show truck west to Eufala, where he caught a Greyhound back east to Savannah. Bubba had arranged a waiting rental car at a downtown diner, one of the waitresses meeting him at the long formica counter with keys. He drove south and met Mel at an anonymous beach hotel in Jacksonville, Florida.

Chain-smoking, only looking Monk in the eye when she wanted answers, Mel interrogated the man. He sat on one of the room's two worn deck chairs, placed each side of a cracked woodgrain formica table on the balcony overlooking the Atlantic. Fingers folded across his abdomen, he listened to Mel's questions. Who had he seen the last night they'd been together? Had he noticed any strange cars on the lot when she left? Any unusual conversations since?

Patient, he answered her questions until she ran out. After a long pause, he finally asked her, "Are you okay?"

Mel balled a fist under the table, pushing the coming tears back down into her chest. "I was kidnapped. Nearly — " Mel's voice caught.

Monk closed his eyes for two, three, four seconds before opening them again. He held his emotions tight, seeing she was about to break. "Who?"

"I don't know. My father was there." Mel watched Monk's eyes widen, the muscles in his cheeks tensing and releasing. "I think it had something to do with The Social."

While Monk held her hand, she explained the kidnapping and the men on the beach. She watched Monk's chest rise and fall in a rhythm as steady as the tide. Without naming him, she told Monk about Bubba, and what she had learned. And then she fell silent.

They both stared beyond the crashing surf, the moon cutting a luminous highway to the beach. Mel smoked two cigarettes and waited for the man to speak. He finally kneeled in front of her — his posture begged her to meet his eyes.

"I know this is your fight," he said. "But I swear, Mel, tell me who. Say anything and I'll do it."

"I know you will." Mel pulled his head close to her chest, holding it there until a tear dropped from her cheek, down onto his face. She wiped it away, trying to smile. "First we find out what we're dealing with. We save Charlie — then we can think about the rest."

In the morning, they drove to Tallahassee, Mel on the Harley, Monk fifty miles ahead in his vanilla Ford.

Mel walked to the carousel, grabbed a gold twist barley pole as it passed and hopped onto the spinning platform. Monk followed. The trio rode the merry-go-round alone, the armed ride jock standing twenty yards over the midway, smoking and watching the crowd.

Happy as he seemed, Mel thought EK looked exhausted. After the kicking he'd given her, she didn't care.

"Melinda." EK folded his paper. He tried to stand but wobbled on the spinning platform.

"Don't, EK. The gesture's enough." Mel sat in the opposite wing chair.

"You notice we're traveling clockwise?"

"I hadn't," Mel said.

"The wrong direction," EK said. "Turks used to train soldiers on these. Europeans, as well. Used them to practice jousting. But they rode right handed, lance in their left. Clockwise. American carousels are just carnival rides. We reversed the direction so people could 'joust' with their right hand. Easier to get the brass ring."

Mel sat silent, arms folded.

"We're riding the wrong way — a European merry-go-round, I'd say."

Mel didn't yield.

EK shifted in his seat. "Melinda. I can only apologize again for your ribs."

"If it didn't hurt so much, I might have forgotten."

Monk appeared behind her. He slid in beside EK, blocking his exit.

EK's face lit. "And you are the amazing Monk. My God, your act."

All business, Monk held the man's gaze. Silent.

"Well, you're intimidating." EK turned back to Mel. "Melinda, I doubt *Cuthbert County Press* is on your reading list, but you might want to make an exception this week. It seems we've lost another pillar of the community."

EK held the paper out for Mel.

"Willy O'Keefe," he said. "Drove off a bridge into Maddox Lake. Drunk driving. You know they say you shouldn't drink and drive. You spill too much."

No one laughed.

"Anyway, Willy O. was Chairman of O'Keefe Industries."

"Is that supposed to mean something?" Mel asked.

"Millions. Willy O. ran the only labor contracting outfit in Cuthbert county. One of the biggest in the state."

"Doing?"

"Slaughterhouse. Sweatshops. Farm labor."

"Work gangs?" Monk asked.

"By God, you speak as well. Yes, work gangs. O'Keefe Industries deals with farms and factories. You need labor making dog food out of pigs' ears? Willy's your man. I heard he supplied a dozen men at $750 a day."

Monk did the math. "That's minimum wage. Where's the profit?"

EK turned to Monk. "There isn't one, your holiness. Not if you're a law-abiding citizen. But then we wouldn't be speaking of Willy O. Common knowledge says he employed more undocumented workers than anyone in the state."

"If everyone knew, why wasn't he in jail?" Mel asked.

"Well-placed friends. Corporate business. O'Keefe greases a lot of wheels in Cuthbert. But here's the thing — it was all about to change."

"What do you mean?" Mel asked.

"Front page. Below the fold."

Mel turned the paper to the first page, folding it to read the bottom half. "*DC Pols to Tour Cuthbert Prison*," Mel read. "What's that have to do with O'Keefe?"

"Nothing," EK said. "And everything. The story *says* they're touring the prison. But really, why would a delegation of US Congressmen make the trip from Washington to Cuthbert just to tour a jail? This was set up by The Committee."

"The Committee."

"A group of locals who run everything. Willy O. was one. And his friend Sarge Cooder. Two Committee men, both dead. Every member of The Committee sits on Willy's board. They're all on the boards of each other's companies — O'Keefe Industries belongs to all of them now. They own everything in the county and Willy supplied the labor. But mostly he exported to the rest of the state. Check the front page again. Headline."

"*State Approves Tough Immigration Law*. I'm not connecting the dots."

"It's a crack-down on hiring illegals. Willy's labor force. That law would have put Willy O. out of business. And most of The Committee," EK said.

"You're saying that led to his death," Monk said.

"No. No I'm not. I'm saying things are more complicated than they appear. The politicians are touring the prison because The Committee were about to lose their cheap labor force — the best thing they had going. They saw it coming years ago. So they got creative. They built a private prison — an upscale jail — and contracted to the state. Holiday lockup for white-collar criminals. Education programs, psychologists, a library. They lost their collective shirts over it.

"So they went for the three-time losers. Blacks mostly. Violent criminals, hard to handle. That got expensive, too. So they finally got the idea to make it an immigration lock-up. Illegals get arrested, thrown in jail for a few years, then shipped out of the country. If they're mistreated, who cares? Who can they complain to? That was five years ago. Now DC's coming down — they're looking to expand. Big money Federal contracts."

"Thanks for the civics lesson, EK." Mel's crossed her arms again.

"I'm just telling you — if you want to catch the brass ring, you have to run the right direction — you need local knowledge — "

"That's why I brought you here," Mel said. "Your local expertise."

"I don't understand," EK said.

"One of your locals. The man from the motel. He brought me a present in Gibtown. He brought me my father."

Chapter 47

"You're describing Dylan Hide."

"Is that who you went to see? To pay off?" Mel asked.

"At The Social," EK said.

"So you knew about my father."

"I didn't know this would happen, Melinda. Not this way."

Before they'd arrived, Monk had offered to sit the conversation out. *Private matter*, he'd said. *I don't have to be here.* Mel had insisted it was okay, but once EK started talking she changed her mind.

Now Monk waited across the midway with the ride jock, both staring as EK and Mel rode backward circles.

"The Committee goes to Gibtown every year," EK said. "It's normal. All the small town mayors and sheriffs on Charlie's route visit at one time or another. Charlie provides *hospitality*. That's how he built his route."

"I know that," Mel said.

"The Committee are different. They don't go for a weekend. They vacation. Two weeks or more. Dylan, too. It drives Charlie crazy, but he puts up with it."

"How did my father meet Dylan?" Mel asked.

"A long time ago, Melinda. At one of Charlie's parties. Dylan and The Committee. Most of the mermaids. And your father." EK threw his head back. "Doing what they went there to do."

"Get laid."

"Laid. Stoned. Drunk. Whatever was on the menu — cocaine, mermaids. Your father and Dylan met. The three of you walked in the room — "

"I was there?" Mel's face drained, ashen.

"You *and* your mother, when she could still walk. Dylan took one look and made a beeline. I watched him introduce himself. And my God, Dylan and your father became inseparable."

"I don't understand," Mel said.

"Like old friends. Brothers."

"It had to be more than that."

"I thought so. It was a puzzle. But finally, I forgot about it. Then two, maybe three years later, your mother died. I came to the funeral — "

"I don't remember you."

"I arranged your adoption, so believe me, I was there. Charlie explained your father had disappeared, and someone had to care for you. So I started the paperwork." He stopped.

"And?"

EK took a deep breath and sighed. Mel could see him deciding how much to tell her. "And when I came back to Cuthbert, I found your father. Working for Dylan."

Mel blinked for a moment. "You found him? And you kept quiet?" Three townies passing the carousel turned to look. She realized she was shouting. She didn't care.

"*Of course* I said something. To Popeye *and* Charlie. It was a terrible situation."

"Terrible — "

"We discussed it. A tough decision like that — "

"But — "

"You have to remember your mother was dead."

"Do you think I'd forget?"

"You were better off with Charlie and Popeye. In Gibtown with the carnies. Better than you could ever be alone with your father."

"It wasn't y'all's decision — "

"Your father was an alcoholic."

"So am I. So are you."

"He moved to Cuthbert to run Dylan's brothel."

Mel threw up her hands. "What do you think Charlie runs. A fucking Sunday School show?"

"Melinda — "

"It wasn't your decision."

" — your father has a very manipulative talent. A horrible ability to hold women — "

Mel started to leave. EK pushed her back down in her seat.

"Damnit, Mel. You want to know. You hear me out."

Mel could feel herself breaking. She wanted to run.

"Charlie is a pimp. You know that. But he doesn't force anyone to do anything — he helps them. This goddamned world, it creates unique people. Amazing, talented beings. And then it breaks them over and over until there's no place left for them to turn. And those are the people Charlie takes care of. He made a home for you. The Mermaid Parade is a home for lost souls. But your father is different — "

"Don't talk about my — "

"You want to know. He is not in Cuthbert to help strays and outcasts. He is a *destroyer*. He harnesses alienation and uses it to exploit. People lose their souls at that man's hands."

"No — "

"Better the cruel truth than a comfortable delusion, Melinda. Your father is a feeder," EK said. "There is no way you don't know that. Had your mother allowed it — and she suffered for her bull-headed insistence — your father would have done the same to you. That man was a feeder and he fed your mother to death."

Mel felt herself weeping. She wanted him to stop. Her fists pushed down on her knees. She squeezed her eyes shut, tears pressed along her lashes.

Goddamnit.

She rose and walked to the edge of the carousel, dazed.

She stepped down, the ground sweeping up to meet her feet. She steadied herself, blinking. She found her balance and walked away, Monk running toward her across the Million Dollar Midway.

Chapter 48

Not now.

She needed him to leave her alone. Mel held her hands up and walked away, moving down the midway. Monk let her go.

She felt dizzy. The Florida humidity surrounded her, made it hard to breath, as though she were inhaling a solidifying resin, locking her in place.

Her phone vibrated in her pocket. Mel ignored it, letting it ring out. After thirty seconds, it vibrated again. Mel looked at the screen — a blocked number. Few people knew her number, but EK was one of them. She looked back.

EK tried to climb off the spinning carousel, one hand on a gold twist, the other waving the air for balance. The ride jock ran past Mel, trying to get to the ride before EK fell. Mel turned to find Monk in the crowd. He followed a few yards back, his hands in his jacket pockets.

If Charlie called, the police station number would be blocked.

She answered the phone.

"*Bubbala.*" Bubba's Southern accent rumbled against her ear. "This is a secure line. We can talk. "

Mel closed her eyes, shaking her head. She didn't say anything.

"Listen, whatever y'all're doing, get back to Cuthbert."

Mel tried to speak, but couldn't.

Monk hovered close, his expression a question mark.

"It's Charlie," Bubba said. "I hacked the Sheriff's network. Don't ask — "

The name brought her back to earth. "Is Charlie okay?"

"Right now he is, but they decided to move him and I don't know where. Sheriff said it in an email. They're moving him tonight. I'm trying to hack the other systems. Vehicle tracking, the prison — it's a tough nut, Mel."

Mel listened, saying nothing.

"The email was encrypted. That he should even bother, I think he's serious," Bubba said. "I found a copy of the encryption key on his computer. He gives an address, but it's not the prison — *50 and Dead End Rd., 2 a.m.* And I don't know if it means anything, but he sent it to *dylan@cuthbertsocial.com.*"

Mel hung up. EK tried to approach her. Monk shielded Mel with a turn of his body. Barely visible, Mel shook her head. Monk yielded, letting EK back in.

"They're moving Charlie," Mel told them. "Two a.m. tonight."

Chapter 49

1:40 a.m.

Mel scanned Sheriff Lew's cruiser as it left the rear yard of Cuthbert Police station. The prison van followed. The transport looked like an old box ambulance, resprayed white save for the big steel bumper under the rear loading doors. One man drove. Mel assumed Charlie would be in the back.

Earlier that evening, she and Monk recced Dead End Road, a quarter-mile red clay and gravel strip running from County Road 50 to the Cuthbert Landfill just outside town. A twelve foot chain link fence surrounded the city dump, corralling a prefab metal building, two Caterpillar dump trucks and a good twenty acres of cast-off — shattered televisions, molding sofas and rusty, bleeding air conditioners.

She'd stationed Monk there before returning to the police station, parking him near the intersection on a hidden patch of dirt behind a clutch of trees to keep an eye on the highway. Sitting in the vanilla Ford, he could watch the gate through a pair of night vision binoculars they'd picked up in Tallahassee.

"They're on the move." Mel spoke into the mic of her handsfree.

"Quiet here," Monk answered.

The night vision binoculars, Monk at the landfill and the open cellphone line were the whole of her plan — there were too many unknowns. They had to be ready to improvise. She'd forced EK sit out the operation — she didn't want to have to speak to him. To depend on him. Mel planned to follow the transport, Monk keeping an eye out for anything suspicious.

The pair had reviewed the logistics with her phone's mapping app. The prison lay two miles past Dead End Road along 50. No dots to connect — just a police jail, a prison seven miles away, and a landfill in between. Mel expected an ambush. Or Sheriff Lew to pull over, shoot Charlie in the head, and claim attempted escape.

Mel couldn't let the transport out of her sight.

At the carnival lot, she'd clipped the wires powering the Harley's lights. Now she hung back, riding in shadow, and watched the Sheriff and his transport slow cruise Cuthbert's dark two-lane streets.

1:45 a.m.

At the city limits, Sheriff Lew pulled onto the soft shoulder, the van following. Stalking the convoy two blocks behind, Mel dipped the Harley into the driveway of an old ranch house, its windows dark and curtained in the early morning.

She eyed the Sheriff as he climbed out of the cruiser and walked back to the transport. He leaned against the van's driver side door, smoking, an eye on his watch.

They waited.

"Nothing happening here," Mel whispered into her headset. "You got anything your end?"

"Nada."

Mel wished she could see Charlie, but she knew unless he stood on a bench, he wouldn't be able to reach the high windows of the transport's rear doors. She wondered if he was handcuffed. He must have been terrified. Mel's heart caught. She pushed the thought away.

"Mel. I've got something." She could hear Monk breathing. "A couple guys just left the building. Walked straight to the gates."

"One of them have long hair? Around his shoulders?"

"No. They're bulletheads. Checking the gates. They're pulling at the lock and chain."

"Wait, they're outside?"

"No, inside. But it looked like they were checking to make sure the gate was locked. They're headed back now. How about you?"

Mel watched the Sheriff start the cruiser and pull onto the road. The van followed. She kept her distance. Looked at her watch.

"We're moving again. Almost there."

1:57 a.m.

They drove a steady pace — 45 mph. After a minute, they slowed again, creeping along the county road.

1:58 a.m.

"Heads up, Mel."

"What have you got?"

213

"Those men climbed into one of the dump trucks. Lights on." He paused, watching. "Engine fired up. About thirty yards inside the gate."

"Are they — "

"Mel, they're driving straight for the gate. Fast."

Through the phone line, she could hear Monk start the Ford's engine. The rental's big motor roared. She heard his tires kick gravel.

"Monk, what — "

"They've crashed the gate. I'm going in."

The Sheriff's convoy rounded the bend, still creeping. A quarter mile from the intersection. Mel checked the time.

2:00 a.m.

Chapter 50

"Take cover, Mel — "

The connection died. Mel heard the groan of wrenching metal. Sound reverberated over the treetops, the crash so close she could hear the Ford's thin hood fold into the dump truck's girded sides, One-hundred-eighty tons of steel bulldozed the gravel road with Monk's ford. A cloud of dust rose over the trees like a last breath.

The first explosion blew as the Sheriff's convoy rounded the bend. The blaze washed the transport with hot orange light. The Sheriff's car slowed, drifting through the intersection before he slammed his brakes. Slower to react, the van rear-ended the cruiser.

Mel squeezed the brakes, trying not to skid. Her thumb hit the engine's kill switch. In the split second as she shot past Dead End Road, Mel looked to her left. The dump truck's second gas tank exploded. Fire shot through the cab, chewing at the blackened bodies slumped over the dash. Monk's Ford lay on its side. Fire licked the car's underbelly, one wheel ripped away, the other cocked at an odd angle, spinning. The passenger door gone. She couldn't see Monk.

She leaned into the bike, wrestling it to a silent off-road stop just right of the prison van. All eyes stayed on the fire. She lay the bike down and jumped onto the transport's steel bumper, pulling herself flat against the loading doors. The transport bolted to a start, rear wheels smoking. Mel clung to the back door, a handle in each fist.

She pressed her face against the rear windows and she saw Charlie in back chained to the floor. He struggled on aborted hands and knees. The truck threw him around its metal box. Only his chains kept him from slamming the walls. Mel shook the door handles, trying to open the loading doors. Their eyes met before the transport sent Charlie skidding sideways across the metal floor. Mel looked down at the road — they were moving too fast for her to jump.

Sheriff Lew's siren wailed ahead of them. Red and blue light flashed the trees on both sides of the highway. An ambulance's siren rose behind her. The convoy turned off the highway. The transport fishtailed around the intersection, nearly rising on two wheels. Mel's fingers went white around the loading doors' handles, blood drained from the force of her grip.

The transport hit a pothole, throwing Mel's legs in the air. She tried to regain a foothold on the bumper, but her legs slipped, dragging the asphalt behind the speeding truck, Mel struggled to hold the door handles. She closed her eyes and brought her legs forward, her jeans tearing at the knees. She planted both feet in the asphalt and pushed off, scrambling one leg onto the bumper, pulling herself back up.

One moment they drove in darkness, the next the van's brakes screamed. Mel's face slammed against the glass, her body pressed into the rear doors. Bright vapor lights washed the truck with an artificial dawn. The van juddered to a stop, the suspension's throwing Mel backward. She tumbled off the bumper, hit the asphalt hard and rolled to her hands and knees.

Mel heard the unmistakable *chuckchuck* of shotguns cocked in unison. She lifted her head. Surrounded by armed guards, raised weapons trained on her chest, Mel surveyed the receiving bay of Cuthbert Prison.

Chapter 51

Mel ran her palms over the back wall of the trapezoidal cell. Embedded deep in a two-inch glass sheet, steel wires criss-crossed the big window, nearly the size of the prison cell's outer wall. At the room's narrow end bars ran floor to ceiling, wall to wall, four feet across.

Squinting through the cell door, Mel thought she was on the top floor. From her vantage point, the building looked like a four-story roundhouse — a wheel laid on its side, prison cells stacked in a circle with one continuous outer wall.

At the wheel's hub, a sentry tower rose half the height of the building, the guardhouse surrounded by glass. She couldn't see anyone in the tower — couldn't see into the tower at all, the glass smoked and mirrored. But Mel recognized the design.

She knew a prison guard could spin a circle and see into any of the cells, the inmates' silhouettes backlit by the stark vapor light pouring through the reinforced window that made up the back wall of each cell.

She guessed she'd been there twelve hours. She lay on the hard cot, listening through the night. Prison whispers filled the big hall, turning it into an echo chamber of English, Spanish, and a handful of languages she didn't know. At morning light, she'd watched inmates march past her cell door on their way to breakfast. The only woman, her cell door remained locked, breakfast passed through a slot in the prison bars. Silent and stripped of their clothes and identity, garbed in a dull and uniform grey, it was difficult to tell where the men were from. After five minutes of the parade, Mel was confident she was the prison's only white inmate, until they brought Charlie.

A trio of guards trundled Charlie to the cell next door, handcuffed to an institutional wheelchair. The man pushing him seemed twice the chair's width. A pair of armed gym-rats escorted, as though Charlie might miraculously rise and break his chains.

Charlie looked slumped and withered since she'd seen him five years ago. His short hair fell thin and pale across his forehead. Where he wasn't bruised, his skin looked dusty and transparent. There was something else she struggled to identify.

Mel watched his eyes widen as they passed her cell. He didn't speak.

Charlie was afraid — something she'd never seen. The prison walls, the sheriff, the gym-rat screws walking him to his cell — they'd turned the man into a strange animal Mel barely knew.

She listened while they moved him into the room, lifted him from the wheelchair and dropped him on a metal cot she assumed identical to her own. She knew he'd despise the indignity of it — the lifting, the prodding and pushing, as though he were a child.

The guards left. The ward's metal door echoed closed behind them. Mel heard Charlie slip down off the cot and shuffle to his cell door. After a moment, he reached around the wall between them. His fingertips grazed the bars of her cell.

"It's you," he said.

His small hand appeared like something beyond nature, as though one man's normal palms had been cleaved along the life line, the fingers discarded. She watched his small, familiar hand stretch around the cell wall. Mel conjured the whole of the man — his soft eyes, his brow's crease, the corner of his mouth rising as he tried to reassure her or make her laugh.

She left her cot and moved to the iron bars. "It's me," she said. She slipped her normal fingers into Charlie's odd hand.

Chapter 52

Mel figured Sheriff Lew bugged the cells. Why else lock them up side-by-side? Mel and Charlie spoke in whispers. They kept an eye on the inner balcony running a circuit around the ward, wary of prison guards.

"Weaze heazave teazo geazet yeazou eazout eazof heazere," Charlie said.

They used carny-talk — a showman's pig Latin — dropping *eaz* before every word's first vowel.

"Seazay theaze seazame feazor yeazou," Mel gestured toward the other cells, putting her hand through the bars so Charlie could see it. *"Neazeither eazof eazus ceazan eazafford teazo geazet meazixed eazin weazith theaze peazopulation."*

"What happened out there?"

"A dump truck — big Caterpillar rig. They tried to ram your van. The truck exploded first."

"You did that?"

"Monk. He called just before it happened. Said a couple of men inside the dump were checking the locks. Making sure the gates were closed. I think they were trying to make it look like a break-in. Kids joyriding in a dump truck. Monk said he was going in. And the line went dead. He drove his car into the truck. He must have aimed for the gas tank."

"Is he —"

"I don't know. I hope he jumped."

She pulled her hands back into the cell. "*Company*," she said, flagging a group of men shuffling back from breakfast, a phalanx of guards behind them. Mel and Charlie scrabbled to their cots and waited for the guards to pass before regrouping by the cell doors.

"I shouldn't have called you, Mel. I'm sorry."

"I'd have heard about it. Bubba would have told me."

"But I called you here. Asked you to come."

"You didn't have to —"

"That's what I'm saying."

"But it's not what I'm saying. You didn't have to ask. I'd have come whether you called or not."

"You have so much to deal with already —"

"The man who raised me is in prison. That's all I know."

Charlie held her hand tighter.

"You look like hell," Mel said.

"Feel it, too." Charlie sighed.

"You worried?"

"No." Charlie paused. *"You?"*

Mel laughed under her breath.

"I'm hurting," Charlie said. *"Physically. That asshole — he was pretty rough arresting me. But it's these cells. The cement floors. Having to waddle around everywhere. I'm not built for it. I never realized how much control I have over my environment — I have money, you know? I get to live in a bubble I made for myself. What's a normal person do?* A normal cripple."

Charlie had always taken a hard line with Mel about what he called *pussyfreaks* — the disabled who weren't willing to flaunt their deformity. She'd never heard him express this kind of sympathy.

"It's one thing, all the verbal people throw at you," he said. *"I never get that — not on the show. Not even from the townies I see — they're all mayors and councilmen, looking for a deal. Imagine some poor fuck who goes into town just wanting to buy groceries or send a letter, except he can't even lick his own stamp. How do they do it? Christ, they're fucking heroes, just getting from morning to night."*

"Tell me what happened in the kooch tent," Mel said.

Charlie told her about Sarge. About Shortie. The arrest.

"Who called the meeting?" she asked.

Charlie lowered his voice, his whisper so hushed Mel barely heard the word. *"Dylan."*

"Dylan Hide?"

"Yeah. He didn't call me himself. He had the Sheriff do it. Said I should meet Dylan on the lot. I told him to send Dylan to my office trailer, but he wouldn't have it. Said the kooch tent or the deal was off. Dylan never turned up."

"What was the deal?" Mel asked.

Charlie sighed. *"The usual. Cash. Hospitality —* "

"Hospitality? Dylan has his own women."

"I thought of that. I don't know."

"What about the vic?"

"Don't know about him either. I've met him — come down to Gibtown with The Committee — but I don't have a story to tell."

"Do you think Dylan set this up?"

"I doubt it." Charlie sounded tired. "I've gone over it. Dylan's crazy. Maybe insane. But he wouldn't fuck around with a set up. If he wanted to kill a man, he'd kill him, and sleep well on it, too."

"The Sheriff?"

"Maybe." Charlie coughed.

"Do you think Cooder had something on the Sheriff? Or Dylan? They set you up for the fall?"

"Maybe. There's plenty to be had on both of them."

Mel thought for a moment, deciding to tell him. "Dylan followed me to Gibtown."

"Did he hurt you?"

"I'm fine."

Charlie didn't speak for a long time. "I'm sorry."

"Why didn't you tell me Dylan knew my father?"

"I was trying. With that photo. We were getting ready for the season and — I don't know — I got a bad feeling. Decided to leave the box for you, in case something happened. In case you came back. I didn't know you'd need it so soon."

"I'd say it wasn't soon enough." She said it and regretted the remark.

Charlie took his time before he spoke again. "Mel, what do you do when you hear gunfire?"

"What do you mean?"

"When you see trouble. Something unjust. What do you do?"

Mel didn't understand where he was going. *"I don't know."*

"You run toward it. When you see trouble, you go there. You're a fixer. Always trying to make things right. I raised you since you were a girl — I know."

"That has nothing to do — "

"It has everything to do with it," Charlie said. *"If I'd told you I knew Billy Barry was alive, and he was in Cuthbert, you'd have come here on your own — "*

"I'm here for you." She heard herself say the words and knew it sounded wan.

"You're here for more than one reason. That's okay with me. But, I sent you to Gibtown to get you away from Dylan, to let you know what you're up against — that should be okay with you, too." Charlie paused. *"That's what family do."*

They both went quiet. Mel wanted to ask. Why Charlie hadn't told her about Billy. How her mother died. Whether EK spoke the truth about her father. The feeder.

Charlie spoke first. "What happened out there? In Gibtown?"

"Forget it, Charlie. Now's not the time."

Chapter 53

Sheriff Lewis Evans leaned back in his chair, his feet crossed over his desk.

EK stared eye-level at the soles of his cowboy boots — too dull for new, too unworn for a man who did his job. Framed photos lined the walls of the office — Lew and the mayor, Lew and the Lieutenant Governor, Lew and the County Fair Tobacco Queen.

EK'd always figured him for a self-congratulatory son-of-a-bitch.

"EK, you have got to understand," Lew smiled wide. He opened both palms to the ceiling. "We're in a period of mourning."

The man didn't chew or drip in a spittoon, but that was technicality — EK knew this man, same as every other shit town lawman he'd dealt with.

"With poor old Sarge dead, well," Lew smiled again. "We're just all broken up. Got us a funeral tomorrow, and there ain't no time for legal proceedings or paperwork today. Can't be bringing the Atlanta boys into this right now — "

"The State of Georgia, Sheriff Evans, is the least of your worries," EK said.

"Is that so? Well, maybe you just ain't been keeping up with the gossip. I took two prisoners last night, both of which was involved in very serious crimes."

"That's speculation — "

"Like you said, I'm the speculator, and right now I speculate I'm holding Matt Clay — him being *the negro* — on suspicion of reckless endangerment resulting in vehicular manslaughter, as well as the destruction of government property. Melinda Barry — her being the crazy bitch — well, that thing'll be lucky to ever see daylight. Obstruction of justice, resisting arrest. And a small matter of desertion of duty from the United States Marine Corps."

"Sheriff, I have to warn you that unless due process — "

"Due process, my sweet ass. EK, when have you ever represented anyone in a court of any kind?"

"As often, Lew, as you've arrested someone for a crime they've actually committed. My clients must be bailed before the court within 24 hours of being charged."

"Well, aren't you something?" Lew took his feet off the desk. He leaned forward, the smile gone.

"You listen to me, and you listen good. You may have been some fancy federal military prosecutor before you growed your hair out and started sucking dick, but you ain't passed no bar exam in the State of Georgia. In *this* state, short of a special dispensation from a Georgia court of law, you got no say in this matter or any other. And you sure as hell ain't got no clients. I do *not* have to bail those two, because I ain't charged them yet. Ain't even in the system and I ain't putting them there until we've had Cooder's funeral. And we are not having Cooder's funeral today."

EK looked the man in the eye. "Then when you do decide to get off your country ass and do something, you might want to think about how deep a shit creek you're wading into. Right now I'd say you're about in over your head, boy. Obstruction of justice and resisting arrest are state crimes. Reckless endangerment and vehicular manslaughter — same local *chickenshit*. But desertion? That's Federal."

Lew looked out the window.

"Same for harboring a deserter. MCO 1620.3," EK said. "*It is the policy of the United States Marine Corps to cooperate with civilian authorities unless the best interests of the Marine Corps will be prejudiced.* Now, you don't want people to think you're prejudiced, do you?"

The Sheriff started to rise, angry. "Goddamnit, if you think that means — "

"That means that within seventy-two hours of you logging Melinda Barry in the system, unless you plan on violating Federal law, Ms. Barry will be remanded to the Naval Consolidated Brig, Miramar, California, where she'll face trial for desertion. And *the negro*, as you call him, gets turned over to Atlanta FBI for harboring a deserter. What that means, Lew, is when you do get around to charging Mr. Clay and Ms. Barry — *and* Mr. Koontz — the FBI's going to have a goddamned good sniff around this high-tech chicken coop of yours. Then they'll take all three of your prisoners and start kicking your chickenshit ass." EK leaned back in his chair, lighting a cigarette in the man's office. Sheriff Lew started to say something, but EK cut him off. "Kick your ass the same way as Dylan, once he finds out you lost his prize to Federal custody."

Lew looked out the window again.

"Or you could release them to me."

Chapter 54

Mel crouched in an oak tree behind the police station. She watched the Sheriff's surveillance cameras sweep the lock-up yard, looking for an opening.

He'd released her close to midnight. Eight hours ago. The Sheriff appeared at her cell door, fists planted on his hips, brooding and silent. Without taking his eyes off Mel, he'd called Charlie's name. "Koontz. Get ready to move."

Mel had shot off the cot. "You can't — "

"You're not in the position, missy," he'd shouted through the bars. "Turn around. Face the window."

"Where are you — "

Evans pulled a taser from his belt holster. He aimed at Mel's chest. "At the request of his so-called *lawyer*, we're moving your freak friend to the medical ward."

"You — "

"Shut up. I said, *Turn around. Face the window.* You hear?"

A guard had appeared with a wheelchair. Mel turned slow, putting her hands on her head. Charlie had gone with the man in silence.

The Sheriff had returned fifteen minutes later, cuffed her hands behind her back and pushed her down a series of hallways.

"I know what you done." His voice a raged whisper. "All of it. You may be getting out now, but don't you start thinking you ain't going to pay. Believe me, missy — there will be a reckoning."

No one had witnessed their path through the empty prison hallways, onto the loading bay out into the pitch black of the parking lot. EK had been waiting, the El Camino idling in the dark.

In the car, EK explained the lay of the land. Mel was free temporarily, released in his custody. Monk was being kept in a *special* ward — "Not for acrobats, you can be sure". EK thought he'd be released in a couple of days, after Cooder's funeral. The situation with Charlie was less certain. "But he's safe in the hospital ward. There are real medical people there."

No charges filed. No arrests recorded. That hadn't reassured Mel.

EK explained the city would shut down for Cooder's funeral. Things might change then. Fast. They had to be ready.

Mel had doubted a whole city would close for the funeral of one man, but as she watched the police station from the oak tree, she saw EK had probably been right — the station, at least, was shuttered and locked, the streets deserted.

The tree was one of a row that ran behind the station. Thick limbs arced across the residential road, kudzu dripping nearly to the sidewalk.

The station remained dark, the gates surrounding the back lot chained and locked. Mel had been in the tree an hour, watching the station, keeping an eye on the three cameras covering the lot. Their lenses swept arcs across the yard, out of sync, each camera rotating at a different speed. Mel figured it was an attempt at creating an unpredictable pattern. A failed attempt. Instead, the out-of-sync motors opened gaping holes in the camera coverage. She spotted two periods in their cycles that would leave her unrecorded for at least five minutes.

Impounded cars and pickups filled the lot. Mel shimmied along a thick branch reaching across the yard's chain-link fence. Near the end she looked back for passing cars. Clear, she dropped down onto the roof of a rusting pickup. Mel rolled onto the ground, crouching between rows of cars.

EK had told her which vehicle belonged to Willy O'Keefe, but he needn't have. Willy's Ram sat next to the station, its right front suspension collapsed, the body covered in mud and drying algae. Mel watched the cameras, waiting for her opening.

The center camera turned just enough that she thought she'd be out of sight. Three minutes, at least. Mel duck walked across the yard, trying to run.

She made a quick circle of the truck, looking for anything. Any kind of clue.

Boiled by the screaming engine, river water had forced the hood open, buckled at the center.

The Ram's headlights were still filled with water. The collapsed suspension had flattened the right front tire, gouging a hole in the truck's big treads.

Mel moved around to the back of the truck, staying low. She spotted a fresh scar circling the truck's towing eye. Probably left by the cable used to winch it out of the river. She leaned in close and found red paint along the bent chrome bumper. Mel guessed someone had rear-ended the truck. She snapped her switchblade and scraped the flake away. Not red paint. Red primer, baked beneath a chip of black auto paint.

Mel edged her way around the other side of the truck. She found the driver's door open, the window broken out. Black sludge poured out of the footwell, sunbaked into a dry river of silt and mud spilled onto the asphalt parking lot. She checked her watch. Less than ninety seconds left, she climbed into the cab. First, Mel popped the glovebox and found Willy O.'s gun, a third gen Glock 19 alongside a soaked box of 9mm Luger. She sniffed the barrel for burn. It hadn't been fired for a while.

Mel rummaged the footwell on both sides. She buried her hand in the soft silt. Nothing. She leaned across the front, searching the space between the passenger door and the seat. Slotted down in the door pocket, surrounded by black sand, she found two teeth fused to a piece of bloody jawbone. Mel picked it up with her fingertips — salt and pepper stubble covered a flap of Willy's pale grey flesh, still attached to the bone. Mel dropped it back on the floor.

She scanned the door frame and found two bullet holes. Mel used the switchblade again, digging out a flattened 9mm slug. She doubted it had come from Willy's Glock.

Mel dropped the slug in her pocket and rolled out of the cab onto the asphalt. She checked her watch. Twenty seconds.

She made another squat run across the parking lot. At the rusty pickup, Mel climbed into the pickup bed, leapt up onto the dented roof, and launched back onto the limb of the old oak.

Chapter 55

One man in Marine uniform stationed himself across the field from Dylan and the rest. Away from the grave. A roll of red fat bulged from the back of his neck, pushing out over his collar. The gold buttons on his black jacket strained, the white belt a binding on the thick man's gut. Dylan figured him for sixty.

The man readied his rifle and aimed at the sky, jerky and unpracticed like a jangling machine about to lose its bolts. He fired — *crack* — the blank's hollow sound feeble and dull.

Not even a proper honor guard.

Dylan shouldn't have give a shit, but it bothered him. The fat retired Marine bothered him. The coffin with the worn-out flag off Cooder's front porch bothered him. The Committee hovering around the hole like a handful of meerkats, eyes bugged out and jumping at shadows. Sheriff Lew bothered him. Dylan didn't know if that son-of-a-bitch was worse when he had his eye on the ball or off it. And that EK bastard stood all by himself under a tree, like he had an invisible cloak, like he hadn't just fucked the whole lot of them. EK bothered him.

The leatherneck fired again. *Crack.*

Fucking Committee. Simpering and weak like a bunch of women. Every one of them too scared to deal with shit themselves. So freaked out, they looked like they didn't even know what was really happening.

But they knew. He'd let them know about Cooder, and they'd probably figured out Willy O. on their own.

And they knew what Dylan knew about them.

Twenty, thirty years. Every one of them had come downstairs at The Social more times than they'd been home. Done more fucking in his club than in their own bedrooms. Young fucking, old fucking. Asians. Niggers. Boys sometimes.

And it was always Dylan with the supply. *Dylan get me this. Dylan how about that? I'm tired of Chinese, Dylan, hadn't you got something Mexican?* Dylan Dylan Dylan.

Now they thought they'd leave their friend behind. Go big time. Like some uptown SOB'd think they was worth the time of day. They wasn't. And it wasn't going to happen neither. Not as long as Dylan lived and breathed.

They knew that part, too. That it'd be over his dead body.

It's time. That's what Willy O. said at that meeting. Dylan had read his face. Heard his voice in his own head. *I love him like a brother, but Dylan's got to go.*

At least Dylan knew about love. Willy O. didn't understand the first goddamned thing. Love was family. Love was men looking out for their friends. Sticking together. Helping one another.

Dylan's got to go. That wasn't love.

He'd show them all some love.

Crack.

Straight from his fucking heart.

Chapter 56

Mel waited in the kooch tent. The mermaid's tank loomed over the space. Light swept through its pumped currents, refracting over the tent's canvas walls. The smell of chlorine soaked the humid air.

EK and Monk walked in through the backstage run. In her relief, a rush of vertigo overtook Mel, adding to her sense that she was underwater.

Monk looked exhausted. Black dirt from the cell floor covered his palms. Bruises tried to hide his left eye. A mean cut weltered beneath his right.

Scabs and stitches pockmarked his forehead. Monk tried to walk normally, but Mel could see pain arcing through his frame.

"Melinda Barry," EK said, flourishing his hand. "Matt Clay."

Mel wrapped her arms around Monk, the man wincing as she hugged him close. She relaxed her hold, pressing her head to his chest. Mel closed her eyes as Monk lay his fingers on her temple, sweeping a strand of hair back over her ear.

Eyes still closed, Mel asked, "Where's Charlie?"

Monk's voice rumbled through his chest. "Prison."

Mel let him go and turned to EK, her face washed in fear. "EK?"

"Prison infirmary, actually."

"Didn't you try — "

"I begged. I threatened. I invoked *habeas corpus* — "

"You're a lawyer — "

"Not in Georgia."

"You're a fucking lawyer."

Monk tried to calm her. "Mel — "

She pushed him away. "No, Matt. Don't *Mel* me —

"They won't release him," EK said. "Sheriff Lew said he didn't have the authority."

"Then who — "

"No one, Mel," Monk said. "That's the point. Charlie is *detained* — "

"But not *charged*. Like the two of you." EK finished Monk's sentence. "In legalese, to constitute an arrest there must be an intent to arrest under authority, a detention in the manner of the law, and it must be understood by the person — "

"You're saying he's been kidnapped."

"By the police. Yes. But it will take a court to establish that — "

"Then make it happen — "

"This is a very complicated situation — "

Balling her fists, Mel let out a frustrated cry, silencing EK.

Monk waited for her to calm before speaking. "Mel, I saw things in there you couldn't have. The ward where they held me, they're not running a penitentiary. It's a prison labor camp."

Mel was silent.

"They held me in a special wing. EK thought I was going to the *black* ward."

"*Black* ward?"

"The whole prison is segregated, by color and nationality, not just levels of violence. EK thought they would throw me in with the black inmates, but they put me in with the immigrants instead. It's a separate section of the prison, away from the circular ward."

EK interrupted him. "They didn't want anyone speaking to him. To tell him what's happening there."

"Where they kept me, no one spoke English. I don't know where they hold the Mexicans, but the men I saw — Chinese, Burmese, Thai — almost all of them were Asians."

"But we know they do immigration," Mel said. "It's out in the open."

"This is different," EK said.

"A group of Chinese men told me. Every man I spoke with paid to come to America — to get in the country illegally. Boats, trucks, sometimes thirty men in the back of a box van, usually across the Canadian border. They pay to get in, then end up working on farms or factories, living ten to a room. Work gang stuff. Eating out of the company store, in debt to a gang boss."

"Like the 20th century never happened," EK said.

"But you knew this," Mel said to EK.

"Not everything," Monk said. "After they work in the camps a while, they get arrested. Picked up on immigration violation. Usually, they're held in Cuthbert Prison, then shipped back home."

"That's normal — "

"But it changed last year," Monk said. "Mass arrests. Roundups. People getting real prison time before they're shipped home. Five years, some of them."

"Georgia passed an immigration *reform* act," EK said. "HB 87. It gave the police free reign. Roadblocks. Stop and search. Arrests on suspicion. The rednecks love it, but there's half a million illegal workers in Georgia — that's a lot of cheap labor. The arrests started and crops were left standing in the fields."

"Not enough pickers," Mel said.

"Factories couldn't keep up with orders. Businesses went bankrupt. So The Committee lobbied the Governor to invoke the Crime Control Act," EK said. "It's a simple law — *all state prisoners must work.* And because the prison is privately run, the work is contracted to private companies."

"Police round up the immigrants," Monk said. "Throw them in prison, then *rent* them back to the same fields they worked before they were arrested."

"Prisoners get twenty-three cents an hour," EK said. "And even that they have to give to the prison for their upkeep. Who knows how much the prison makes. It's a privately-held company — they don't have to open up their books. And families back home don't know about it. They're still using the same route trying to get into America. It's an infinitely renewable labor force."

"Slave labor," Monk said. "Charlie's in serious danger."

"He's handicapped. They can't put him in a field," Mel said.

"They won't. Him working isn't the problem," EK said.

"It's what he knows. Charlie. You, me. We've seen it ourselves. Been told the stories. Now we know, we're a threat," Monk said. "This is the link no one understands."

Everything clicked in Mel's head. "It's an end-to-end operation — a trafficking ecosystem. The people who arrest the immigrants — "

"*And* the people who rent them from the prison back to the field — " Monk said.

"*Are the people who trafficked them in the first place,*" Mel said. "The people holding Charlie."

EK nodded. "Sheriff Lew. The Committee."

Chapter 57

"You knew all of this."

EK sat on a front row wood seat in the kooch tent, his back curved, palms against his forehead. Folding into himself. Mel shouting.

"The day I drove down here — you knew before that — "

"I didn't — "

"You could have stopped it, couldn't you?" Mel paced forward and back, start and stop, fingernails digging into her palms.

"Melinda, I — "

"Tell me you couldn't have stopped it. Look me in the eye." She kicked the chair next to him. "Look at me."

"I couldn't stop it."

"Bullshit. *You knew.*"

"Not everything." EK held both palms in front of him, shaking his head.

"Really?" Mel started to walk away, frustrated. She made it two steps before she turned back, rushing EK, jamming her finger in his chest. Her teeth clenched. "Let me review events, in case you need some detail."

Monk stood with his arms crossed, his voice quiet. "Mel."

"No, Matt. He knew every fucking bit of it." She turned back to EK. "You knew I was coming before I got here. You weren't surprised — "

"Charlie told me — "

"You knew the victim."

"We all knew Sarge — "

"You know the Sheriff. The Committee. The other dead guy, you hinted that was murder before I found the bullets. Before I found a piece of his face. And the man that almost raped me — *you fucking sent me to him.*"

EK rose, defending himself. "Charlie sent you to Gibtown. He didn't know you'd be followed."

"But you did, didn't you?"

"For the love of God." EK threw his hands in the air. He sat down again. "Monk, will you talk — "

"You knew my Dad — " Mel stopped. She shut here eyes. EK and Monk waited. Mel's voice dropped to a whisper. "You knew my father was here, and you sent me on a goose chase. You made me follow you. You made me beg — "

"Melinda, it was not my intention — "

"I don't care about your fucking intention." The words luffed into the tent's soft canvas walls, so quiet now Mel could hear blood in her ears. Her breathing. "Tell me what you didn't know."

"How can I — "

"Easy, EK. Think of the things we've been getting arrested for, shot at, manhandled. Now ask yourself which bit you didn't know. Anything?"

"I was trying to protect you."

"*Anything?*"

Monk stepped toward her. "Mel."

"No. No." Mel fumbled her self-control. "Where is your father, EK?"

"He's dead — "

"That's right. Dead. And what would you do to get him back — "

"I'd — "

"Anything. You'd do *fucking* anything."

"Mel — "

"The man who raised me is stuck in a wheelchair in prison. You knew everything and you have done nothing but *get in my fucking way*. So here's what you do now, you get him out. You're the one who knows how — "

"I'm not sure — "

"Then get goddamned sure, EK. Skin a dog, paint some bacon. Do whatever you do to get your fucking spirits juiced. Get. Charlie. Out. Because if you don't, I swear I'll tie you from a fucking lamppost and — "

"Melinda — "

"*Make it happen.*"

Mel walked out of the tent. Monk started to follow.

"Don't," EK said. "Let her be."

Monk kept walking.

"Let her go, Monk," EK called. "It's just hitting her — she's scared."

Monk stopped. "Of what?"

"She's lost her father again. She doesn't want to lose Charlie."

Chapter 58

Milo told Sheriff Lew to meet him at the Eufala Country Club along the George Reservoir, just over the Alabama state line. Milo was a no golfer, but he didn't give a shit. They couldn't meet in Cuthbert — Eufala was a safe half hour down the road. Plus he figured between the fairway and the reservoir, he could keep an eye on the horizon. Keep an eye out for Dylan.

Lew hit his ball off the tee, ending his swing with a top-toe flourish, like he thought he was some kind of pro.

Together, they watched Lew's ball sail over the fairway and roll ass-kissingly close to Milo's last shot. The two of them started the long walk down the fairway.

No one had seen Dylan since the funeral, not even Lew. Milo'd tried calling by The Social, despite the *Closed* sign. One of Dylan's cars sat out in the parking lot, but the kitchen help told Milo Dylan wasn't in. Hadn't been for days. Milo couldn't remember the last time Dylan had disappeared, but he remembered it'd been messy.

Once they found the balls, Lew fished in his pocket for a dime to use as a marker. Milo tried to find the right club.

He pulled out an iron, then a putter, and finally gave up. "Fuck it, Lew. I can't play this game. Let's just walk."

Lew shrugged and picked up his ball, pocketing the dime.

Milo's heart hurt, his breath giving out on him. He could feel a headache coming on from the sun. He wished he'd brought his gimme hat from the truck. "You figured out what to do about that Lobster fella?"

Lew scanned the horizon, looking over his shoulder. *Jesus.* Milo thought a man could've been in a jet plane and still known Lew was about to talk about something he wasn't supposed to.

"Accident, I imagine," Lew whispered. "EK forced us to put him in the prison hospital. Maybe someone'll give him the wrong dose of medicine."

Milo stopped and wiped his forehead. "Well Lew, I figured that's what you'd say, but it ain't the way we're seeing it. We done met about this, and we think it's about time for all this to stop. We got a planeload of DC brass coming in, same time as this thing's turning into one hell of a shit sandwich. So we don't need no worries piled on our woes. Last thing I want to be explaining to some DC asshole is why a man who wasn't even on the books just died in our infirmary. From a *accident.*"

"But no one knows he's there."

Milo gave the man a look.

Lew shrugged. "I guess I see your point."

"They *do* know," Milo said. "EK and that woman and her Afro-American friend knows. All them carnival people, too. We can't go around middle of the night disappearing people — this ain't Costa Rica or whatever. We got to be surgical."

"That's what you said before you sent Sarge after Dylan. *We got to be surgical.*" Lew grinned. "That would be just before Dylan cut his throat."

"I could do without your smartass remarks, Lew. And you keep in mind when you open that mouth of yours, Sarge was a friend of mine." Milo could feel the sweat down his back. "Where's the goddamned golf cart?"

"You left it. Said we got to walk."

Milo pulled at his shirt. Sweat dripped into one eye. "Look, I know you're close with Dylan. We all growed up together. And Dylan's been good for all of us — hell, we probably owe him. But we ain't kids no more, Lew. We're exposed, and we got to do this like men. Dylan, he ain't acting like a man no more. You can't run around all hot-blooded, killing people just cause they looked at you funny. We need someone to man up and take over. We can't have a mad dog running around."

The two men stared across the green. Lew held his tongue, waiting.

"Damnit, Lew, I'm offering it to you." Milo watched the man for his reaction.

"I'm grateful," Lew said. "Mighty grateful." He paused, drawing out the moment, staring out across the fairway. "Thinking on it, though, I can see how Dylan could still be useful."

"How's that?"

"Forgive me for speaking poor of your friend, but Sarge wasn't no killer. He might have been back in the day, but he's just a businessman now. Was, God rest him. You can't send a possum into a gator fight. But I'll tell you something, Milo. You can sure send a gator to a possum party."

"What the hell are you talking about, Lew?" They crossed a water hazard, Milo struggling up the white picket bridge. He needed sense out of the man, not more bullshit.

"What if we let Lobster Boy out?" Lew said. "Where's he going to go?"

Milo stopped at the top of the bridge and gripped the rail with both hands. "Back to the carnival, I guess."

"That's right. Straight back to every problem we got, right there on the carnival lot. All our troubles, in one place. And Dylan'll be watching."

"You saying he'll go after them?"

"You said it yourself. He's a mad dog. He ain't run away, he's got his hunt on. Dylan's out there watching, and all we need to do is focus his attention. We get all our problems together, they're his problems, too. We manipulate it so everyone's problems are in the same place at the same time — "

"Your possum party."

"Then we sit back and let the gator come," Lew said. "Probably take him out while we're at it."

"And if Dylan don't show?"

"He'll show. That woman's there, he'll show."

"And what if he don't, Lew?"

"Then I'll handle it. Can of gas and a pack of matches. There won't be no accidents. We'll have something bigger than that. Something where afterwards, people just shake their heads and say they're shocked. *Shocked.* But they ain't surprised."

"And what would make folks say such a thing?"

"A tragedy. A great circus fire," Lew said. He grabbed the handle on his golf bag, turning for the clubhouse. "You know that saying, Milo? *One man, one problem. No man, no problems?* You leave it with me. I'll see to every problem you got."

Chapter 59

Dylan watched the old queer through the two-way mirror. EK had knocked on the door, ignoring the sign saying they were closed — closed for the first time in the life of the joint. EK blocked the door with his foot soon as the bartender opened it. Asking for Dylan.

Closed. Dylan shook his head.

The barman tried to put him off, gesturing with open palms, but EK'd pushed past, headed for the office. Making a ruckus. A couple of the niggers had come out of the kitchen. Now they tried to hold EK back without assaulting him.

EK made for the mirror, shouting and waving his arms. Shouting at *him*, Dylan figured. Convinced he was there.

Dylan couldn't hear a word through the glass, the office silent except when Jimmy gurgled in his wheelchair in the corner. Jimmy's one eye wandered around the room, out of control, his head a white swaddle of gauze, spotted here and there in crimson and a color that wasn't quite yellow.

Billy'd found some back-alley doctor to bandage Jimmy up and smack him out on heroin.

Dylan didn't want him in a hospital. Without his jaw, Jimmy couldn't talk, but he could damn well point a finger. Stella slumped on the couch beside Jimmy, her head lolling, chin against her chest. A string of drool reached down from her bottom lip, aimed for her crotch. Dylan looked at the rubber tube knotted around her arm.

Couldn't stay out of Jimmy's supply.

The niggers were having a hard time out in the club. EK'd broke loose and turned on the pair. He moved from table to table, smashed candle holders and ashtrays, losing it. Doing what a man does when he's got no options. No place left to turn.

The niggers had their arms out making a loose circle, treating EK like some kind of bush animal.

Dylan punched a button on his desk. Ten seconds later, a pair of heavy footsteps lumbered up from the basement. His door flew open. Two red-faced bulletheads hustled into the room, breathing heavy.

Dylan pointed at Jimmy. "Boys, you see old Jimmy there?"

They nodded, looking from Jimmy to Dylan, confused.

Dylan moved his finger to the two way mirror, jabbing it. "That's the queer's fault. Mostly."

He watched the men's jaws clench like a couple Dawgs gunning for War Eagle. "You ain't got to kill him, but if you do, take it out to the truck stop." They ran into one another, fighting for the door.

Dylan raised his voice to let the men hear him as they ran through the kitchen. "How's he lived so many days, suffering like that? Testament to the power of the human spirit."

He watched through the mirror as the first fist slammed EK's jaw, knocking him on his ass. Jimmy gurgled again, struggling to breath. Dylan smiled at Stella, paralytic on the couch. When the mood took him, he was going to have to put both of them down.

Chapter 60

"Door's locked. Not answering his phone, either."

Mel climbed off EK's porch, slipped the handset into her pocket and pulled the helmet back on. Waiting in the drive, Monk straddled the Harley. Mel gripped the shoulder of his jacket and threw her leg over the taillights, settling into the passenger pegs. She saw Monk wince, his body still hurting.

Monk stared at the porch. "Is that where it happened?"

"Yeah." Mel cursed herself, silent voices punishing her for her words.

"Where to?" Monk asked.

"Police Station maybe."

White shells sprayed behind them as they tore down the long driveway and turned onto the county road.

"You can't beat yourself up about it," Monk shouted over his shoulder.

"You about to say *He's probably fine?*"

"EK's not stupid," Monk said. "But he's probably not fine."

Mel leaned forward and wrapped her arms around Monk's stomach, careful with his ribs. They sped up the Interstate onramp. Monk gunned the Harley, slipping in between pairs of rushing headlights. Mel thought she was probably a better rider, but back at the carnival lot she'd decided to hand Monk the keys. From the elevated viaduct, she scanned the parking lots of gas stations and chain restaurants lining the service roads. Searching for the El Camino, finding nothing.

"You think there's a tie between Dylan and the prison?" she asked.

Monk thought about it, riding in silence.

He finally spoke. "Instinct says yes, but it's hard to know. I can't get a handle on Dylan's business."

"The Social's not serving cupcakes," Mel said.

Silence again. Monk considering. "Strippers don't always mean prostitution. Or trafficking. Stripping's a gateway, but it's pretty legit these days. Not like when we were growing up."

"Speak for yourself," Mel said. They were about to pass another exit — a service road leading to a lone truck stop. Mel scanned the big parking lots.

"Right. You grew up with Charlie and the mermaids," Monk said. "But there's miles of grey between the mermaids and Dylan's operation."

Mel could see the problem for Monk, locating the dissonance between Charlie's business and Dylan's. She felt his admiration for the man jar against the reality of prostitution.

"*Violence* is the difference," Mel offered. "EK's right. Charlie's not taking money from widows and orphans, he's helping them. Social freaks and people in trouble — he finds them a place — like your broken stones. But Dylan and my father. The damage they do — " Mel stopped. "Monk. Over on your right. You see it? The truck stop parking lot."

Deep in the lot, five men corralled a sixth, crawling across the ground. Concealed by semis, covered from every angle except the interstate, the men formed a beatdown circle, taking turns on the man in the middle. Mel was sure it was EK. A seventh man sat behind the wheel of a dirty yellow Freightliner school bus, parked and watching. At the center of the circle, EK struggled to his feet, swinging wildly with his cane. One man kicked him in the small of his back, knocking EK to his knees again, the gnarled rod flying from his hands. Two others moved in, cocked their fists and delivered.

"You think that's EK?" Monk asked.

"Does it matter?"

"No." Monk throttled the Harley down the offramp. They turned onto the service road, Monk leaning into the handlebars, pushing the bike low into the road's turns. He shouted to her over his shoulder. "We need surprise. They see us coming, they'll kill him. If we drive into them, we'll hit EK. But — "

"What're you thinking?"

"You ever stand up on one of these?"

She hadn't. "Are you saying we jump?"

"With the helmets. Like cannonballs," Monk said. "You mind getting your bike scratched?"

Mel slapped the back of his jacket. "Let's do it."

Monk swerved into the parking lot and aimed the bike toward the men. Mel held his jacket collar and pulled her feet up onto the seat, checking her grip. In one quick motion she was standing, knees bent.

Monk downshifted and pulled back on the throttle. The Harley's roar echoed back at them, reflected off the parked semis surrounding the men.

Chapter 61

Mel clocked the speedometer before she jumped. They were doing 35. She spotted her target and tried to time it by instinct, reminding herself her ribs were a vulnerability. She gripped Monk's jacket, set her direction and pushed off the seat.

She spread her arms, trying to sail head first. What should have been a precision sortie felt like a disaster at the end of a bowling alley. Her body wheeled horizontally, parallel with the ground. She spun sideways, chopping into the circle of men like a helicopter rotor set loose in a crowded stadium.

She heard the crack of her helmet split the closest man's head. The impact shot down her vertebrae, stunning her. As she tumbled over the man, Mel wrapped an arm around his throat and drew his bulk into her trajectory, slowing her fall. His feet jerked off the ground. Mel tried to twist her body in the air, balancing momentum against the man's weight.

They crashed into a second man, his fist raised, ready to deliver EK a finishing blow. The three went down. Mel landed on the second man before rolling out across the dirt. The whole thing lasted less than two seconds.

Burning rubber screamed fifty feet behind her, Monk spinning the bike around for another pass.

Mel whipped off the helmet and looked back at what remained of the circle. EK struggled on all fours, drooling and coughing, facing her. Blood dripped from his mouth, his face unrecognizable. Three men formed a half-circle to EK's left. Monk's best shot was the man in the center, furthest from EK.

Mel heard the Harley's throttle open, drinking fuel. She ran toward the closest man, helmet swinging. Still on the ground, hands and knees, EK ducked his head.

Mel let loose. The helmet crunched the man's face, shattering his nose. She leapt straight up, driving a heel into his chest. He fell backward, tumbling over EK's back. Mel landed on one foot and pushed off sideways, giving Monk space.

He flew off the bike feet first. An impossibly long jump that erased gravity. Monk shot toward both men. His right leg crunched across the throat of the man furthest away as he slammed his helmet into another man's temple. Both hit the ground. Monk twisted midair and touched down momentarily, facing Mel, beyond the men's fallen bodies. Still driven by momentum, he pushed off, arcing into a backflip, trying to control his fall.

Mel heard a pistol crack behind her. Hot metal zipped past her ear. Midair, Monk began to spin and twist. Blood sprayed an arabesque around him. His body limp, the flip broken, he cartwheeled into a dead stop.

In a single motion, Mel pulled the OTs-38 from her jacket and turned. Three self-silenced bullets hit the man behind her — a double-tap to the chest, another to the forehead. Already dead, his body fell backward into the splatter of his own blood.

Heat shimmered off Mel's Russian pistol, ready in her left hand as she turned a circle in the silent parking lot, checking the seven men splayed around her.

Chapter 62

EK collapsed forward landing on his elbows, his nose mashed into the gravel parking lot, a downward dog mewling a pool of blood. Monk lay still beside him, eyes closed.

Mel saw two of the bulletheads were still conscious — one three bodies away. The other scrabbled beside Mel on his back, reaching in his jacket pocket for a pistol. Mel lifted one leg high to gain leverage before she fell into the man. Her weight drove a sharp elbow into his ribcage. Two ribs snapped with the impact, one piercing something deep in his body. He coughed blood, spewed from the side of his open mouth. Mel snatched the weapon from the man's hand.

The second faced her, armed. He raised an automatic, pointing it at her head. Still on her back, Mel rocked her head and shoulders forward and pushed her pistol between raised knees. Three quick shots. One to each wrist — the weapon scattered across the lot — and the third to his ankle. The man went down, howling. Mel rose and pistol-whipped him into darkness.

She collected every weapon she could find, then moved to Monk's side. "Matt?"

Eyes closed, he tried to draw air through his nose.

He exhaled a noise somewhere between a cough and a laugh. "I knew you could fly," he said.

"Jesus, Monk." A dark slough of blood seeped beneath his shoulder onto the parking lot. She snapped her switchblade and cut Monk's jacket away, tearing at the shirt beneath.

A single bullet wound opened a muscled knot below his shoulder. Mel slid her hand under his shoulder blade, hoping for an exit wound. She found it behind his broad left pectoral, along with a second entry point in his bicep — the bullet passed through chest muscle, deflected off the ribcage, reentering his arm. She couldn't feel a second exit point. Mel found the bloody leather patch she'd cut from his jacket and slipped it into Monk's mouth.

"Bite down."

Monk drove his teeth into the hide, knowing what to expect. Mel probed deep in his arm muscle near the entry wound, careful to avoid infecting the cauterized hole. His bicep radiated the bullet's heat. Monk arched his back, one knee rising. "Sorry, baby," Mel said. She pulled the hand back. Mel shed her jacket and stripped her t-shirt, ripped it in half and used the cloth to lay pressure on his inner arm. "Bullet passed through your pec, sideways into your arm. It's lodged, close to the bone. You're losing blood."

Monk pulled air again. "EK," he whispered.

"Hold this." Mel let Monk find the cloth with his hand. "Keep the pressure up."

She barely recognized EK. A flap of skin peeled away from one of his cheekbones, pulp and torn muscle exposed beneath.

Through a slice in his other cheek, Mel could see clenched teeth losing anchor in his pale gums. Blood shot through one eye, ready to leave its socket, The pupil wandered in his skull. The other eye puffed along the lids like slips of pupating flesh, an extra pair of lips set wrong on his face. He couldn't move his jaw — probably broken.

"Mel." Monk called to her. He lifted one arm and pointed across the parking lot. "Company."

She turned, letting the Russian pistol lead her line of sight.

An old man in overalls and a gimme cap limped toward them from the school bus. He wore a metal brace over one denim-covered leg. "*Qué chingados,* lady. Don't shoot."

"Back the fuck up," Mel said.

"Men are coming from the diner. You got to go. Come on, I'll take you to the hospital."

"No," EK mumbled, his teeth clenched. He scrabbled for his cane, just out of reach. "No hospital."

"We won't be safe," Monk said to Mel.

"I'll take you anywhere, okay?" the man said. "But you got to go, *pronto.*"

Mel knew it was true. "Who are you?" she asked.

"Gabe Orozco," he said. "I drive the school bus."

"I just killed a man. Why are you helping us?"

"Because of this bastard." He kicked one of the unconscious men in the head, the clink of his leg brace accenting the blow. "*Hijo de puta,* he made me this way."

Monk raised his head. "Let's go, Mel. We don't have a choice."

Chapter 63

They made it onto the interstate without a tail. Mel didn't think that would last long.

She'd stretched Monk out in the school bus aisle between the rows of seats, EK near the front. Sitting up hurt EK's ribs, but Mel wanted to keep his head elevated. He gripped his cane across the back of the the seat in front of him, dizzy from the beating.

"Put it to the floor, Gabe," Mel said.

"Lady, I'm trying. It's as fast as she goes." Gabe battled the engine's governor, fighting the upper limit on their speed.

Mel called Jalinda. She picked up on the first ring.

"Girl, where are you? Monk gone missing — didn't even make his show tonight —"

"He's with me. Is there a doctor on the lot? We need a show doc, no townies."

"We got the vet. He got X-rays and a lab and all. You sick — "

"Monk's been shot — "

"Oh my God — "

"You've got to stay cool and listen."

"Oh my God — "

Mel raised her voice over the noise of the bus. "You cool?"

Mel heard her swallow. "I'm cool."

"He'll live, but you have write this down."

"Okay."

"Monk has two bullet wounds, one straight through. No organ damage. The bullet's lodged in his left bicep, but it's near the brachial artery. B. R. A. — "

"I can spell."

"He's conscious, but losing blood. We need to establish a blood type — "

"I'm O negative. I can give blood to anybody."

"We need X-rays, too. EK's with us — broken ribs, a broken jaw, maybe his wrist and a possible concussion. I think there's internal bleeding — the danger is hemorrhage. We need all hands on deck. The vet have a tent?"

"Out back of the kooch."

"We're ten, maybe fifteen minutes away. And Jalinda, call a *Hey Rube*. Time to circle the wagons." Mel hung up the phone.

EK raised his head. "You have to leave me. Drop me off," he moaned, his teeth clenched against the pain of moving his jaw.

"What?"

"Leave me. There's no point."

"EK, we don't have time for drama — "

"Give me a weapon — I'll slow them down — "

"Not going to happen."

EK put his forehead back down on his arms. "Melinda, I'm sorry. I was trying to help you. I did it wrong."

"Shut up, EK. It hurts when you talk."

EK tried to smile, but winced at the pain.

Mel's phone rang.

"*Bubbala* — "

"Bad time, Bubba," Mel said.

"Listen, I'm in. The whole system. Very high tech. The prison, vehicle tracking, Sheriff's office. Video, even — "

"Bubba — "

"Listen to me! They're releasing Charlie — "

"Now?"

"Right now. I can see everything. Even his cot. That prison's a nightmare."

"You have video in his cell?"

"He's been moved."

"Where?"

"On the loading dock. Right this minute. Looks like they're going to put him in the Sheriff's car."

Mel tried to bend her head around what she was hearing. "What do you think?" she asked.

"What's *to* think?" Bubba said. "You see a rat, you smell a rat, you're standing in a trap."

Mel hung up the phone.

Chapter 64

"At the light, Gabe," Mel said. "Next to the Wal-Mart."

The old man hit the brakes, the traffic light flicking green-yellow-red as he rolled to a stop outside the Wal-Mart parking lot. Mel pitched through the back door. She slammed it behind her and slapped the side of the bus. "Go, go."

The bus pulled away, ignoring the red light — a midnight caution against nonexistent traffic. She'd left EK holding the compression cloth, staunching Monk's bleeding.

Mel ran across the empty parking lot, wary of the gang of cars surrounding an Applebee's fifty yards down the road. She circled the strip shopping center's beige outer wall, rounding the corner for the back lot. A bread delivery van stood empty at the loading bay. Mel shot out the driver's side window with the Russian OTs-38 revolver. Loaded with self-silenced SP-4, crackling glass and a single ricochet were the only sounds to give her away.

She opened the panel van's door, hot-wired the ignition, snapped the steering lock and pulled away from the bay, lights out, heading for the prison.

At the county road, Mel rang Bubba. "You said you hacked the tracking system. Where's the Sheriff?"

"Just turned off 266 onto County Road 50. Charlie in back. Where are you?"

"50 and Highland. Chicken joint on the left."

"Headed your way. Pull in and wait."

Mel parked in the empty lot. She shut down the engine, wary the exhaust would betray her presence. Cuthbert's streets were deserted. This late, the town offered two choices — the Applebee's, or The Mermaid Parade's midnight show — each on opposite ends of town. The middle was a no man's land.

Mel waited less than a minute before the cruiser drove past, riding slow on the four-lane street. Sheriff Lew drove — she watched him talk. His mouth worked overtime, his right hand gesturing over the back seat. Charlie sat in back, anxious eyes risen just above the window line, a desperate child seeking escape.

Mel watched the cruiser ride another block and started the van. She pulled onto the road and drove in darkness, the highway's dim streetlights creating an irregular rhythm of light and shadow sweeping the van's interior.

The cruiser turned left at Town Hall Square, driving north on 216 for the county fairgrounds. Mel waited until the car was out of sight, then pulled into the intersection and followed.

Two blocks down 216, she spotted two men sitting in a pickup, parked and facing north along the right side of the road. Mel slowed down and flipped her lights on. She drove past the pickup, killed the lights again, and gunned the engine to catch up with Charlie and the Sheriff.

Four blocks from the lot, she saw it again — two men in a car. No lights, engine idle. Mel kept driving. Just before she passed them, she whipped a quick right onto a residential road circling the fairgrounds. She saw it a third time — a truck on each side of the road, both facing north, two men in each. Mel drove over the crossroad and called Bubba. First she checked Charlie's location.

"They're pulling onto the fairground parking lot. You lost them?" Bubba said.

"I got diverted," Mel said. "You tracking any other vehicles?"

"Nothing," he said. "Mel, you think you ought to get back to Charlie?"

Mel crossed another intersection — another pickup. "I got something here. The lots surrounded. Five parked trucks so far, pair of men in each. I'd bet there's more."

"Jesus, Mel. Call a Hey Rube — "

"Done."

"I'm going through the Sheriff's files. Some bad shit there. Things I don't want to know — "

"Get to the point, Bubba."

"He bought a bunch of equipment on eBay — shipped it all overnight. Old Nokias. Low amp wire. Battery casings — "

"Cell phone triggers?"

"Plus three cases of instant cold pack. Unless he's handing them out to prisoners, he bought them for the ammonium nitrate — DEA don't trace cold packs. This ain't no hobby, Mel. He's building bombs. You got to get everyone out of there."

Chapter 65

Mel called EK. No answer. She tried Jalinda.

"Oh my God, Mel, those two are in such bad shape — "

"They're already there?" *Shit.*

"At the vets. I'm tending EK. Doc say he ain't got no hemorrhage. He's got Monk unconscious, getting that bullet pulled out of his arm."

"You call a Hey Rube?"

"Did I? Run up and down the lot yelling 'Hey Rube, Hey Rube'. The agents pulled down their shutters, but they's four, five thousand townies on the lot. I got half the ride jocks trying to move them off — other half's circling the midway. No ins, just outs."

"You got to tell them I'm coming in. Driving a panel van — "

"Most of them, they ain't got no cells, Mel."

"You seen Charlie?"

"Is he coming?"

"Sheriff brought him in. They're in the parking lot. Get two ride jocks out there and carry Charlie to the kooch tent. Whatever he says, you get him inside."

"Okay."

"And tell the doc he's got five minutes to bring Monk back around. I don't care what's in his arm, doc's got to wake him up. I'm coming in. I need everybody on their feet in the kooch in five — "

"Mel, I — "

"Five minutes." Mel hung up the phone.

She drove past the fairgrounds entrance and found a midnight traffic jam, towny cars lined bumper-to-bumper, a string of headlights back to the parking lot. Shirtless boys partied in the beds of pickup trucks, whooping at high-haired girls dangling their summer legs through the sunroofs of teen muscle cars.

Near the show entrance, Mel saw the Sheriff's red and blue bar lights flash the exiting crowd. *Five thousand on the lot.* Mel guessed only a few hundred had made it off the midway so far. The show's lights burned through the midnight sky, some of the rides still spinning. She watched the ferris wheel's swinging buckets, still packed with townies. The big silver wheel turned achingly slow half circles, emptying seats one at a time, the ride jock keeping the rig balanced. She wondered how many bombs Evans could have built from a few cases of cold packs.

Mel heard a scream and slammed her brakes. A handful of teen-agers shouted in front of her car, nearly run down while she watched the midway. She ran a hand over her face. The group were headed *toward* the lot. She put the car in park and rolled down her window. She leaned out and tried to wave them back. "Get out of here. It's closed."

One of the kids flipped her off. "Learn to drive, stupid bitch!" They laughed and ran onto the parking lot.

Mel put the car in drive and maneuvered through the exiting traffic. Further around the lot, she watched the Swinger turn neon circles. The ride jock gunned the engine rocketing the chair swings nearly horizontal over the red-painted metal fence surrounding the ride. Near the end of the midway, a dozen children climbed screaming from sparkling fiberglass boats and miniature fire trucks, the jock emptying the kiddy ride and shutting down the lights. Mel watched a couple sweep their children into their arms and move onto a grab joint for candy apples and popcorn.

If Jalinda had really called a "Hey Rube", not everyone heard the message.

She kept driving, circling the lot, looking for an opening. Silhouetted by the scream of carnival lights, Mel spotted ride jocks stationed every fifty feet, armed with baseball bats and tire irons. No one would get past them — not even her if she didn't recognize someone who returned the compliment. Mel drove until she was sure she didn't know any them.

Damnit.

Mel set her jaw, downshifted the van and put her foot to the floor. The truck picked up speed. She clutched and threw the big center stick into fourth. Over the field, she could see the school bus parked behind the vet's tent, the kooch just beyond.

She swerved onto the field, downshifting again. The rear-end fishtailed. Mel battled the steering wheel, fighting for control. One hundred yards to the bus. She whipped the van straight, then downshifted again, gears grinding, lights off, punching the engine. Two ride jocks heard her coming before they spotted the van in the dark.

Run away. She didn't want a fight.

Mel shifted up. The men ran toward her. *Shit.*

Fifty yards now. She'd have to create a distraction.

Mel slid the driver's side door open. One of the men waved a tire iron over his head and ran straight for her. She threw the van into neutral and rose with one firm hand on the steering wheel. Planting a foot on the inside running board, she gripped the door's edge with one hand, and yanked the wheel hard left with the other.

A slow-motion wave swept her brain. The front axle snapped, hammering the truck's nose straight down. The rear of the van lifted behind her. Mel pushed off and started to dive away, the big truck gearing for a roll over the dark green lot. The flip started too soon — she'd mistimed it — the truck twisted in Mel's direction. She wanted to roll out in the grass, but shot up instead, thrown by the truck, arcing fifteen feet above the ground. The truck rolled ahead of her. Mel tucked her legs into her arms, trying to gain control of the flip. The van hit the ground a second time. Mel rolled out across the grass, absorbing the impact over her back. The fall knocked the wind out of her. She leapt to her feet, sucking air. Ice stabbed her chest.

The truck caught fire, the heat forcing the ride jocks to retreat. Mel felt the shock wave as the gas tank exploded. Screams rose from the midway. She ran for the kooch tent, her path lost on the distracted men.

In the distance, she saw Jalinda help EK walk to the kooch tent. Light poured from the vet's entrance, silhouetting the pair. Monk wasn't with them.

She started to call the Jalinda's name, but stopped dead. Mel hit the deck, ducking in the tall grass and weeds. Opposite the kooch, beyond Jalinda and EK's line of sight, Mel's eyes traced the dark outline of an old American car, its front bumper bent into itself. A cross-haired ornament dangled from the crunched black hood. Fear shot through her shoulder blades, pulling her scalp taut.

Lying flat in the weeds, Mel scanned the backlit carnival lot, searching the horizon for Dylan Hide.

Chapter 66

Mel heard the ride jocks shout in the distance, their voices nearly drowned by the fire roaring around the bread truck.

"Hey Rube!"

Carny-code for 911. Townies took it for a greeting — carnies knew it meant trouble on the midway. Time to man-up.

"Hey Rube!"

Closer now. Still hidden in the tall grass, Mel stole a look over her shoulder. She'd been spotted.

The men rushed her at 10 and 2 o'clock, one swinging a baseball bat, the other a tire iron. On her feet, Mel drew both pistols — the OTs in her left hand, the Airweight in her right, hoping she wouldn't have to shoot. Even pissed off, the ride jocks were friendlies. But she couldn't afford debate — couldn't afford to give Dylan her position.

Mel flicked on the laser-sight above the OTs' trigger. The red beam fired through the night sky. She aimed the pistol at 10 o'clock's face.

He froze, blinded, dropping the baseball bat. He threw his hands over his eyes. Two o'clock spotted the laser dot flash across 10 o'clock's forehead. Mel clicked both pistols' safeties and flipped the weapons. She caught them in the air — the two pistols becoming wood and hard rubber bludgeons, hollow steel barrels for handles.

Mel ran straight for 2 o'clock. He took a single step back, but Mel was already airborne. She bicycle kicked the man's chest. He fell. Mel landed beside him. Like a drum roll, she rapped out four pistol-grip blows to his sternum before backhanding his temple with the Airweight's rubber grip, knocking him unconscious.

10 o'clock hauled ass.

Mel ran for the kooch tent. Two more ride jocks entered the tent chute, Charlie flung over the larger man's shoulder, arms and legs flailing. Mel started to make for the trio until she spotted Sheriff Lew.

His face lit blue from a smartphone backlight, Lew hunkered down behind the veterinary tent, watching Charlie and the ride jocks walk the chute. Mel changed course and ran toward the man. Halfway between the kooch and the vet tent, Mel saw Lew's jaw set. He dropped an index finger onto the white phone's screen.

"Charlie — "

The vet tent flashed white, lit by the explosion behind her.

The shockwave blew Mel forward into the canvas wall. Heat scorched her back. The roared scream of one-thousand townies arced over the kooch tent from the midway. Mel shook her head and crawled to her feet, woozy from the concussion. She saw Lew's face brighten. His smile crept toward his earlobes. He started tapping the phone again. Another bomb.

The jammer. Mel fished the black-faced block of plastic from her jeans pocket.

Lew shifted his gaze to the opposite end of the midway, focussing on the entrance. His index finger hovered over the phone's glass face.

Mel flipped the jammer switch as Lew tapped his phone's screen.

One long second passed. Another.

Nothing happened.

Lew lifted his finger and poked the glass again, a puzzle cracking his face. Mel found her feet and charged the man, firing. Air exploded in front of the Smith & Wesson. Her first two shots missed. Eyes wide, Lew heard the shots from the snubby, turning on Mel.

A third silent shot found its target, its burning lead blowing a hole through Lew's hand. At close range now, her fourth shot caught Lew's shoulder, spinning him toward the ground.

Mel brought her fist down across the man's windpipe. She followed the blow with a knee to the hunkered man's temple. Mel raised the OTs to finish Lew with a backhand.

Crack.

A shot behind her, followed by a second.

Crack.

Two more rang from the kooch tent, faster and closer together.

Mel heard Jalinda scream.

The stench of fire and ammonia saturated the air. Flames sluiced the huge canvas sheets of the kooch tent, reaching for the limp red flag licking down toward the centerpole.

Fire swirled a jetstream vortex around the chute. Something dark burned a path through the canvas tunnel, moving toward her. A man, tall and bulky, his body a black stain wrapped in fire — the ride jock who'd carried Charlie. He flailed forward, running, stumbling, spinning to escape.

A fifth shot split the air. Jets of fire and blood punched through the ride jock's back, spouting from his chest. The man fell. Flames melted his charred body into the ground.

Mel forgot the Sheriff and ran for the gunfire.

Chapter 67

A horizontal whirlwind of flame gasped through the chute, pulled by cool air surrounding the mermaid tank. Standing at the entrance Mel braced herself. Hot backlot wind threatened to push her into the fiery tunnel.

Thirty feet to the end of the chute — without protection, she'd incinerate in half that distance. Mel turned back, battling the gale, bolting for the vet tent.

Inside the makeshift hospital, the veterinarian buzzed around an oversized operating table, cloaked in cold light. Monk lay unconscious, wrapped in a bird's nest of tubes and plasma bags, the skin around his gunshot wound flayed and pinned.

Mel yelled, waving her arms at the entrance. "Fire! Get him out of here."

The vet spun, glasses dangling at the end of his nose. "Fire?" He turned back to the operation. "It's fucking Fallujah out there."

"Where are the animals?"

"Cleared. Jalinda called a 'Hey Rube'," the vet said. "They're safe in the trucks."

Mel rushed the table. "You have to get Monk out — "

"Don't touch him." The vet turned on her, scalpel in hand. "He can't be moved. That bullet deflected off his ribs, but it took a fistful of bone shrapnel with it. His brachial artery is surrounded by fragment. I need another half hour here — "

"You don't have it — "

"Tough shit. I finish. Then we get out."

Mel knew she had to wait.

"I need burn blankets. Charlie, Jalinda — they're trapped in the kooch."

The vet didn't look up. "Water Jel blankets. Orange tubes by the door."

Mel found the orange plastic tubes and emptied one, throwing a blanket around her shoulders. She opened another and wrapped her guns, wary the heat might ignite the bullets' gunpowder.

Mel slung two more tubes over her shoulder and ran for the chute.

"Come back alive," the vet yelled behind her. "I'll need help moving him."

Mel stopped at the chute entrance. She turned her back on the inferno and sucked three deep breaths, a long-distance diver prepared for an immersion in flame. Mel turned again and ran into the hot squall.

Chapter 68

Fire scorched the fine hairs in her nostrils, an acrid smell turning against the flesh in her nose. She held one blanketed arm over her eyes, running blind, hoping she wouldn't collide with the burning canvas walls. She stumbled over the dead ride jock's charred embers, nearly hit the ground.

The chute seemed like an infinite death tunnel, longer when measured from inside. Mel willed herself to keep running. Twenty steps and she was clear, fire blowing at her back.

"Whatever you got there, you may as well drop it," Dylan said. "Before I get around to telling you."

Dylan stood imminent within the main entrance. Burning canvas flaps whipped behind him like glowing red wings.

The second ride jock lay dead at his feet. Charlie kneeled over the fallen man, claws in the dirt, Dylan's Chubby pointed at the back of his head.

Backlit by flames, Mel barely found the man's eyes.

"You're outnumbered," she said. "Two of us — one of you."

Dylan swept the Chubby across the tent. "Have a look around — maybe stay awhile."

Mel scanned the room. Stationed on the other side of the kooch tent, Mel's father trained a shotgun on Jalinda and EK.

A slow-burn chewed the fire-retardant walls behind them. Flame crept across the canvas, the entrances hellgates. The tent sucked heat through the openings, the air difficult to breath.

"We'll all die in here," Mel said.

"*We'll* die." Dylan laughed. He threw his head back. "Honey, I'm dead already. Been dead since I set foot in this titty revival joint. It's just taking them sons-a-bitches a lot longer to kill me than they intended."

Mel felt his eyes run over her body.

"Throw out whatever you got there, starting with them guns," Dylan said. "That's me telling you."

Mel unwrapped the pistols and threw them halfway toward Dylan. She pointed her chin at the orange canisters over her shoulder. "I've got fire blankets."

Dylan shrugged.

Mel threw one of the canisters toward Charlie. Dylan's face didn't change, but the Chubby shifted two inches before he fired. The orange canister shot away to one side. The bullet ricocheted, burying itself in a wood seat five feet from her.

"Listening's not really your thing, is it?" Dylan said. He shoved the gun's hot barrel into Charlie's neck. "Think you can hear me now?"

Mel tossed the blankets in front of her.

"Good girl. Glad we understand one another."

Mel pointed to her father. "What's he doing here?"

"It ain't polite to speak that way about your own father," Dylan said. "Not when he's in the room."

"Why's he here?"

"You and me's got some business to tend to. Some negotiating," Dylan said. "I thought Billy might be useful."

"Is that right, Billy?" Mel said. The man didn't answer.

"*Daddy*. Is that right, *Daddy*," Dylan said. He shifted the gun against Charlie's neck. Mel almost winced at the burned ring of flesh it left behind. "I want what's coming to me."

"Money?" Mel asked. "I have all the money you could ever — "

"I — want — what's — mine!" Dylan's voice screamed over the burning canvas. With one hand wrapped around Charlie's shirt collar, Dylan picked him up, digging the Chubby into his temple. Charlie's short arms flailed. Dylan marched across the tent to Billy and threw Charlie in the dirt at his feet. "You fucking move, I fucking kill her."

He turned and smacked his pistol across Billy's head, knocking him back. Dylan snatched the shotgun as the man fell. He smashed the butt down across Billy's back before turning the barrel on him. "Crawl, fucker. Crawl to Mommy."

Billy scrambled over the artificial sawdust. Mel backed away. "Stop moving, Melinda." She saw that Dylan could kill them both with the shotgun spread. She stopped.

"Now fucking tell her," Dylan said. "Tell Mommy what Daddy wants."

Billy simpered. He turned his head away, a dog shamed by his own shit.

"Tell me what?" Mel said.

"That you're promised," Dylan shouted. He pressed the double-barrels deep into Billy's neck. "Tell her Billy. Tell your daughter that she's fucking promised."

Chapter 69

"You were just a girl." Mel watched her father collapse into the earth around him. Hands ran through his sticky hair. Sawdust caked his eyes.

"Your mother died," he said. "I didn't mean for her to. But she was gone.

"We were together — I don't know how long. And we made you. My beautiful baby. Your Momma loved you."

Mel felt the heat on her back. Flame climbed a rope around the centerpole. The fibers melted, zipping hot tears into the ground.

"She wouldn't stop eating. She forced me. Made me buy her food. Build her trailer. She wanted to make a show. I tried to talk her out of it, but it's all she wanted.

"She wasn't going to live forever like that. I knew it. She hadn't walked for years. She was dying. And I had to take care of you. I had to figure out what to do.

"I couldn't perform no more. What would happen to you? I prayed on it, honey. I asked for help. A sign of how I could walk through the valley. All I thought of was you."

A strip of the canvas wall collapsed. Flame splashed across the ring igniting the old wooden chairs, an audience of fire.

"Then Dylan come along. Like some miracle. *Here is your answer, Billy Barry. Here is what you have been looking for.*

"Dylan offered right there. He said *Billy, your woman ain't got long. And you got a daughter needs raising.*

"He said *I got a joint, and it needs running. Y'all come live with me. We'll do it together.*

"But everything's got a price. At first I thought this was The Binding of Isaac — to turn my daughter into a child-bride so she could have a decent life. But the more we talked on it, the more I saw things different. I saw it clear. It was a good life for you. And for me, running Dylan's operation downstairs at The Social. Even then, it wouldn't be for long. And one day, we could leave. Just you and me. So I tried. Tried to make you love your Daddy more."

"It was to help you — to help you love me like you'd need to love Dylan. But you never did. You wouldn't do it."

Mel felt dizzy, oxygen sucked from the room. She could feel black smoke creep into her lungs, infecting her breath. Pain shot through her arteries, pounding her temples.

"And then your Momma died. She died too soon, and I had to go. I couldn't bring you with me. You weren't ready. I had to leave you behind.

"But Charlie took care of you, so it's okay. I know I made a mistake, but it turned out right. Now it's just you and me, baby. You and me. And Dylan'll take care of us.

"Come with us, baby, and everybody goes home."

Dylan held his arms wide, the shotgun swinging. "I'm just here for what's mine."

Chapter 70

"No!"

Mel planted a foot on her father's bent knee and leapt over him, launching at Dylan with both hands. Dylan stepped sideways. He snatched Mel's arm and pulled her past him, hammering the shotgun into her stomach below her sternum.

Mel cried out, rolling across the ground. On hands and knees, she vomited into the sawdust. Dylan threw the shotgun down, smiling.

"Bites a bit, don't it?"

He walked three steps toward her, then buried his boot in her gut.

Mel took the blow, clinging to the man's leg. She rolled out to her right, pulling him over her. Dylan pitched into the sawdust. On her feet now, Mel rushed him.

He rolled onto his back as Mel dived at the man. He brought both feet up and caught her hips, kicking her body over his head.

Mel landed hard, face to the sky. She rolled back onto her shoulders, kicked both legs and arced onto her feet.

Mel seized a burning chair, charcoaled wood scorching her palms. She held tight, swinging at Dylan. He threw his arms over his head.

Fire and ember rained around him. Mel swung the chair again. Dylan threw a punch and shattered the chair back, slamming Mel hard on the chin.

Stunned, she fell backward, twisting, catching herself on the row of chairs. Fists tight, Dylan walked toward her, shoulders forward.

Mel waited, her back to him. At the last moment she twisted, kicking a sideways heel to Dylan's nose. He fell, hands over his face. Blood poured down his white shirt. He found his feet, shook his head and roared, running toward her.

Mel dove forward, rolling into Dylan's legs. He hit the ground face first. Mel shifted into a squat, hands out beside her, and sidekicked Dylan at the base of his neck. His head whiplashed before snapping forward again. Still behind him, Mel drove a foot into his temple. Dylan sprawled, rolling onto his stomach, his arms folded under his hips. He didn't move.

Mel bent over the man and grabbed his long hair with both hands. She pulled his head back, ready to pound his face into the ground. Suddenly alive, Dylan spun and plunged his switchblade deep in her thigh.

Mel howled. She staggered backward. Dylan backhanded her with the knife's blunt end. The blade followed, carving a red slice from her cheek. He planted a fist in her belly and brought the blunt end of the knife down on her thigh, ripping at the leg wound.

He punched her again. First her temple. Her mouth. Mel felt a tooth loosen. Stunned, she tried to block his blows, Dylan's strength mooting her effort. He shifted the knife between his teeth, grabbing her throat with both hands. Mel felt herself start to black out, the power of his grip starving her brain of oxygen. Mel kneed him in the groin. She saw Dylan's eyes widen, but his hold tightened. She felt herself floating, falling. She kneed him again. His fist loosened. Again. For an instant he relaxed, stunned by pain.

Mel threw both hands up between his arms and knocked them away. Her fists behind her head now, she pounded down on both ends of the knife. The switchblade sliced Dylan's cheeks ear-to-ear, splitting his tongue. He fell back, blood spurting into the sawdust. Mel swept a backward roundhouse kick to the man's head. He staggered. With one leg, she leapt off the ground and bicycle kicked him under the chin. Dylan's head flew back — Mel heard his teeth snap around the steel blade. Blood gushed from his face. He fell backward, hitting the ground with a dull thud.

Mel dropped on him, leading with a knee to his ribs. Unconscious, his body kicked, but the man didn't move. She kneeled on his chest. Buried a fist down in his face. Shattered his nose. Another to the side of his head, blood pouring, Mel's fist flailing.

"Baby." She heard her father's voice. She hit Dylan again. "Mel, baby."

Mel felt Billy standing over her. She looked up. Pistol in hand, hammer cocked, he pointed the weapon at Dylan's head.

"No," Mel shouted. She knocked the Chubby away, rising. Mel brought her elbow back and smashed her father across his jaw. "No." She punched him again, backing him away. She pushed him into the burning chairs.

"You don't get to kill anyone." Mel hammered his face, opening a cut above his cheek. She felt the bones in her hand splinter. She hit him again.

"You don't get to fucking save me."

Chapter 71

"You don't get to save anyone."

With her good hand, Mel punched her father twice. He fell backwards into the chairs, an explosion of fire rising around him. He hit the ground, and jumped up again, batting away flames. "It wasn't true. He made me say that."

Fire worked at the big wooden centerpole close to the tent top. A glowing red chunk gnawed at the core. The pole swayed, threatened to collapse. Flames spread across the canvas ceiling.

Mel pushed her father again. "Don't fucking lie to me."

"He told me he'd kill you, I swear it. I lied to save you. You know I wouldn't do those things."

Mel knocked him down again, picked up a chair, broke it across her father's back.

"I swear," he begged. "Baby. I love you."

"Quit lying, Billy." Spattered past his shredded tongue, barely intelligible, Dylan's voice reached Mel from over her shoulder. "Time to die."

Dylan pointed the Chubby at her father. Mel leapt, trying to put her body between the two men. The gunshot pounded her ears. Billy's head exploded inches from her face. Mel felt the sound of a dying animal rise from her chest. Dylan shifted his aim to Jalinda. He fired again. Jalinda screamed. Her left leg exploded across the canvas wall behind her. Dylan aimed at Charlie.

Mel launched at Dylan. She tried to kick the gun away. He fired and missed. The gun flailed in his hand, bullets punching the canvas walls. Mel heard screams from the midway outside. She grabbed the Chubby, wrestling Dylan for it. They rolled across the sawdust, Dylan pulling off random shots.

Mel heard a groan from the tent top. Above them, she caught a glimpse of the tent as they rolled again. The centerpole started to collapse. A slow motion sheet of fire fell from the tent's peak, ready to suffocate them.

With the strength of a death grip, Dylan pulled at the gun. He pushed the barrel toward Charlie. Mel's hands wrapped around his. Her splintered bones crackled. Pain loosened her grip.

A slice of burning canvas fell next to them. Dylan tried to kick the flames away. Still clutching the gun, Mel used his distraction, pushed off with her feet and flipped over Dylan headfirst. She rolled past the pistol and landed flat on her back, she and Dylan's heads nearly touching. She wrestled the weapon closer, aimed for the big mermaid tank. Mel jammed her thumb against Dylan's index finger, wedged it into the trigger and forced off three shots.

The big tank's glass strained against three sharp cracks, followed by a heart-stopping snap. Mel heard the tsunami before it crashed down on them — fifty thousand gallons of water driving a tornado of razor-sharp glass.

Caught in the wall of water, she lost her grip on the Chubby. Glass shards sliced at her eyes. She tucked her chin and covered her head, gasping for breath. The back of her wrist opened. Blood pumped into the chlorinated current. Billy's lifeless body tumbled past her own, pulled by the tow.

Momentarily weightless, Mel felt herself wash onto the dark midway. She swept past Charlie and the others, safe at the side of the tent. Townies yowled, running from the flood. She thought she heard Dylan scream. Still pushed by the tidal wave, she dropped back to earth, tumbling to a stop in the mud and dirt.

Mel found her feet. Water poured from her jeans and vest, splotched crimson with blood. The tent fire sputtered, doused by the wall of water, the canvas flaps and centerpole ripped away. Mel saw EK head for the vet tent, struggling with Jalinda in his arms. She couldn't see Charlie anywhere.

She found Dylan pinned to the front of the clown head ticket booth. An eight foot shard of glass pierced his chest, buried deep in the painted smile behind him. His face sliced open. Blood drained, his body moved in fits and starts, convulsing against the glass spear. Mel ripped off her leather belt, wrapped each end around one of her palms and gripped the glass shard. She twisted. Slow. Tearing Dylan's heart. Careful not to break the glass.

His body kicked. A gush of blood poured from his mouth. Dylan's head fell. His chin dropped to his chest.

Mel spit on his lifeless body and walked away.

Chapter 72

She found Sheriff Lew on his knees behind the veterinarian's tent, hunched over a shiny black PVC tube, tapping at his smartphone.

She snatched his handcuffs from the black holster attached to his belt. Shocked, he spun on her. Mel slapped the cuffs down across one wrist. The ratchet spun around his arm, biting into the pawl. She kicked the phone out of his hand.

Lew tried to hit her but Mel caught the blow. She twisted his fist back, snapping the small bones in his wrist. She wrenched his arm behind him and cuffed his hands behind his back.

"The first rule of munitions," Mel said. "Put distance between yourself and the ordinance prior to detonation."

"My men have the lot surrounded," Lew said.

"You think I can't handle that, or haven't you been watching the show?" Mel picked up the incendiary. "Improvised. Nice."

On his knees, Lew's face twisted. "You'll never make it out of here alive."

Mel kicked the man in the face. He splayed across the ground, cuffed hands beneath his back. Mel stood over him. "Neither will you." She shoved the bomb down the front of his pants, tightening his belt around the black tube.

"You ignorant bitch." Lew grinned, his mouth bleeding. "Too stupid know what you're doing. That bomb don't even work."

"I know." Mel grabbed him by the collar and the belt, pulling him to his feet. She found the jammer in her pocket and shoved it in his face, turning it for him to see. "But I imagine I can fix it."

Lew's face started to crack. "You've killed people. I can get you out of here. Put in a good word," Lew said.

"We negotiating?" she asked.

"I'll wipe the database. Clear your record."

Mel pulled the man's revolver from his holster, holding it up against the carnival lights. She checked the chamber, clicked the safety, pulled the hammer back. "I'll clear things up myself," she said. "Right now."

Mel flicked the switch on the jammer. Its red LED winked out. She watched Lew swallow.

"Run," she said.

"I can help you — "

"Same as y'all helped her before?" Mel heard Charlie's deep voice as he wandered up behind them. Lew's shoulders started to shake. "Same as y'all helped me?"

Charlie reached up, gripped the incendiary with his claw and wedged it further down Lew's pants, jamming it into his balls. Lew whimpered.

"He any good at building these?" Charlie asked Mel.

"Care to find out?" she said.

Charlie nodded. "You heard the woman. Run."

Mel shot the ground between Lew's feet, grazing his instep.

Lew bolted, limping for the woods across the empty backlot. At ten yards, Mel put another bullet near his heels. He fell, spinning onto his back.

Mel wiped blood away from her eye. "I'm having trouble gauging distance. You want a try?"

She handed the gun to Charlie. He fired. The shot grazed the ground, closer to Lew's head. The man rolled onto his stomach, struggled to get up. Took off running again.

Every twenty yards, they took turns shooting the ground in front of the fleeing man. At one hundred yards, Lew started to scream — a desperate animal wail, unintelligible.

At two hundred yards, Charlie bent down and picked up the man's phone."You're my daughter, Mel," he said. "And you always will be, no matter what you do." He handed her the phone, gesturing over his shoulder with a claw. "Thanks for saving my life."

"My pleasure," Mel said. She gave the phone back to Charlie. "I think you should do the honors."

Charlie smiled at Mel.

He pressed redial.

Chapter 73

They held the carny wedding in Cocoa Beach in September.

The season wrapping up, The Mermaid Parade had made its way down Florida's East Coast, ready to cross the state for Gibtown, the Gulf of Mexico and Winter.

Arm-in-arm, Mel and Monk watched Charlie and Jalinda ride once around the carousel, a ritual carny promise that the couple would stay together through the winter and into the next season.

EK officiated, his face still bandaged. The show's costumiers had fit him out with a Mardi Gras-themed hat, purple and green streamers hiding the white gauze covering his healing cheeks. He read from his mother's family bible.

EK was carny now. He'd joked with Mel that with every member of The Committee under FBI investigation, Cuthbert's appeal had waned. EK sold his home, left town and joined The Mermaid Parade, Charlie's new lawyer Lieutenant.

As incentive, EK got to run his own museum show, displaying the pickled punks alongside his own stuffed chimeral sculptures.

Jalinda wore a hand-made wedding dress, generous with her bosom, tapered to a white satin fishtail fit tight around her one remaining leg. Charlie had promised her, one leg or three, she could be a mermaid as long as she wanted.

After the reception in the new tent, Mel and Monk strolled the beach. They watched the moon rise over the darkening Atlantic sky, Shortie following behind. They made love through the night, Mel exploring the scars across Monk's body. He told her he'd be out six more months, but the vet had promised he'd fly again, if only a little at first.

In the morning, they walked the beach again, slower this time, down to Mel's motorcycle parked among the palms of Ocean Boulevard. When they reached the bike, Mel kissed the man, pulling his warm body against her own.

"Where will you go?" Monk asked.

Mel shrugged.

Monk kissed the new scar on her cheek. "I don't suppose you'd think about what I said."

Mel felt her throat tighten, warmth at the edge of her eyes threatened to trickle down her face. She tried to smile. "I'll think about it every day."

She watched Monk laugh to himself, his brown eyes sad and bright and wise. "Just remember, you don't have to roll solo."

Mel smiled and broke away. She threw the small backpack over her shoulder, waved goodbye and rode alone down US1.

<u>Fahrenhistas</u>

The pre-release version of this book was initially available on Amazon with no clues as to the author, the title or the subject matter. The book was uploaded with a plain brown paper cover and readers were invited to take a leap of faith and put their trust in us.

These are the first 100 people who did just that and in doing so earned their place in Fahrenheit Press history forever.

Thank you Fahrenhistas – we told you we wouldn't let you down.

@bibliophilebc (Kate)
@bluebookballoon (David)
@beester_01 (Beester B)
@defsmith
@destinylover09 (Sonya)
@dhyanic (Dhyani)
@gordondon (Kyle)
@grabthisbook (Gordon)
@karendennise (Karen)
@marie123julie (Julie)
@welshlibrarian
@zummerset_here (Phil)
Tom Abba
Liviu Babitz
Tara Benson
Dan Benton
Tanya M. Bird
Baldur Bjarnason
Craig Breheny
Sacha Brinkles
Rosanna Cantavella
Lee Carson

Scott Cohen
Anna Crew
Ania Dabrowska
Mar Dixon
Lisa Edwards
Janet Emson
H Evans
Derek Farrell
Sandra Foy
Bill Gleeson
Abbie Headon
Ali Hope
Dean Johnson
Laura Jones
Susan Kemp
Jackie Law
Steve Lockley
Ian Lovatt
Raluca Lungu
Ian MacWilliam
Sheila Mansley
Brian Martin
John Mitchinson
Andrew Mosawi
Nick Muggridge
Mike Murphy
Vinay Nair
H.C. Newton
Kate Noble
Andrew Patterson
Poppy Peacock
James Pierson
Lana Preston
Laura Prime
Nick Quantrill
Sue Ransom
Vikki Reilly

Judith Richards
Neil Richards
Carl Robinson
Isabel Rogers
Stephanie Rothwell
Jan Russell
Holly Seddon
Albana Shala
Hannah Shorten
Julia Silk
Ben Simpson
Justine Solomons
Helen Stanton
Ted Smith
Teri Smyth
C.M. Thompson
Gary Thrower
Jonny Thumper
Kate Ward
Brendan Wright

Acknowledgements

The lyrics from the song *Burn Again* used in Chapter 4 are reproduced with the kind permission of *Blind Pilgrim*.

The song is taken from their *Say My Name* EP available now on Spotify and Apple Music